Roads Ahead

edited by
Catherine O'Flynn

**Tindal
Street
Press**

First published in October 2009
by Tindal Street Press Ltd
217 The Custard Factory, Gibb Street, Birmingham, B9 4AA
www.tindalstreet.co.uk

Introduction and selection © Catherine O'Flynn 2009
Stories © the individual authors

The moral right of Catherine O'Flynn to be identified as
the editor of this work has been asserted by her in accordance
with the Copyright, Designs and Patents Act, 1988

A CIP catalogue reference for this book is available
from the British Library

ISBN: 978 1 906994 00 6

Printed and bound in Great Britain by CPI Bookmarque, Croydon

FSC
Mixed Sources
Product group from well-managed
forests and other controlled sources
Cert no. SGS - COC - 2061
www.fsc.org
© 1996 Forest Stewardship Council

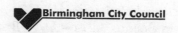
Birmingham City Council

Contents

Introduction

When I was seven I started helping out in my dad's sweet shop. This help largely consisted of reading comics, eating pear drops, smiling unconvincingly at the jokes customers made that I didn't understand and, very occasionally, serving someone.

One of the first things I learned in the shop was that standing behind a counter imbued me with knowledge in the eyes of customers. It didn't matter that I gave no sign of actually possessing that knowledge and happened only to be there because it was more interesting than watching the test card on television. I apparently knew something they didn't. Grown-up men would ask my advice on birthday cards for their wives, old women would seek guidance on boxes of soft centres, and children, invariably older than me, would approach the counter, push a hot ten-pence piece towards me and say the code words: 'Ten p mix-up.'

The ten p mix-up, for the uninitiated, describes a transaction in which the customer purchases ten-pence worth of sweets, the selection to be made by the shop-keeper. I imagine a ten p mix-up today would be a fairly forlorn affair, consisting of only two cola bottles or a solitary foam banana, but back in the late seventies, when Mojos and Blackjacks were half a pence each, ten pence could buy you enough raw candy to keep you buzzing and twitching right through assembly and screaming out onto the concrete at playtime.

At first I couldn't understand why customers didn't select the sweets themselves, but I gradually learned that the thrill of the mix-up was exactly in this handing over of the confectionery reins to someone else – the excitement of letting another choose. I soon found myself enjoying the unfettered artistic freedom the new role offered. I'd stand in front of the sweet stand, opened paper bag in hand, facing my audience of one, their anxious mouth-breathing audible as I prepared myself. The selections I made were based on a hasty assessment of the customer's profile and certain arbitrary connections suggested by it: gobstoppers for thugs, Highland toffee bars for the visually impaired, sherbet fountains only for those who looked like they could handle them responsibly. Occasionally I might check a preference before throwing something in, but largely I trusted my intuition and entered a kind of heightened confectionery trance, my hands moving quicker than my conscious mind.

It was a job without formal channels for customer feedback, but I take the fact that I was never beaten up on the streets for a bad mix as the greatest endorsement of my selection skills.

I was reminded of all this when Tindal Street Press invited me to help them choose stories for this tenth anniversary collection. I felt similarly daunted and unqualified – the fear of a kicking from bigger kids never really goes away. What made the invitation irresistible wasn't a clammy ten-pence piece, but the promise of finding new writers and stories to love.

Writers aren't often invited to submit material. They're

more used to being explicitly asked not to and told that, if they do, their work will just be shredded, or recycled, or made into paper planes: but on no account read. So Tindal Street's unusually open and welcoming invitation precipitated a high number of submissions.

The twenty-two stories we chose have a wide geographical range, from the eerie light of an empty Blackpool Sea World Centre, to a submerged New York where mermaids idle on the roof of the Empire State Building. From the dusty trails of a dude ranch in the American West, to the piss-stained steps of a London tower block.

Naturally, their subject matter is as disparate as their settings, but certain themes emerge to create unlikely pairings. A violent Brummie debt collector and a schoolgirl bully are both disconcerted by a shifting balance of power. Loss, isolation and a disintegrating reality lead a young woman to retreat to a bath of ping-pong balls and an old man to hurl shotgun cartridges at the carcase of a dead cow. Dying or dead relationships haunt cocaine-fuelled nights on the streets of Buenos Aires and hushed lunchtime conversations in a Shrewsbury bistro.

Perhaps inevitably, terror, real or perceived, and the war upon it, plays a part in some of the stories here. A young man tries to discover the truth behind his lover's war crimes in Iraq. A Nigerian mother barters with the military for the release of her allegedly terrorist son. A solicitor remembers her seventies Birmingham childhood and the Irish labourers her father employed.

Conflict on a smaller scale rears its head in a roadside tussle between two women over a discarded chest and a deranged husband and wife offering unforgettable entertainment from a railway platform booth.

Most of the authors here are under thirty-five, but there is perhaps less sex, drugs and rock and roll than might be expected. There are strangely powdery cocktails in a Middlesbrough nightclub, but there are also plastic cups of tea in a Jewish retirement home. Instead of imagining the lives of their contemporaries many of the writers are drawn to the young and the old. Little girls abandoned by their parents; adolescents suffering family get-togethers; a man resenting the guests at his wife's wake; and an old woman cast adrift in time and place.

Tindal Street Press launched ten years ago with the publication of *Hard Shoulder*, another anthology of fiction by young writers. I'm not sure if it's typical Brummie self-deprecation or a keen sense of irony that led the imprint to choose a dead-end sign for their logo. Whatever the reason, only a publisher secure with its own track record of uncovering new voices and launching literary careers could get away with that and at the same time dare to call this new anthology *Roads Ahead*. Welcome then to the cul-de-sac that opens out in twenty-two directions to unknown destinations.

Catherine O'Flynn
July, 2009

The Chest
Kathryn Simmonds

I'm walking back from the job centre, having a good sniff at the air, looking at the trees to see how many I can name, and I'm just trying to decide if this particular one is an elm, when I stop: someone's left a chest on the side of the road. I circle it, admiring the grapes carved in curlicues around the sides. It looks like mahogany. There are a few scratches on the top and the varnish along the bottom is scuffed, but it wouldn't take long to fix it up. I lift the lid to assess the inside. Solid. It's amazing what people will throw out.

The houses on Kingdom Road aren't small – you've got to walk a good twenty paces up the drive before you get near the doorbell – so if there's any chucking out going on, they've got the stuff to chuck. In the past I've had a couple of paperbacks that were balanced on a wheelie bin, and there was a Hoover that didn't suck very well, but I've never seen anything like this. The only problem is there's no way I'm going to get the chest home by myself, and if I leave it here someone else is bound to have it. There's only one bar of energy left on my mobile and a few pence credit so, talking very quickly, I get the number of a taxi firm and ask them to send me their roomiest car.

Five minutes go by and I'm still congratulating myself on my luck, debating whether I should put the chest on eBay or make space for it in the living room. There's a clump of white campion growing near the roadside, so I stoop down to examine it and a few more minutes pass. The sun's out and the sky is a lovely patchy blue.

I'm just thinking where I might get hold of some varnish when an old-fashioned estate pulls up and the woman driving it turns off the engine and gives me a look like daggers. I wonder if she owns the house and isn't throwing out the chest at all but moving it inside, so I give her an innocent smile and step away slightly. Her curly hair is tied up in a scarf and when she gets out I can see the rest of her outfit: pantaloon trousers and some sort of Indian smock thing. She isn't from India, though; she's about forty-five, middle-class hippy type, the sort you see going in the health food shop.

'Excuse me,' she calls, walking towards me. Any pretensions about love and happiness and sharing the hippy vibe are right out the window because there's an edge to her voice like she's caught me doing something illegal. 'Excuse me, but I've come to collect this.'

Now, in my experience, what most English people suffer from is embarrassment, a big dose all round, but by the sounds of it this woman has missed out on her helping and had doubles of superiority instead. I take up my previous position, leaning on the chest, dead silent, giving her the look she's giving me. You can see her working out how to play it. She takes a few steps nearer and puts her wrist to her forehead as if the sun's in her eyes, which it isn't because it's only March and even though it's sunny we're not getting the glare where we're standing because of all the trees.

'This. I saw it earlier and I've come to pick it up.' She motions to her car.

In the meantime I've had a moment to think about how to play it too, and have decided on 'council house and violent', which is probably what she expects anyway.

I give a sigh, like I can hardly be bothered to reply. 'Well, unlucky for you, innit?' Innit is not one of my words.

She steps right up to the chest. 'Look,' she says, going into social worker mode, because I might be carrying a knife for all she knows, 'I was walking past and then I went to get my car. I've only been gone for a couple of minutes.'

'I've been here ten and I ain't seen no sign of you.'

She looks at her watch like it's playing tricks on her. 'It was a matter of minutes,' she says. 'I only live a few streets away.'

'Losers weepers,' I say and glance over my shoulder because I'm hoping the taxi is going to scoot round the corner, but of course there's no sign because when do taxis ever come early? Only when you're still rushing to do your hair and get your lipstick on.

When I turn back it's clear from her face that my last remark has got her going. There's a vein throbbing in her neck.

'This is ridiculous,' she says. Then, trying to pretend I'm not there, she puts her hands around the corners of the chest that I'm not leaning on. But I clasp my arms around it like it's my only child and social services have come to take it away. She says 'ridiculous' again, and tries to drag her end of the chest towards her car, but my weight keeps it from moving very far. She stops. Her face is blotchy pink and the scarf has gone skew-whiff. Up close, I can see that she must have her hair done at a salon because the colour looks expensive, not like the cheap stuff my mum uses, where the shade never matches the one on the box.

'Can't you accept that I saw this first without making a spectacle? Look, there's my car!'

We're fairly evenly matched, about the same size I reckon. 'I'm not making a spectacle. I'm minding my own business waiting for my taxi. You're the one who's got her knickers in a twist.'

That really winds her up. 'People like you,' she says.

'People like me what?'

I know how the sentence ends. I know she wants to say 'are just plain thick' or 'are what's dragging this country down' or some of that other shit. But she doesn't because she doesn't want to hear herself saying it out loud, even if it's what she's thinking. Bet she doesn't know an elm from an ash.

'Finders keepers,' I say.

'Oh, for God's sake, this is mine.' She makes another assault on the chest. Because I'm not expecting it, I stagger sideways and lose my hold. She's dragged it a couple of feet before I can get back to it. A man from the house across the road is pretending to put his rubbish out but actually he's having a good stare, and I don't blame him. I would too.

'Will you, for God's sake, let go?' she says. God again.

'You don't own this, love.'

The word 'love' is worse than if I'd sworn. Her eyes go small with fury. She reaches into the pocket of her pantaloons and takes out her phone and, with one arm holding the chest, uses her free hand to dial. She talks quietly, but I can hear.

'Daniel. Daniel, it's me. Listen, I need your help. No, now. No, no, nothing like that. Listen, it's urgent, could you drive to Kingdom Road? Can't you cancel the meeting? It's important. It's −' At this point she's conscious of my face too close to hers for comfort. 'I can't explain now. Please, Dan. Well, tell them to get someone else to go. Oh, for fuck's sake, Daniel, *one little thing*. No no, don't worry. Oh never mind. Yes, I know you have to work for a living.' The phone goes back in her pocket.

'Oh dear,' I say, which fires her up, making her give an almighty tug. She's trying to drag it, and all that anger is making her pretty strong, but with my weight on it, the chest isn't moving properly. We're head to head, both of us leaning over; my arms gripped around one side and hers around the other. That's the moment when she lunges forward and bites my fingers.

'Aaagh!' It's the shock more than the pain that makes me cry out and I jump away from the chest as if it's red hot. She takes her chance and starts shuffling madly, but in the same moment a car pulls up beside us and the driver gets out like he's one of the Sweeney. About time. I'm standing there shaking my hand and I can see this woman's teeth marks on it, tiny purple crescents in my skin.

'Pick up for Leanne?' says the driver.

'That's me,' I tell him, still waving my hand around.

'You all right?' he asks.

'She bit me.'

Scarf Head is huffing and puffing and by now the blotches on her cheeks have turned red.

'You *bit* her?'

'Oh piss off, will you? This has nothing to do with you.'

This is obviously the wrong thing to say. I shake my hand for effect.

'I think there's blood.' There isn't any blood. 'She could have rabies.'

'You're the one who's mad,' she screeches.

'She's taking my chest,' I tell the taxi driver, helpless.

'Right,' he says and goes to open the boot. The car is pretty clapped out, but it's big: a hatchback with plenty of room inside.

'Come on,' he says to me, striding over to Scarf Head who's dragged the chest nearer the boot of her station wagon. He's a hefty bloke and, without looking at her, he takes one side of the chest and I take the other, though I'm not really feeling any of the weight because he's got it all, and together we carry it to the taxi.

She knows the game's up, and even though she's livid she can't do anything to stop us. She tells me I'm a thief and I should be ashamed, which is quite funny, because I've never tried to take a chunk out of anyone in my life. There was a girl at school, I had a hank out of her hair with kitchen scissors when we were in home economics one time, but that's because she said something about my mum. But I wouldn't do that now. Not at the age of twenty-seven, never mind forty-whatever she is.

The taxi driver has a friendly face. There's a swirl of hair on the front of his head from his male pattern baldness.

'You don't see something like that every day,' he says as we pull off. 'Thought it must have treasure in it the way you two were carrying on.'

'No, there's nothing in it.'

We have a chat about this and that. I like to take advantage of talking to people, because when you're unemployed you can get out of practice. Now and again I've started conversations with myself – 'What are you having for tea, Leanne?' – but you've got to nip that in the bud because it's a one-way ticket to ding-dong land and before you know it you'll be wearing men's shoes and poking around in bins.

*

When we get to my flat we park up close to the steps and the driver helps me carry the chest through the main double doors. Fortunately, I live on the first floor. It's quite awkward manoeuvring the chest around the corners, but he's good-humoured about it. I unlock the door and we get it inside.

'Thanks for that.'

'Phew,' he goes, pretending to wipe the sweat off his brow.

'How much do I owe you?'

'Call it two fifty.'

There's no way it's only two fifty. 'Are you sure?'

'Yeah, you've given me a laugh – the sight of you two in the middle of the street like that.' He smiles. 'How's the hand?'

The purple crescents have dissolved into faint pink marks. 'I'll be all right.'

He pockets the money and is about to go, when he glances out of the front window.

'Hang on, there's your friend,' he says.

Sure enough, when I look round she's standing on the verge at the front of the flats, glaring. I follow him outside.

She doesn't move when she sees us.

'You come for another bite?' I shout over. No response, just the evil eyes. I put my index finger to the side of my head and make the international sign for 'nutter'.

'Want me to have a word with her?' the driver says. But he doesn't get the chance because all at once she's striding over.

'You shouldn't have done that,' she tells me in a trembly voice. 'You shouldn't have done that. It wasn't yours to take.'

'Well, it wasn't yours, was it?'

'Yes it was. It was mine and you took it.'

I don't think I've seen anyone look so angry, except maybe the time I borrowed my sister's best pair of jeans without asking and broke the zip on them.

'What's your game?' says the driver.

She looks at him in confusion, like this is the first time she's ever seen him, then looks back at me the same way.

'Bloody hell,' I say to myself.

Her voice is quieter when she speaks again. 'You took it from me,' she says. Then her bottom lip gives way and she does something with her eyes so that her eyebrows go up like a dog's when it's begging. She makes this half-whimper sound and then she's crying, right there in front of us, standing on the scrubby patch of grass beside the car park. Proper tears. Her shoulders are shaking, and the tears are coming down her face one after the other, and she's letting them come, not even trying to stop herself. A strand of snot is dripping from her nose. The sound she's making is awful, goes right through me. I can't stand it when people cry.

'Come on, it's all right,' I tell her. But it isn't all right; she's completely lost the plot. 'Don't cry.' But she keeps crying. The taxi driver shakes his head.

'Come and have a cup of tea,' I say.

'D'you think that's wise?' asks the driver.

'Yeah, she's all right.'

I feel bad for making the nutter sign at her. A tiny little bit of me even feels guilty for having the chest off her, but what else was I going to do?

'She'll try and take that chest again.'

I look at her. 'No she won't.' She's trying to stop herself now; she makes two big shuddering sighs. Her face has softened. Her shoulders have drooped and she looks saggy, like a balloon with the air gone out.

'I'm taking your number plate,' the taxi driver tells

her. 'So you better not try anything.' She nods, but it's obvious she's lost her fight.

'Come on,' I say. 'Come inside for a minute.'

I lead her into my flat and guide her to the settee. She perches on the edge of it, fiddling with a tassel on her Indian smock, her eyes pink-rimmed and starey. It's quiet, just the two of us, so I flick the radio on and a blast of 'Don't Stop Me Now' by Queen comes out, Freddie Mercury hollering about Mr Fahrenheit. I turn it off again, but the music has woken her out of her daze and she looks around as if she's just realized where she is.

'I don't know what got into me,' she says. 'I'm sorry.'

I'm not sure if she's sorry about the biting or the crying or both.

'Don't worry about it,' I say and duck into the kitchen to fill the kettle, give her a couple of minutes to straighten herself out, put a few biscuits on a plate like I'm somebody's mum with a visitor. I can hear her in the other room blowing her nose, but I stick where I am, concentrating on pouring tea, wondering what I'm supposed to say to her.

'There you go.' I set my best mugs down and take the armchair.

'Is your hand all right?' she asks.

'Yeah, it's all right.'

She takes a sip of tea. 'It's a nice flat.'

'Thanks.'

Probably not what she expected; no nylon carpets and overspilling ashtrays. The walls are painted white – the landlord paid for the emulsion because it saved him a job – which has the effect of making the place look fresh, and bigger than it actually is, which isn't very big; a living room, kitchen, bedroom, bathroom without a bath. There's not much on the walls: a Chagall print, two sepia posters of Paris from the twenties, and three postcards of amaryllis flowers I framed myself. I don't like clutter, it gets on my nerves. I like things to be clean and organized.

The chest is still where the driver left it, at an angle beside the telly. We're both pretending we can't see it.

'Feeling better?' I ask her.

'Yes. Thank you.'

I'm stumped then, beginning to think this tea drinking was a mistake, and there's no music fuzzing up the silence between her and me, so the atmosphere is a bit on the awkward side. Just as I'm wondering what to say next she says, 'I've been under quite a lot of strain recently.' Right, I'm thinking, haven't we all, but she's not finished yet, she wants to try and set things straight. 'I lost my job and things have been rather difficult.'

'Sorry to hear that,' I tell her, which is what you say.

'They called it rightsizing the business.'

'My sister works in HR. They've had to lay people off by the dozen.' Angela's the high-flyer in our family; she works for a big hotel chain.

'I was there nearly fourteen years,' says Scarf Head, taking another sip of tea. 'They carved up my job between two of my colleagues. One of them was about your age, I helped train her when she arrived.'

I give her a nod, let her know I'm listening.

'She was fresh out of university, didn't have a clue.' She fixes her eyes on the carpet. 'And they got me to knock her into shape.'

'I'm not working at the moment either.'

'No?'

'Waiting for something to come up.'

'Anything in particular?'

'I don't know exactly, I've done all sorts.' I leave it at that.

'It's good to be adaptable. That's part of my problem, I think. I was in a niche profession.'

Adaptable, that's one way of putting it. I've adapted to the pub, the biscuit factory, the chemist's, the fish market, the department store and the doctor's surgery. Finally thought I'd got somewhere with the last one: posh Simon and his one-man-band PR firm. Until it went bust. He blamed it on the recession, but the truth is he didn't have a clue, with his floppy hair and stripy suits and no idea how to write a press release.

'I hope you find something,' she says.

'Thanks.'

'It's difficult out there, isn't it?'

She makes 'out there' sound like outer space. But I can't see why she's worrying so much. I've had a glance at the rings on her wedding finger, a thick gold band and an engagement ring with a fat white diamond in it. I doubt she's ever seen the inside of a job centre. Not like the women her age I've seen signing on, not as if she's going to be in there asking for a crisis loan.

'I keep applying,' she says, 'but nobody wants to see me for an interview. I've thought about removing my date of birth from my CV.'

'Something's bound to come up,' I tell her, 'and you've got your husband to . . .' I was going to say 'take care of the bills', but it doesn't seem right to allude to the scene earlier, not now we're sipping tea together. 'I mean . . .'

'Oh yes, my husband,' she says, and that angry note is back in her voice. 'At last he can have me at home all day making jam while he goes out to slay dragons. I have to ask him every time I want to buy a new pair of shoes.'

I drink some more tea because I don't know what to say to that one.

'What do people do all day if they don't go to work?'

she asks. She looks at me intently, like I might have the answer she needs.

'I don't know, whatever they like I suppose.'

'What do you do?'

'Go for walks. Read. I've applied for a beginners' class in botany at the adult education college. You get a concession if you're unemployed.'

They have loads of courses at the college; she could do one in Indian head massage, or yoga, or stress management. She nods, but she doesn't seem like she's interested. I can tell her mind is still fixed on the graduate who's got her job.

'What do you like doing?' I ask her.

'Working,' she says. 'All I need is to get back to work and then I'll start feeling like myself again.'

'Just got to wait for the right thing to turn up,' I tell her.

She nods, but she's not really hearing me. I know how it is, there are those mornings you'd like to put on your work clothes and get out of the flat, even if it's to a job you can't stand, because it gives you the day off from worrying about your life. But you've got to keep your balance or you'll end up in a mess, and then what? Before you know it you're in the street taking bites out of strangers over a piece of furniture you don't even need, just so you can feel like you've won something for a change.

I ask her if she fancies another cup of tea, hoping she doesn't, and she says she ought to be going.

'Thanks,' she says at the door. 'You've been very kind.'

I wish her good luck with her job hunting. When she's gone I put the stereo back on and experiment with different locations for my new chest.

It's a couple of weeks later when I see her near the post office, walking a dog, a great big red setter flopping along the pavement. She's on a mobile phone, looking very intense.

There's a moment when I'm sure she notices me, but in that fraction of a second we both look the other way, her picking up her pace to get round the corner, me taking a renewed interest in the trees. She's jabbering away, probably trying to fix herself up with another job doing whatever it was she did in her niche profession. We keep on walking like we haven't seen each other, like we're complete strangers, like we've never even met.

Devotion

Anietie Isong

The leader of our union – the Ibok Women Progressive Association – imposed on herself the task of praying before and after our meetings. But her prayers were never short. Last gathering, she prayed for so long that by the time she finished, everyone had fallen asleep. Even Mama Victor succumbed, and she was a deaconess in St Saviour's Church. Three weeks ago when I prayed, the whole plea lasted just thirty seconds. Our leader chided me afterwards. She took me aside and opened her Bible (she always had a small one in her handbag) to the place where Paul the Apostle asked Christians to pray without ceasing.

After the day's meeting, the women peddled gossip.

'Edima, did you hear that Barrister Okon has imported a brand new *Tokunbo* car from Germany?'

'I heard that the councillor is going to the US next week.'

'Architect Ebong is sending his first daughter to study in Spain.'

'Where did you hear that?'

'Ah, do you doubt me? Have you forgotten that I am the BBC of this community?'

'Not that I doubt you. It's just that . . .'

'That girl, that architect's daughter, sleeps with every man who smiles at her. Last night, she did it with five men. Did you hear me? Five men in one night. I saw it with my two eyes.'

'It's a good thing she is going to Europe. Let her take her smelly buttocks away from our husbands.'

'And our children too. Imagine if the harlot gets hold of your fifteen-year-old boy.'

Mama Sammy was the chief story teller. But I knew her tales were filled with salt and pepper – the lies that seasoned the saga. She was the only one of us who frequented the capital city and her stories were often about government policies.

'I can tell you that they are planning to introduce a housing tax,' Mama Sammy revealed. 'You just wait and see. Everyone in your household will be taxed. You, your husband, child, even your dog will be made to pay. As long as you have a roof over your head, you will pay. Mark my words.'

Nene, my cousin, called the gossip session the real meeting. As she mingled with the other women, I watched her closely. I noticed, for the first time, how bony her hands were, how all the veins that ought to have been covered with healthy flesh stood out like a school child's drawing. But Nene was not an old woman. It was too much hard work that had aged her. As the bread winner, Nene supported her home with sales from *akara* and other petty goods. As in my own case, her husband had left her for the world beyond.

'Are you all right?' I asked Nene, when she'd disentangled herself from the women and we were making our way towards our homes.

'I am all right,' she said and laughed.

But there was something in the sound, something hidden, which troubled me greatly. Near the town square Nene let it out: 'I think Nsima has joined the Ibok Youth Movement.'

She said it quickly, as though the words scalded her tongue. She spat the words out as one would spit out hot yam. And she did not look at me. I wanted to slap her hard and tell her to stop playing games with me. Instead, I told her to go and wash her bad mouth with soap. Last week, gunmen in speed boats attacked an oil field. Three foreign workers, including a Briton, and four Nigerians were taken after a three-hour gun battle with the army. The Ibok Youth Movement was blamed for the attack. How could my thirteen-year-old son be a member of such a dreaded militia?

'You should open your eyes,' Nene said. 'Open them wide to see what your son is doing. I have told you before that I don't like the company he keeps. He hangs around with some bad boys.'

At home, I found refuge in the easy chair that had been worn smooth by many bottoms' many years of sitting. The yard was quiet. I shut my eyes. Perhaps my cousin was right. Why hadn't I suspected all along? Those times Nsima said he went for football training, why hadn't I checked it out with his coach? I remembered one night he came back, limping. He'd told me then that he was injured on the football field. I believed him. These things happened. Even professional football players got injured. There were times that he screamed at me. Times that he raised his voice and sang of change in the community. I thought it was all part of growing up without a father. I rarely saw him do his homework and it never occurred to me, then, to check with his teacher. I sighed and struggled to my feet and then stumbled into my tiny kitchen to prepare a meal for him.

When Nsima came back, I stood and watched him eat. I watched the *garri* travel from his hand to his mouth. I watched him and felt a lump rise in my throat. My son. My only beloved son. He was the only thing in this world that was real for me. I had the sudden desire to build a wall around him, to protect him from the terrors of the land.

'I am really enjoying the soup,' Nsima commented.

I smiled. It was bitter leaf soup. I had put in just the quantity of red pepper that he liked.

After he'd finished his meal, I started my 'interrogation'. He didn't try to deny it. He just looked at me and sighed.

'Why, Nsima? Why have you joined the Movement? You want to disgrace me, eh?'

He stared at me then and I gasped at the transformation in my son. The mildness was gone from his eyes. In its stead was stony resistance. I pinched myself. I pinched myself hard.

'We need a change in this land,' Nsima said. 'The Ibok Youth Movement will make the government sit up and address the poverty in this region.'

'A change?' I exclaimed. 'Do you know what the government does to militants? They execute them by firing squad!'

'Mama, we are not militants.' Nsima's voice was heavy with disdain. 'We are just a pressure group that wants to control the resources of this land.'

I tried to control my indignation. 'A pressure group that blows up oil pipelines? A pressure group that kidnaps innocent foreign workers, eh?'

I made him sit beside me, on the raffia chair. I held his hands. Last week, the army had arrested ten suspected militants. The militias were tortured and left to die. I thought of my son in the hands of the soldiers. I thought of him begging for mercy, while they beat him with rods and guns.

I made him swear by the Bible that he would stay away from the Movement. I prayed for him, too. I called upon the God of Isaac and Jacob and David to lead my son not into temptation. My son did not immediately repent. I begged Nene to have a word with him. My cousin came and spoke to him about a mother's love, reminded him that he was an only child, that everyone in the family looked up to him. I also took him to Bishop Emmanuel of New Man International Ministries. The man prayed for Nsima. Then he made him swallow a teaspoonful of anointing oil.

Nsima started to take an interest in my business. When he began to help out in the shop, I taught him the basics of trading. He soon memorized the prices of bread, soft drinks, juice, butter, eggs and tomatoes. The shop was not far from my home, so I usually closed late. Because he could easily have been fooled by some sweet-mouthed customers, I put up a notice near the counter: 'No credit today. Come back tomorrow.'

I was confident enough to leave Nsima alone in the shop while I went for the next general meeting of the Ibok Women Progressive Association. We had a special guest – Lady Smith, wife of the Honourable Commissioner for Special Duties. She arrived in a convoy of four cars and our leader promptly gave her a royal welcome.

'A woman of substance,' our leader praised. 'A worthy wife, mother and an idol for many women in this community, shall we not applaud her kind gestures?'

As the lady smiled and fanned herself, I watched her closely. I noticed how light-skinned she had become. I'd known her before this transformation in her complexion. Only last year, she was one of the 'unknown' mothers of the community. She worked as a teacher in St Paul's Primary School. Her husband's sudden appointment had reversed her fortunes. Three months after she'd moved into the government quarters, she adopted the title 'Lady'.

When Lady Smith eventually spoke, she chose her words carefully. She spoke about her determination to help women in the community. She spoke about the Women Development Centre that the state government would soon build. She concluded by handing out handbags to us.

'It's a little gift,' she said. 'But it is of good quality. Imported from China; you will not find this type in the local market.'

The women clapped and cheered while the lady's aides distributed the cheap handbags. Somebody said, in a very loud voice, that Lady Smith had chosen the perfect gift: she needed a new bag to match her blue shoes that her son who lives in London had sent her. But I did not move from my seat. I did not reach out to grab the bag that was passed to me.

'Sometimes, you can be very annoying,' my cousin told me as we walked home after the meeting. 'Why didn't you collect the bag?'

I wanted to tell her that I didn't care about the lady's handbag and her bleached face. I wanted to tell her that the lady and her husband were stealing government funds to enrich their pockets. The local magazines fed us with these stories. The week before I'd read in the *Nigerian Mirror* that a governor's wife had used public funds to entertain friends at her mother's birthday celebrations. I knew that Lady Smith's handbags were bought with stolen government funds. But I held my peace and hurried home to check on my business. It was a wet night. I hiked up my skirt as I dodged the puddles.

Nsima had sold ten cups of *garri*, a crate of soft drink and five sticks of cigarettes. He had a Midas touch, that

boy. It gladdened my heart to see such good sales. I was
going through the sales, making sure that everything was
carefully recorded in the blue book, when I heard the
siren. It sounded like the loud wail of my neighbour's cat.
I froze as a military truck rattled to a stop in front of the
shop. Five soldiers leapt out of the vehicle. The military
men had guns as long as the bamboo trees that grew
behind the communal pit toilet.

'Where is your son?' a soldier asked me.

'Officer, is there any problem?' I asked.

The slap numbed me. The officer who had hit me
looked like a teenager. How times had changed! In the
old days a boy of nineteen could not raise his voice
against an older person. The soldiers found Nsima
hidden behind the sack of *garri*. They knocked my son
unconscious and then they bundled him inside the
military truck.

'They have killed me, oh!' I wailed, as the truck pulled
away. 'The calabash of my happiness is gone . . .'

News of the arrest spread like an outbreak of cholera.
Several members of the union rushed to commiserate
with me. Some came and sat and said how God would
not abandon His children, how I must not stop praying.
Others came and talked about the desecration of the
land, about the death of peace and the birth of terror.

Three days later, when prayers and talks did not
produce my son, the leader of our association suggested
that I visit the army barracks.

I shook my head slowly. 'I don't know where they took
him to.'

'I hear they are in Port Harcourt.'

Our leader subjected me to a prayer session, but she
also loaned me some money for the trip. Friday, the
driver of Young Shall Grow Motors, gave me a ten per

cent discount on the fare. When I got to Port Harcourt, I was surprised at how easy it was for me to meet the captain in charge of my son's arrest. His office had the touch of modernity. On the mahogany desk was a framed photograph of a boy.

'You Ibok people think you own this country, eh?' the officer asked in an unmistakable northern accent. 'You enjoy playing games with people's lives. You want to turn Ibok into a war zone, eh?'

I said nothing to the soldier. I just watched his eyes. I heard him say something about the oil in Ibok belonging to the Federal Government of Nigeria.

'When will that sink into your silly heads?' he barked. 'The oil companies have the full backing of the government to operate in that region and the military will deal with anybody or any group that tries to terrorize the oil workers. This Niger Delta belongs to us all. Do you hear me?'

'Please let my son go,' I begged.

The soldier laughed. It was a most startling sound, like the spurt from an exhaust pipe.

'Why should I let your son go?' he asked. 'He is a member of the Ibok Youth Movement, isn't he? He is a terrorist. He must be sent to jail.'

'He is my only child, please. His father died while he was still young. He –'

'You should have taught him to hate terrorism! You should have taught him to obey the laws of the land.'

Then he picked up the picture from his desk and turned it towards me. 'That's my son,' he revealed. 'I teach him to obey me. I teach him to respect the law. He is my son so he obeys me.'

I studied the picture. It was his son all right; the resemblance was there. He must have been Nsima's age. I felt a pang of jealousy and rage. That boy had a father and a good life. What did my son have? I took my eyes away from the picture.

'Please let my son go,' I begged again.

I stared at the soldier. He stared back at me. Neither of us said anything for several seconds. Then he smiled the strangest smile I have ever seen, vindictive and mocking. He reached out a hairy hand and touched my chin.

'You are a very beautiful woman,' he whispered. 'I like beautiful women. You and I can play a harmless game and your son will be released this afternoon.'

I thought of my son in the torture room. I imagined the screams that escaped from his lips. I thought of my late husband, the last man who touched me, seven years ago. I thought of the terror in Ibok, in Nigeria. And then I sighed.

The soldier didn't move from his seat. He only smiled his mocking smile and patted the table.

'Don't be so bitter, my beautiful lady,' he said. 'The key to your son's release is in your hands. This little game of ours won't take very long.'

I gave in.

The man was surprisingly gentle and it was over in five minutes. He gave me some money, too.

'I am not a bad man,' he said. 'I swear to God. Had it been some other soldier, *kai*, your son would have been dead. But me, I don't kill. Your son will be released shortly.'

On our journey back home, Nsima didn't say a word to me. The bus was filled with traders and students. I sat beside a young mother whose breath stank of rotten egg. Though I tried to steer my face away from her, she always managed to move closer and comment on the recent hike in transportation costs. I was pleased when she alighted at the next junction and a student promptly took over her seat. I scanned the young man's face and wondered if he, too, was a member of some militant group; if he, too, had seen the insides of a prison.

'Praise the Lord!' someone suddenly screamed. 'Praise the Lord!'

For the remainder of the journey, we were forced to listen to the sermon of an itinerant preacher. The man spoke about the end times, about the second coming of Christ. His message was punctuated by cries of 'Amen', 'It is well' and 'Jesus'.

'My brothers and sisters,' the preacher cried, 'we live in evil times. A time of lawlessness, when a man's life is so easily wasted in some trivial encounter over a worthless matter. But that is bad news. The good news is that we are the children of the Most High God and we will be protected from all evil. Can I hear an amen?'

'Amen!'

At home, news of my son's release had spread before we'd even alighted from the bus. Many mothers rushed to rejoice with me. Some came with great words. Others came to sing.

'Our God is alive,' my cousin said. 'I knew that your son would be released. I saw it in a vision. The good Lord revealed this to me.'

She ate all the rice that I offered her. I wanted to ask her if the good Lord had shown her that there would be plenty of food to eat. When the last of our guests had left, my son decided to talk.

'They beat me, Mama,' he said. 'The soldiers beat me so hard I could not cry.'

'Oh, my poor boy! My poor son!'

He showed me the wounds. They were patterned like the mould that spread across my bathroom walls. I cried as I bathed them and rubbed his back with Power Man, an ointment that my cousin had given me. The balm could cure anything from rashes to eczema. Afterwards, I held my son. He fitted in my arms. The shock of holding him made me feel as if my arms had been empty since he'd been away.

'God punish them,' I cursed as I massaged my son's youthful shoulders. 'God block their arses with clogged blood.'

I settled back into my business. The god of prosperity smiled upon me. I stocked up my stall with new goods. I even bought a new refrigerator, as I was tired of customers complaining about my 'hot' drinks. I put the old one up for sale. The first person who priced it was a retired court messenger. He offered to pay a paltry ten naira.

'Get out of my shop!' I yelled at him. 'It is your mother's fridge that you will buy for ten naira. Thief! If they sent you, go and tell them that you did not find me.' I immediately swept away his footsteps with a fresh broom.

The fridge was eventually bought by Koko, who taught physics at the community school. He thought the item would be an excellent piece of apparatus for his poorly equipped laboratory.

Then, two weeks after my son's arrest, people began talking. I heard it first through my cousin.

'They are saying that you paid the army one hundred thousand naira for your son's release,' she said.

When the rumour did not die, the Ibok Women Progressive Association held an emergency meeting. I was summoned before the executives.

'We have been hearing a lot of stories,' our leader said. 'It worries me, the way these things are being passed from mouth to mouth.'

I stared at her head tie. I could never get mine to look like hers. I did not have the skills and the patience to do it.

'You know, we all love you very much here,' our leader continued. 'It is my wish to believe that the rumour is untrue, that what they are saying is complete nonsense. But –'

'It makes sense to me,' the deputy leader cut in. 'Ten youths were arrested that night. It is only your son who has been released. Why is this so?'

I watched the treasurer rummage through her books.

'I have the records of all the payments that you have made to the union,' the woman said. 'If you paid one hundred thousand to secure your son's release, then you have been lying to us about your finances. You have been cheating the union. Mama Nsima, you did not contribute towards the building project. If I remember clearly, you paid nothing, too, towards our gala night.'

The leader crossed her legs. 'This is your chance to defend yourself. What have you got to say?'

It's been six months since I left Ibok. Six months since I insulted the executives of the union and fled. Six months since I settled in Calabar. Now I live next door to a church – SALVATION IS AVAILABLE MINISTRIES. The presiding bishop calls himself the Mighty Man of Valour. I know, from the way some of the church members are looking at me, that it will not be long before they come over to my doorstep to invite me to their weekly vigil.

Table Rock Lake
David Savill

Back from second tour you finished building the cabin. Just out of Pittsburgh, you said. So I flew from Arkansas Northwest Regional to the City of Bridges and found you two hundred miles across the map. Hired a teeny new Ford compact with a teeny new engine. Would have hired an Explorer if I knew how far. Hell, would have hired a freaking RV. Just out of Pittsburgh turns into just out of Punxsutawney turns into just out of Clearfield and the road never stops climbing and when night falls the hills are darker than the sky. Come midnight on Route 80? I'm still passing rigs in a convoy must be sixty strong, a long chain of lights like a landing strip and only the air beating between trailers to keep a man awake. Then the road you off has no electric. Road turns into tyre-tracks of damp autumn leaves. Tyre-tracks turn into creek where I call you from a cell and say, 'I knew you was country, boy, but this is *real* country, they still hanging niggers round here?' And you say, 'Question is, how far is Abel Jones prepared to go for a short-ass redneck?'
   Plenty far, Kyle Karilcek, plenty far.
   Your first kiss is all Big Red gum, then right out we make love on the bearskin rug. One of those things every man should do in his life. Make love to a hot white boy on a bearskin rug in a maple log cabin, smell of sawdust

and wood polish. In those days, you still had the army buzz-cut. Muscles in your back ripple like milk and I'm holding onto the teeth of the bear. Then the petrol generator starts to die as I'm getting to it. The lights flickering fast until the electric is gone and the blue moon filling the cabin like a movie theatre and you looking every inch like Tom Cruise.

'Gotta fill the tank,' you said.

Already did, scout. Already did.

The cabin. There was a place worth driving to. Journey worth taking the time for. Two years now. Two years since the cabin and four weeks since I heard from you and here I am in Florida trying to find out what happened.

Mom said one time how Florida may be south but it ain't southern. She's right about that. Remember when we had no money to speak of? When me and you was all about the Papa John's chicken strips and *CSI Miami* on Friday nights? Well, true enough, Miami's a place feels full of murder. Place fit to make a man act guilty even though he ain't. Heat like a blanket everybody hiding under. Outside the airport heat so strong I gotta shake the air conditioning off my back.

Shake off the southern boy, too, because Miami is full of wetbacks from Havana in hundred-dollar suits driving Escalades with chrome spinners and here's Abel Jones from Arkansas trying to find Budget. Top of the car park must be six hundred vehicles shining like a solar panel on a barn roof but *can't satisfy your order* the kid from Budget says. They all out of the cheap rent Chevrolet compact. *All out of everything except this V12 Dodge Viper.*

V12 Dodge Viper in red.

'Well, ain't that a shame? I hear you say free upgrade, boy?'

*

Let me say it, Kyle. We should have had one of these. Holy Mother of God Bless You Jesus for I Have Surely Sinned, low down, cockpit wrapped in a whole prairie of leather. The freeway is up before I know it and Miami just a wrong way glint in the rearview. Signs overhead saying no place I know. Don't know the sea from the swamps. Don't know Miami from dick.

In the glove box there's a plastic map of Florida and the place called Vero Pines where the newspaper said the colonel lives – about a hundred and fifty miles too far for my liking. Flat, dumb, skinny state of snowbirds and Spaniards gave America to Dubya. I know we agreed never to talk about politics, Kyle, but here's where you are plain wrong, dog: look down from space and Florida's just one big John Thomas pissing all over Cuba. Cheap real estate signs on Route 95 following me all the way to midnight in Vero Pines where there ain't nothing but a cop car going slow over the rail tracks making *sure* I know they checked the black man driving a V12 Dodge. Making sure I know my place round here before they turn into tail lights and slip back into the swamps.

And Vero Pines? Vero Pines is just a closed garage and one solitary 7-Eleven. Not the kind of place I see your colonel rooting down.

I pick up a box of Pepperidge Cheddar Goldfish, Premium Saltines, four case of Sam Adams, jar of Strawberry Fluff, Colgate Regular, carton of Parliament Ultras and tub of Advil. No one around here neither. Nothing but the growl of Harley engines and Quincy Jones brass running up and down the aisles. Over the counter, TV shows an old episode of *Chips* and the white kid says *sixteen dollars ninety-seven*, without taking his eyes off a beat.

I hand him a twenty, tell him keep the change but even then the dumb-ass don't know where Sunleaf Park is at.

'Sunleaf Park?' kid says.

'Gated community,' say I.

'Round here's all gated, dude.'

'Big one, lotsa money.'

'Round here's Indian River Shores, dude. Everyone's money round here.'

Kid with a mouth don't close and a yellow zit in the hairs of his upper lip and blue-grey eyes. Blue-grey eyes like stones. Like hopelessness. Like the kids from high school pay me to produce their hopeless bands. Pay me to spit and polish their dreams.

Then he looks at the phone in my hand and says, *Got the net on your cell? Y'all could look it up.*

And guess what? The dumb kid's right. But past midnight's too late. I think of you and what you would do and I know for sure you don't want me disturbing nobody at night. So I park up beneath a banyan tree and dip a Saltine cracker into the Fluff. Suck it down past the bad wisdom tooth then chew on a couple of Advil. No wisdom in a tooth like that and I'm laughing or crying, Kyle, I couldn't tell you which. Laughing or crying as the man on the radio tells how these are the end of days. How Bush is leading us into the final battle and the Lord did say what the Lord did say. And maybe it could feel like the end of the world here in this black, croaking swamp thinking I will never hold you again, but I have to believe it's only the beginning. Have to seek refuge in some hick station called Eagle Rock playing 'Look Out Cleveland' by the Band. Kind of white boy music got soul. Live production still. Live production that reminds me of a time before I met you. Before you ever moved into town, dark eyes and a past.

Back in Fayetteville, Mom's congregation had a white boy band play with the gospel choir. Old boys kick out the Doobie Brothers when people taking their leave. Me?

I'd stay just to watch the drummer. Drummer the bass player's son. Handsome boy pumping the skins and biting his lip over the crack of the snare, focused on something I couldn't see. That was all I knew of love before you. Nice little white boy two grades above me played pitcher in the high-school team. Though now I think about it, wasn't the boy I loved so much as what his eyes could see and I could not.

And I fall asleep in those eyes still, radio on and the leather cabin of the Viper smelling like a baseball mitt.

'Put the handle into your shoulder,' you said.

'This what they teach up at Fort Riley?'

'Recoil on that son of bitch'll knock your face off.'

'I do believe you care, honey. Say – are you my best boy scout?'

'Shut up and shoot, you old nigger.'

I look at you, grinning your wide Polish grin. And I want to kiss you like the first time we kissed, do it all over again.

'You know I voted gun control, Kyle, this here is against my religion.'

'And I paid my subs to the NRA already. Now shoot.'

When I aim the gun at a tree, the tree takes on some personality. So I try and shoot nothing, but the wood ain't nothing but trees. The shot canons through like a movie shot. Birds breaking out of the branches, the whole deal. Pulls my shoulder like a bitch too. I never told you that.

Never told you how frightened I was that first time up at the cabin. New state more like a new country to me and no doctors in nowheresville Pennsylvania. Last place I passed ten miles back and even that an empty rocking chair of a place with plastic-sheet windows, old '62 Chevrolet flatbed on bricks, logs under tarpaulin. Next to this, our cabin is shiny new. No ending this place, but a new beginning for us. All hooked up inside with a flat-screen TV, washing machine, dryer, Jacuzzi. Everything you said a pretty boy like me would ever need. When I asked you where the money came from you said family.

'Family money,' you said.

Think on that, Kyle – *family money*.

Three years together and even then you never told how the money was made out of insurance. How your dad blew his own head off on Table Rock Lake.

Here's the luck of it. Finding a person these days is easy. On my cell, bring up Sunleaf Park courtesy of Google maps. Then wait at the gates for this Prius to come out and open sesame.

'Excuse me, sir. Know where Colonel de Andre's residence might be?'

And the cute old kids with their golf clubs tell me straight off the bat. Number 5011, just past the lake with the fibreglass storks and round on over the humpbacked bridge is where. Chalk driveway snaking through candy green grass to a big place of battleship grey. Big double garage where luck has surely found your colonel because every tree in the neighbourhood was taken by the last hurricane that strolled through. All except the colonel's poplar, which makes me think of 'Strange Fruit' and how the roots of southern trees go everywhere and deep.

Then, chewing on a couple of breakfast Advil and eyes watering, I swim to the colonel's door. When I knock can't even feel the wood against my knuckles.

'Can I help you?'

And here he is. Your colonel. Man don't expect a colonel talk so soft. Don't expect a colonel to be a short-ass brother. Brother in a salmon pink polo shirt and knee-length shorts. Brother looks like a Tiger Woods doll. Man like an Obama key ring.

Not the man you told me about.

'Yes, sir, I do hope so. I'm a friend of Kyle Karilcek's.'

'Sergeant Karilcek?'

'Yes, sir.'

The colonel breathes in through his nose and keeps the air in his chest like he's deciding what to do with it.

'That your vehicle cross the road?'

'Yes, sir.'

He runs them brown eyes over the big red fuck-you of it all.

'Got any ID?'

I show the colonel my driver's permit.

'I'm sorry,' the colonel says and shuts the door.

Sorry for what? I knock again. Sorry because he won't let me in? Sorry because he don't who I am? I rap my questions on the door but no one is listening. And what if I wasn't a friend? What if I was a wife? A husband? What if the name on my driver's licence had meant something?

What then?

I walk back down the drive, turning on the pavement to look at the colonel's house. No side passage to speak of. White picket fences meeting the walls. But this is the end of the estate and over the shingle roof don't look like there's nothing but swamp and trees. So I drive round on the toy town road, prowling, feeling just like the nigger those cops were looking at in Vero Pines. And, sure enough, there's an unfinished road leading into the swamp, the concrete foundations of a newbuild on one side, but nobody around and an overgrown plot of land for sale.

The tangleweed here is up to my waist, so thick I can't see where I'm putting my feet. Dragonflies jump ahead of me hoping I'll give up; dragonflies too lazy in the heat to jump anything but one flower at a time. They make me think of dolphins skipping the prow of a boat and it's like I'm dreaming, the back porch of the colonel's place listing. Veranda and patio and kidney of perfect green grass cut out of the chaos. But I keep going forward, breaking through the weed like I'm wading water for land. Just as I think I'm going to cut free something cold grabs my foot and pulls me head first.

'I'm fixing a shake,' the colonel hollers from the kitchen. 'Good and chilled. Bananas, wheatgrass, splash of apple juice, tomato juice, carrots. My own recipe. You want one?'

I can swim all right. But the water in the break channel at the end of the colonel's lawn is black with warm mud. So when the colonel comes out on the veranda with his golf bag I'm already there for some fifteen minutes of burning sun. Standing waist deep, unable to move, like a scarecrow in the floods.

'Shake sounds fine,' I say, folding the colonel's pink towel best I can, though everywhere is covered in the mud like a volcano exploded. I brush it off a hand-stitched cushion that says, *A Home is a Heart and a Heart is a Home.* Cushions all over this room like the dolls on a girl's bed. The colonel has a carpet of deep purple shagpile and air conditioning. Feels like walking on a cold moon after the heat outside. Open-plan lounge like a show home. Everything big and comfortable. You know how I don't sit right on couches? Well, the colonel's eats me up. There's a marble fireplace where my trainers dry. On the mantel, pictures of the colonel's two kids clutching graduation scrolls. Picture of his wife looking like she owns it all and damn proud she is too. I guess the colonel must have put himself away somewhere. A man's room where he can be a man.

'You play golf?' Colonel shouts over the blender.

'They're building a golf course in Springdale.'

'Springdale?'

'Outside of Fayetteville, Arkansas.'

'That where you met Sergeant Karilcek?'

And I'm trying to think on what you said to me, Kyle. What you said about the colonel first time you came back from interrogation school in Arizona. Came back talking like the man was King, Marvin Gaye and Jay-Z rolled into one. *You can't lie to the man*, you said, *and you don't know when he's lying.*

'Yup. Building a golf course,' I say. 'A public swimming pool, too. Building everything now there's North West Regional. Arkansas is the fastest-growing state. So they say.'

Colonel gives me a glass of something brown and I'm looking at the sport socks pulled high to his knees like a boy and thinking, *you* ever notice how the man has a damn fine pair of calves?

Then he points the remote at a TV so big I hadn't even seen it.

'I'm going to TiVo the game,' he says. 'Then we can talk outside.'

You were better at keeping our secret in company. Me? Sometimes I had the urge just to take off all my clothes like some antsy kid at Sunday service. To hold your hand across the table in the school canteen. To put my arm around you on the second-floor porch at Big D's that time some college kid shut the doors and the party throbbed like blood in my ears. And, yeah, I wanted to kiss you at my uncle's funeral right there over the open coffin and the body powdery black like a dusted cough candy. Right there in front of all those people who thought they knew me.

'Speak!' you whispered in my ear at parties, harsh sometimes. 'Where's your goddamn tongue?'

But when I got moon-eyed like that my power of speech was gone.

You? You didn't play it that way. I knew the punch of your fist in my shoulder as well as I knew your kisses. In school, on the street, round my home, you were somebody else. In five years I never saw your own mother, not even the inside of your own home. Out on the playing field you'd take me down just like any other player.

What use is a black man six foot five can't play sports? Can't run with a football, can't shoot a hoop?

Being mean in public was sweet nothings to you. You said that at heart Abel Jones was a fat, confederate white boy.

The colonel hits a golf ball and I hear it twice. The hit, then cracking in the trees. When I look down from the blinding sky the earth tips up, like the swamp will swallow everything.

'Here, tee up. Have a shot,' he says.

Then, I kid you not, Kyle, Colonel de Andre of the 5th Battalion Fort Huachuca – the colonel whose face I've seen in the *Herald* and looking grey as death on Fox – is standing behind me, hands on my hips, telling me how to swing.

I watch the ball scamper eagerly over the sleek lawns and plop in the black water.

'Shame about Sergeant Karilcek,' he says. 'Have you spoke with him? Since the court martial?'

'Well I –' Funny how when you're after the truth seems like a good time to lie. But then I can't lie, Kyle. Not about that. 'No, sir. Kyle has refused my calls.'

The colonel taps the toe of his trainers with the club. Like he's seeing how tough they are.

'I believe you are from Fayetteville, Mr Jones. I believe

you know Sergeant Karilcek. What I don't know – is what I can do for *you*.'

'You can tell me what happened,' I ask, straight up just like I know you'd want me to. The colonel swings and this time he clears the trees and the swamp and though we listen there is no sound.

'You know about the conditions of a military tribunal I am sure,' the colonel says. 'No press, no talking. If you didn't know that you wouldn't be here. I also appreciate how far you have come, Mr Jones. But I am not at liberty to discuss Sergeant Karilcek's case.'

They always talk that shit about liberty. At Fort Riley. The attorney's office. *Not at liberty to talk.* Only people have liberty are the press to tell lies over what Kyle Karilcek did.

'Sergeant Karilcek's *case*,' Colonel says again, looking after the ball weary, like it's up there in the sky just waiting to be whistled back down. 'Well, his *case* maybe not but I can tell you something. Sergeant Karilcek was an excellent non-com officer, Mr Jones. One of my boys. I protect my boys out there and I protect them back here. Even retired.'

The colonel turns a fresh ball in his fingers and I remember you saying how the best way to get information is to keep it shut. Just keep your mouth shut and make room with listening.

'There was a man, Mr Jones. Non-combatant Iraqi man worked in the Burger King in the Green Zone. Muslim not worried about handling meat that isn't halal, not a dangerous man you might suppose? Well, it was my mistake to suppose.'

'Suppose what?'

'I guess Sergeant Karilcek might have told you something about hearts and minds. Going out every week to try and win them? Going out every week to meet with muftis, imams, local businessmen? Hell. Anyone who would meet with us and that's not too many.'

Hearts and minds? Closest I ever came to Iraq was waking in the cabin surrounded by all the dark Pennsylvanian forest, you moaning into your knees.

'Mr Burger King set up such a meeting for us,' Colonel says. 'Told us how his village elders wanted to talk. And all went dandy until on the way home an RPG took out my lead vehicle. Took out a boy from Tennessee, two from Kentucky, one from West Virginia. *My* boys . . . well, the game was up for Burger King. Man like that we arrest and interrogate. Not pretty, Mr Jones, but there it is. He knew all right. But he wouldn't talk. None of them ever talked. So, here's *my* story. Not Sergeant Karilcek's. Mine. Story of a man with twenty-two years' experience as an interrogator. Story of a colonel soon to be Battalion Commander. I take that man, Mr Jones, man with a wife and kids for all I know. I half drown him in a barrel and when he's taking his last but one breath I put a gun to his head and fire a blank across his ear. Man died of shock. As I'm sure you've read in the *Herald*, Mr Jones. What I'm telling you ain't news.'

'Seen it on the web, sir.'

'So you also *seen* I handed in my stripes.'

The colonel dispatches another ball, short into the trees this time, then leans on the handle of his club like an old man with a stick.

'My point is this. You take a boy like Kyle. And no offence, Mr Jones, but a boy without much schooling? You give him six weeks' training at Fort Riley then put him in a jail full of men he believes are killing his friends. You ask him to pick up body bags so full of bits you *can't* pick 'em up. Then ask him to go babysit the suspects some more? Kyle sitting there every day weighing up how much a jailed man is worth? Worth for a boy from

David Savill

Kentucky, boy from West Virginia, boy from Arkansas, Mr Jones? What would you do?'

Kyle he said. Not Sergeant Karilcek. So I knew for sure it was you sitting there in the jail watching those men.

You were the new boy in school. We skipped class together. Hooked up in Rogers where there still ain't nothing but a crossroads, one train a day and a federal bank. I remember the old Camry smelled all sickly sweet of the Marshmallow Fluff I spilled on the back seats. We took off up Prairie Creek all the way to Beaver Shores, found somewhere quiet on the edge of the lake where we could hear leaves falling in the dark. Somewhere two boys from a school in the south were allowed to be. We were no more than seventeen and I loved you weren't from round these parts. Loved the smell of elsewhere in your clothes and wanted a part of it. But boy you don't talk about family. You don't talk about friends.

When you said, *Dad's gone*, I took it for what it meant round Fayetteville. Took it that Dad got up and quit.

Five years those leaves were falling in the dark. Five autumns and we were out fishing on Table Rock Lake again, talking about getting to the cabin, back to back, lines doing sweet nothing in the water. You were off the third tour of duty and I was still horny for every ripped muscle. Felt your voice sounding in your chest.

'Always wondered what happened to Pa's boat,' you said.

'Your pa took his boat?'

'*Someone* took the boat . . .' you said.

'Boat got stolen?'

'No. Cops took the boat maybe. Courthouse or some-one took it.'

Then you spat in the water and I wondered had I ever seen you spit before. Even then you couldn't tell it

42

straight. Pretended I must have known. I couldn't understand how you said nothing and you couldn't understand what there was to understand.

Afterwards we docked under the trees, walked up your land and I asked one last time if I could meet your mother. You didn't deign respond. Silence could mean no. Silence could mean yes. Had to love Kyle Karilcek to know what was what. Had to be the kind of man who followed Kyle Karilcek to Pennsylvania and lay around in his cabin all day. Lay around naked counting up the cuts and bruises on a soldier boy's body. The welts on hands and swollen fingers – from boxing with the boys you said, and I never questioned it. Because I must have learned to love silence, Kyle. To love the kind of silence *you* made. And I must have stopped wondering what stories those bruises told.

'Harleys all the way,' the colonel says and pushes the bike out of the garage where chrome takes fire in the sun. 'Pleasure of my life.'

Now I see the man's garage is just full of boxes. Full of boxes of clothes, books, films, computer shit. Exercise bike in bubble wrap. All the colonel's things. And for the first time I get it.

'Ride whenever I can,' he says, putting on the helmet. Then he sees where I'm looking at the boxes in the garage and says, 'Be riding a helluva lot more pretty soon.'

The colonel is going to lead me up to 95.

'Kind of you, sir,' I say without hearing.

Kind of you, I say and convoy behind the man without thinking. He looks even smaller top of the Harley, your little Obama key ring. Shirt filling like a flag and knees up either side like a boy riding a chopper. The Dodge is hungry to go but I have to admit I am glad of someone to follow. Glad to be on the end of someone's rope.

Across the railroad track the colonel signals and waves for me to pull over into the car park of the 7-Eleven. When I stop, he gets off the bike, crunches over the forecourt in his boots and leans over the roof until I let the window down. Then the colonel looks at me, just eyes in the helmet.

'Meant to mention it. Kyle did talk about you, Abel. That's how I know you are who you say you are. Kyle talked of you fondly. Talked of you a lot. And that's a matter of fact.' Then he taps the roof of the car, crunches back to the bike, kicks her up and is gone in the dust.

After a while of watching the road I feel the rope break and it's just me in Vero Pines. A crossroads and a stop light and a railroad like Rogers but nothing left tying me to someone who knows you and knows what you did and loves you still.

I watch the kid at the 7-Eleven take out the trash, kid with blue-grey eyes like hopelessness, like stones. I watch him and try to imagine you talking about me. Try to imagine what you would have said about the man who loved you ever since you were a kid from someplace else. Try to imagine what might have happened if I made you talk.

Six of the Best
Iain Grant

There are four calls on the scrap of paper.

The first call is easy: two Housing Association potheads in Balsall Heath. I explain the situation, take their benefit books and tell them Mr McIlwraith will give them what's left over after he's taken his cut.

Second call: Lefsay Barbers on the Stratford Road. The man's got fuck all in his shop worth repossessing. A sink, a mirror, one pair of scissors and some clippers. We get nowhere until I spot the can of disinfectant in the corner. Seventy quid in notes and coins appears by magic. As I leave he screams, ethanol tears in his eyes, that what I do is *haram* and moneylenders like me will burn in hell. I tell him he should have thought about that before borrowing off Mr McIlwraith.

Third call and not yet lunchtime: some chav family in Druids Heath, the very tower block from which that brainless boy threw a ginger tom four times in a row. How desperately sodding dull must your life be to throw a cat off the roof, take the piss-filled lift down to the ground, pick it up, go back up in the lift and repeat the process three more times? Kharlo. That was the cat's name.

The chav-dad goes through the classic stages: denial ('Ain't us, mate, we just moved in'); anger ('Listen, mate,

I'll fucking deck ya if you don't piss off'); depression ('You don't know what it's like, mate'); and bargaining ('Mate, I can give you fifty if you can wait till Tuesday'). I tell him I'm not his mate and walk out with the Nintendo Wii, which is already wrapped up for Christmas.

Fourth and final call: a backstreet terrace in Moseley, a narrow house towering over brutally trimmed box hedging. An old woman in a tightly buttoned cardigan answers the door.

'Mr Pendleton?' I say.

'Do I look like I would be Mr Pendleton?' she says, looking down her nose at me. She's a tall old bird.

There's something familiar about her severe, high-cheekboned face. I reckon she was quite a stunner in her youth.

'Is he in?' I say.

'Who?'

'Mr Pendleton.'

'There's no Mr Pendleton here.'

'Yeah, right,' I say in blunt disbelief. 'However, it says here that Mr Pendleton of –'

I look at my scrap of paper. I'd read the address as 51 Grange Road but, looking again, I think that five could be a lazily unfinished eight.

'You'd better not be lying to me. I'll be back if you are.'

As I turn to go, she says my name.

'What?' I say.

'You're Laszlo Bellaby,' she says.

I frown at her but when I see the chunky amber necklace under her cardigan I realize who she is. Her red hair may have turned almost completely white but I can see the old poise, the self-assurance in her stance.

'Miss Swan,' I say and am suddenly awash with old fears.

She snorts and shuts the door.

*

Back at the flat, I tell Chantelle. Chantelle's on her hands and knees, scratting around for something under the bed.

'So she was your old teacher?' she says. 'Have you seen the pink pull-along anywhere?'

I throw myself on the bed, beer in one hand, and place the day's takings on the windowsill. Chantelle sighs as the bed springs creak.

'She never taught me,' I say, 'but she was one of the heavy hitters at St Paul's. God, she was a nasty piece of work. You borrowed the pink case to your sister.'

'Tits,' says Chantelle with feeling and comes out from under the bed with a big shapeless canvas bag.

'She gave me the cane,' I say, remembering it for the first time in years. 'Well, six of the best with a wooden ruler.'

'Caned? Bloody hell, Laz. How old are you?'

Chantelle is twenty; chock-full of Melanotan injections and the stupidity of youth. I slap her arse as she turns to go out the door with the bag and I make a decision.

I ring the doorbell. I don't step back. I put on my collector's face and prepare my accusations.

Miss Swan answers, a pair of black-handled scissors held lightly in her hand.

'He's still not here.'

I mentally stumble. 'Who?'

'Mr Pendleton.'

I shake my head. 'I'm not interested in Mr Pendleton,' I begin.

'You were yesterday.'

'But not today. Do you remember me, Miss Swan? Remember me well?'

'Absolutely. But don't take it as a compliment. I just have an excellent memory.' Her gaze meets mine. 'Yes, even now.'

'You hit me.' I load those three words with well-practised menace.

Her eyes look to one side for a moment and then she smiles at the memory. 'Oh, yes.' She looks me up and down. 'Someone told me you were in prison.'

'I was. Three-month sentence.' That was five years ago. Ancient history to me. Maybe not to her.

'So?' she says with a shrug, the scissors rocking in her grip.

'So, I'm not happy about it,' I say, a little louder.

She laughs at that and then shrugs again. Her ugly amber beads rattle. 'Maybe you ought to come in.'

I stand awkwardly in her living room as she makes tea in the back kitchen.

'I've been retired ten years now,' she calls out as though that explains everything.

I survey the room with the automatic eye of the illegal debt collector. Portable television, colour: twenty pounds. Three Lladro figurines on the mantelpiece, one chipped: two hundred pounds. IKEA coffee table: five pounds. Three framed art prints, two Gainsboroughs and a Constable: ten pounds the lot. Sofa, somewhat old, with embroidered arabesque: ninety pounds. High-backed armchair (her favourite seat, I can tell): fifty pounds. I wonder if there is any silver or crystalware in the sideboard. Possibly.

There's a two-foot-high stack of catalogues down the side of the armchair. Argos, Littlewoods, Grattan, even Woolies. They're the only books in the room. The topmost catalogue is open to a page of garden toys. On it rests the black-handled scissors and a number of images that Miss Swan has snipped from the catalogue: a boy on a swing, two children in swimming costumes running round a sprinkler, a playhouse with a cheeky face peering out of one window.

'It's been fourteen years since I last saw you, by my reckoning,' she says, emerging with a teacup in each hand.

I take one.

'Sit,' she says. 'Sit there.'

She slips into the armchair and slurps her drink. I perch uneasily on the edge of the sofa.

'You told the careers adviser you wanted to be a mechanic,' she says.

I say nothing.

'But you're not. What are you?'

'I'm a debt collector.'

'Like a bailiff?'

I flex my fingers and make a fist with my free hand.

'Not like a bailiff,' she says brightly and smiles. Her ancient teeth are small, receding things, almost sharpened to points, like the teeth of a gin trap. 'You're a loan shark.'

'No. My boss is a loan shark. I'm the collector.' I make a point of gazing round the room. 'I take what I want to settle old debts.'

'Then it's a good job I don't owe you anything.'

I open my mouth to speak, but she's there first.

'In fact, you've probably never stopped to think of the debt of thanks you owe your teachers.'

'Thanks? Thanks?'

'Mmm. For us teachers, it's our job to care, but I know I always wanted the best for you.'

I frown. She's senile. She doesn't remember me properly at all.

'You hit me with the ruler!' I say, looking at her narrow wrists and wondering how they could have wielded such pain. 'On at least seven occasions. Physical punishment.'

'What for?' she asks, though she clearly already knows.

I shake my head. 'That's not care. You didn't like me.'

'No,' she admits. 'I didn't like you. I had *sympathy* for you. I knew about your dad, for one. How is your father, by the way?'

'Dead.'

'And how do you feel about that?'

'I don't,' I say firmly.

'Good. There are two kinds of teacher, you know. The first kind do it because they care for the future of young people. The second kind do it for the money. The first kind usually – *usually* – turn into the second kind before the end. The second kind quickly discover there's no money in teaching. Now, your job: constant surprises, a spot of danger, mingling with the scum of the earth . . .'

'We're a pretty nasty bunch,' I say.

'Not you!' Miss Swan tuts. 'I mean the fools who borrow from you. Anyone stupid enough to enter such Faustian pacts deserves to lose their money!'

I don't know what Faustian means, but I didn't expect her to approve of my chosen profession.

'And what do you do when people won't pay up?' she asks.

'You don't need to know,' I say.

'I do. I do, Laszlo Bellaby.'

'Well, it's about choosing the right tools for the job,' I say. 'An intimidating silence is often enough. The false threat of court action works wonders. Repossession of obviously sentimental items works even better.'

'But you do hurt people,' she says. It's not a question. Nor a bald statement. It's an expression of desire.

'I have hurt people,' I concede.

'Tell me.'

'I don't think I ought to.'

I have no idea what I ought to be doing right now. Where are the accusations I had lined up in my mind? This is not the direction I imagined our encounter taking.

She huffs and sits back in her chair. 'You think your bully-boy antics are too shocking for old ladies? You think my frail heart will give out.'

'No . . .'

'No. I'm an old bird. Gristle and sinew. I can take it, so tell me.'

She's in control of the situation and I can't work out how. It's as though the last fourteen years haven't happened.

I give her the basics: the kind of people my employer lends to and how we extract the payments. I tell her about the weak and vulnerable and how I turn the strong and secure into the weak and vulnerable. I expect her to be fearful, disgusted, condemning, but, no, she listens intently, rapt, as though my account is a fascinating radio play she's happened to tune in to.

'Remarkable,' she murmurs when I'm done.

Something has passed between us and I'm not sure I like it.

It's dark now. She gets up and turns on the lamp behind her chair.

'I've enjoyed your company,' she says.

'You have?'

'You may come again and we'll talk some more.'

'I . . .'

'Next Sunday. Three o'clock sharp,' she says and then adds, 'I'll lay on a little tea if you like.' She coughs uncomfortably. 'Now run along.'

She might as well be sending me back to class.

*

Chantelle has gone when I get home. Chantelle, with her endless prattle and as much stuff as she could get into a shapeless canvas bag.

Gone.

Something has passed out of my life and I'm not sure I like it.

I go back the following Sunday at three o'clock sharp.

Miss Swan has made a plate of fish-paste sandwiches and a pot of tea and has lit the gas fire in anticipation of my arrival.

On the coffee table in the living room is an open scrapbook, a Pritt Stick and a mammoth pile of catalogue snippets. Is she compiling her own catalogue digest, the ultimate catalogue? Is she composing a story created from cut-out images; a tale of husbands and wives in cheap, casual clothing, of happy children with too many toys?

'I didn't think you'd come,' she says.

I shrug.

'Why are you here?' she asks.

I look around the room, seeking inspiration from the nicotine-yellow anaglypta, from the eyes of Gainsborough's *Blue Boy*. 'I don't think you understood.'

'Understood what?'

'Understood why I came back here last time.'

'You had something to say to me then?'

I want to say it. I am big and you are small. I am muscle and an iron will bereft of mercy. Once upon a time I lived in fear of you, but now I am the monster and you can be nothing but the victim, you dried-up bag of old bones. I want to say it. But the words do not emerge. Her eyes, those sharp predator's eyes, hold me in check.

Her cup tinks against its saucer as she rests it in her lap.

'I know why you're here.'

'Really?'

'You've come to confess.'

'Fuck that,' I say and, for the first time in fifteen years or more, I feel a childish thrill at uttering a swear word.

'Or to boast,' she suggests.

'Why would I do that?'

'Because you're a naughty man. And you know it.'

Naughty. Naughty. What a word.

'I'm not naughty, Miss Swan. I am a fucking evil bastard. I do deeds that you couldn't comprehend. They'd stain your soul just to hear them.'

'Really?'

I look at her, the red gaslight glinting off her spectacles. This is what she wants: the horrors.

She's baiting me now. I know it, but rise to her challenge nonetheless.

I give her a horror. I tell her the story of the Briscoe brothers who had reneged on a debt. I tell her how I gave one a jar of pickled chillies and the other a thorough beating and how the beating only ended when the jar was empty. I wring every last detail from it – the vomit, the broken bones, the burst duodenal ulcer, the stitches – and I don't stop until Miss Swan is moaning softly and her teacup is rattling in its saucer.

Eventually she gathers herself and sets her cup down on the hearth with shaking hands. She's breathing heavily now, her amber necklace rising and falling atop her bosom.

I wonder if I've overdone it. 'Are you all right?' I ask.

'Yes,' she replies, her body still quivering with excitement. 'Thank you.'

Her cheeks are flushed with colour. I saw them like that years before, when she was standing over me, ruler in hand.

My gaze drops to the scrapbook and the stolen images.

Snippets of other lives, unreal stories of a suburban idyll pressed between pages that smell of cheap glue.

I stand up.

'I'm sorry, Miss Swan. I shouldn't have come. This is wrong.'

She stands, too, and puts her hand on my wrist. 'You may come again and we'll talk some more.'

'I don't think that's a good idea.'

Her long fingers clutching my wrist are like twigs, wrapped in sagging, liver-spotted, ghost-white skin.

I look around and see for the first time what my debt collector's eyes had failed to notice before. There are no personal photographs in this living room. On the wall there are the Gainsboroughs and the Constable, but no silver-framed wedding photos or fading pictures of older relatives. On the mantelpiece, where there should be a gaggle of gap-toothed grandkids in their school uniforms, there are only the stylized, long-limbed figurines.

Miss Swan has nothing from her own life in this room. She has her images of other people's children. And she has me.

'Please,' she says. 'I would like you to visit me again.'

I look at our hands, touching, and pull away as if burned.

On Thursday, I stand on a twelfth-floor balcony of a Kings Norton tower block playing Frisbee with a debtor's collection of early eighties vinyl.

For each excuse he offers me, I fling a rare 2 Tone twelve-inch out into the grey skies of Birmingham. I'm doing it alphabetically. I've worked my way through Bad Manners (from 'Lip Up Fatty' to 'That'll Do Nicely') and I'm starting on The Beat.

The debtor breaks down and begs for clemency after I've sent 'Too Nice To Talk To' to its doom.

Just to drive the message home I carry on until 'Save It For Later'. It seems the right place to stop.

I take the story of my day back to the empty flat above Spice Traders. I lie on the bed and drink beer and play it over and over in my head. My hand lies flat on the quilt at the spot where a round, tanned arse used to be.

I check my watch. It's three o'clock.

I ring the bell and step back. Her expression when she opens the door is one of cocky self-confidence. She fingers her amber beads.

'I thought you weren't coming,' she says. 'I haven't put the tea on.'

'I'm here now,' I say.

She smiles with pleasure and maybe with gratitude, that gin-trap smile.

'Do you know what I found this week?'

I shake my head.

She reaches into the windowsill by the door and produces a twelve-inch ruler. Its edges are rough and worn. The numbers and divisions almost completely faded.

'I *was* a naughty boy,' I say.

'So you've come to confess.'

I arch an eyebrow.

'Or to boast.'

I follow her into the house and through to the living room. She was lying, of course. The tea is already waiting.

Since Charlie Hadn't Come
Chris Smith

Dry-stone walls rose like towers up the steep and craggy hillside, patches of mist slithered across peaked summits, Herdwicks and Swaledales wandered through the fells. An aged cottage jutted from the side of the Old Man of Coniston. In red chalk on the paving stones in front of the door it was written:

ALBERT REYNOLDS, THIS IS YOUR FARM. DON'T FORGET
TO CLOSE THE DOOR.

The words were faded and difficult to read.

Inside, Albert was sitting on a broken armchair. Tufts of white stuffing, like the hair from his ears, stuck out from the chair's legs. He was wearing the rust-coloured dressing gown that Charlie had given him for Christmas. In the pocket of the dressing gown there was a list of things Albert needed to do before he went to bed: brush your teeth, go to the toilet, cross the calendar, blow out the candle, close the window. They were simple things, but they were important things.

Albert had a tumbler of whiskey in his hand, no ice; the freezer was broken, or he hadn't paid his electricity bill, or he didn't have a freezer. He didn't know. His eyes were fixed on Martha, who was standing in his living room, scratching her head against the coffee table. Martha's homeland bordered onto Albert's cottage and was marked by an orange star dyed into her grey wool. Her itch seemed insatiable; it was hard to get at, somewhere between her ears, not quite reachable. She pushed the pile of *Farmers Weekly*s onto the floor. The latest issue was dated some weeks before, the same day as Charlie's last visit. Martha bent down and tested the front cover with her tongue. Then she tried to chew through the whole paper. Albert mumbled at her, or tried to talk without remembering to open his mouth. She ignored him. Albert stamped his foot, making a pathetic clonk on the wooden floorboards. Martha turned away and carried the paper with her through the kitchen and out the door. She stood on her favourite spot on the grass by the wall.

Since Charlie hadn't come, Albert had ignored a lot of things. He ignored the rats that scurried from the kitchen, past his feet-filled slippers into the hallway. Since Charlie hadn't come, he'd ignored the cow's carcase at the bottom of the stairs. The cow had been there for two weeks. She'd wandered in while Albert was asleep in his armchair and made her way up the steps. Then she'd chewed the guest room's heavy velvet curtains, pulled them off their rail, and stood for a long time on the landing. Later she'd walked into Albert's bedroom, looking for something else to eat. Seeing that there was no grass on the floor she'd made her way back to the stairs.

Now, the rats had scratched through her tough Friesian skin and eaten away at her flesh. Her neck was bent at an unlikely angle. Her eye sockets were filled with maggots. Above her body a calendar was Blu-tacked to the wall. A red marker hung next to it on a string. A carefully marked cross filled each day leading to Sunday, where it was written:

ALBERT REYNOLDS, GET DRESSED FOR CHARLIE.

Since Charlie hadn't come, the upstairs had become an aviary; bird shit covered the single bed, the worn carpet. Since Charlie hadn't come, the cow continued to rot and Albert's grey stubble became a white beard.

Charlie was Albert's brother. He worked in a bookshop café in Windermere, selling flapjacks and tea for £1.50. Every Sunday he would visit Albert. He'd get a bus to Coniston and walk up the track beside the beck to the base of the Old Man, Coniston's conical mountain. Albert's door was never locked, but Charlie would knock and wait. He would hear Albert scurrying around the house, his Sunday shoes clattering on the wooden floorboards like clogs. When Albert opened the door he would have islands of stubble on his face and shaving foam in his hair. His white shirt would be inside out or have a charred circle where he'd tried ironing it with a hot saucepan.

Charlie would bring food; they'd have tea and go for walks. Last time Charlie came Albert had answered the door wearing only a dinner coat and shoes. He tried to boil the kettle without any water and then made tea without any teabags. Charlie patiently wrote him a note, with an arrow pointing to the right pot:

ALBERT REYNOLDS, HERE ARE THE TEABAGS.

After Charlie had helped him make the tea they went for a walk in the hills. Albert could still name all the sheep in the valley; it was one thing he never seemed to forget. There was a small waterfall that Albert always headed for; it had a deep pool in the shape of a basin. It was the only place Charlie could get Albert to wash.

Back at the house Charlie returned things to their right places. He replaced notes. He cleaned and tidied. Before he left he filled in next Sunday's box:

ALBERT REYNOLDS, GET DRESSED FOR CHARLIE. DON'T
FORGET YOUR SHIRT AND TROUSERS.

Since Charlie hadn't come, the window in Albert's bedroom hadn't been closed. A damp semicircle on the side of the bed made the urine stains look fresh. But the bed hadn't been slept in since Charlie hadn't come. Since Charlie hadn't come, every couple of days Albert would stand upright, and each time his body would be more withered, less human. He would prance into the kitchen and defecate in the sink.

Albert's food supplies had either been eaten or had rotted since Charlie hadn't come.

Albert looked at the door in the kitchen and saw that Martha had come back in. She walked over to the empty fireplace and stuck her nose in the cold, grey ash. She recoiled with a snort and sent a small puff of dust into the air. She ambled across the room and nibbled the corner of the rug beneath the coffee table. Albert picked up a shotgun that was leant against his chair and pointed it at Martha. He pulled the trigger; there was the gentle tap of metal on metal. He didn't know where the bullets were. He looked down at the coffee table, which had a message scratched into it:

ALBERT REYNOLDS, YOUR HOUSE SUPPLIES ARE KEPT IN
THE BASEMENT.

Albert had to walk around the dead cow to get to the basement door. There was a sign pinned to it saying:

ALBERT REYNOLDS, PUT THE TORCH ON THE NAIL. DID YOU SWITCH OFF THE TAPS?

A torch hung on a piece of string from a nail. Albert walked down the steep steps and stood on the basement floor. It was cold and black. He opened a wall cupboard and found a box of shotgun shells and a tub of grease. On the way back he paused to look at the cow at the bottom of the stairs. In the living room he took a shell from the box and threw it at Martha. She ran out of the house. There were now only three shells left in the box. He loaded two of them into his shotgun and put the last one in his mouth like a cigar. He shouted at the cow.

'Where is Charlie?' He paused for an answer. 'If you don't answer me or leave my house in the next five seconds I'm going to blow my feet off.'

He counted to four and fired; the recoil of the gun sent the bullet through a large window at the side of the house. The window shattered. For a second it hung like a spider's web and then it fell in shards to the floor. Albert got up and walked back towards the cow, holding the shotgun in both hands and ramming the butt into his shoulder. The shotgun didn't have a sight, but he looked down the length of the barrel anyway, walking towards her as he lined up his vision. He tripped over her hoof and landed on top of her, dropping the gun as he fell. It bounced down the basement stairs and landed on the floor below. Albert crawled to the door and looked down into the dark for a brief, silent moment before backing into the living room and scratching his head against the coffee table. Then he started chewing the papers on the floor. He stared for a long time at a picture of a sheep and then ate that too.

He crawled into the kitchen on his hands and knees and

looked out the back door. A note, which he couldn't see, was pinned to the back of the door. It read:

ALBERT REYNOLDS, YOU ARE NOT A SHEEP.

The view was still stunning, but cigar smoke clouds were forming on the horizon. It was going to be a wet evening. Albert went back inside, took the tub of grease from the coffee table, and smeared the dark, bile-coloured paste all over his head and his body He rubbed some into his hair. Then he crawled back though the kitchen and into the yard, where the red chalk had faded since Charlie hadn't come. By the edge of the wall Martha was chewing Albert's favourite patch of grass.

Sea Life
Keelie Walker

In the daytime, in the tropical section, the walls drip with
sweat from humid tourists. The walls are supposed to
look like, what? Something volcanic, or some kind of
coral reef? They don't. They look shit. They look like
cheap, sweaty, rough, purple plastic walls. It's cooler now
but my body remembers the heat and crowded bustle of
a normal working day. I prickle with sweat and my
Airtex T-shirt sticks to the slowly healing tattoo across
my waist and lower back.

I take my fourth cup of coffee of the night, in its navy
mug with a red Sea World Centre logo, back towards the
birthing tank that was specially installed for our latest
project. As I walk through the tunnels, the filters and
neon lights on either side hum an electric chorus. After a
while, the noise seems to join up in the middle and close
in on me. The main lights are off and I'm careful as I step
across the wooden bridge by the piranhas, because it's
designed to buckle and bounce and make you think
you're going to fall into the stagnant water below. Like a
lot of things in this town, it plays on the old trick of
making people feel that little bit more alive for having
come close to something dangerous but then lived to tell
the tale. These days, Blackpool's moved on from
fairground rides and sideshow freaks to date rape drugs

and punch-ups outside kebab shops. Then there's those fucking hats and the tat spilling out from stalls on the prom that spring up overnight in the season. That's not all Blackpool has to offer, but it's what most people remember and it's what half of them come here for.

The bridge creaks.

I grab the handrail.

Bob – that's an in-joke here; any of the fish that don't merit a *Gazette* headline-grabbing name, like 'Hector the Hectapus' or 'Tootsie the Sex-Changing Grouper Fish', are all called Bob – looks at me sideways with one dead, black eye. I fucking hate piranhas. It's like they've no soul. Most of the other exhibits here – starfish, jellyfish, even sea monkeys – have a bit of character about them, and plenty of them are basically plankton. At least with them there's a bit of light and a sense of motion. Piranhas just lurk in the dark with their hoods up, like a pack of teenagers outside a corner shop, just waiting for someone to get too close, to look at them the wrong way. They make the hair on my arms stand up and not in a good way.

I step over the dodgy bit of the bridge and head through the winding corridor, past the back-lit, rounded aquaria of jellyfish and the bioluminescent shapes of the 'Creatures of the Deep'. I pause for a while to look in at the seahorses until the weirdness of their spiky shapes and long snouts makes me feel funny inside.

Watch any sci-fi film: there's no freaky creature from the depths of imagination that's not already been outdone by nature.

I carry on down to the shark section.

In the slightly less sweaty, white plastic Roman-amphitheatre-style-arena where visitors gather to watch the sharks being fed and listen to our resident bio-expert Mark doing his speeches about new attractions and the breeding programme (until the kids get bored and start crying and want to rush off to the gift shop or the pool where you can poke a starfish), I'm startled by a sudden splash. It's Droopy, one of the smaller white sharks. We call him that because of a fin problem caused by his being kept in captivity, but we're not allowed to tell the tourists that: we've to tell them it's genetic, or whatever.

Thank God, there is some balance, though – which means I can justify working here. We do great conservation stuff, some of the best in the world. We've won awards for it. It's the same at the zoo. But you can tell that for some people it's just another place to bring the kids to shut them up for an hour or two while having a moan about the entry prices. But I love those moments when you catch a child – or even a jaded parent – learning something new and realizing or remembering that the natural world is a pretty amazing place.

Droopy's splashing about at the top of the tank. I wonder if he knows that it's me walking past, or if he just thinks it's feeding time again, because he's seen the shadow of a person pass by.

I mumble at him to stop showing off, like I always do – we're encouraged to act up for the grockles – and I feel a bit sorry for him. I carry on through the archway. Here the sharks swim over your head, above magnified glass so that they look much bigger and closer than they really are. Three-metre sharks, my arse. The divers who go in to clean the tanks'll tell you different. One day I was standing at the far end watching a young dad carry a small, screaming girl out of the magnified bit. As they joined mum at the other end she gave him a withering look. 'I told you, you shouldn't have taken her in there. I told you she wouldn't like it.' And dad looked at her triumphantly. 'She loved it. She's crying cus she didn't want to leave.' A girl after my own heart.

*

Once I'm through the roped off section and behind the curtain, I put my cup down next to the birthing tank, take off my silver bracelets, the matching ones Ellie and I bought together, instinctively look round to make sure no one is watching me this time and reach over into the warm water to run my fingertips over Adelaide's back as she swims by near to the top. Her skin feels like wet sandpaper or a cat's tongue. I slide my arm slowly out of the water thinking that I'm probably not supposed to touch her, not when she's this close to giving birth. I wonder if sharks do that thing that mice do, where they eat their babies if they feel threatened. I remember the sick horror one day at primary school when I discovered that Snow White had eaten three and a half of her babies, because that kid with a hook for a hand wouldn't stop tapping it on the side of their cage. Wobbegong sharks are only supposed to bite when they feel threatened and if they do, they don't let go. But for some reason I'm more scared of a piranha that's completely sealed inside a tank than of Adelaide. If she was going to bite me, she'd've done it before now. I know for sure that she recognizes me; she doesn't swim to the top for anyone else.

I sit on the floor, lean my head against the thick plexiglass and gaze in at Adelaide, watching her swim hundreds of miles in just a few feet of water. The darkness in the rest of the building intensifies the translucent glow from her tank. The magnified light starts to make my head throb and my eyes feel uncomfortably swollen, so I look away.

Blinking away the rippling patterns of light and dark around me, like when you've accidentally looked straight up at the sun, I start thinking about Ellie and the argument we had this morning. The words of the argument are stuck in my head on a loop, like one of those songs that you can't even remember when you last heard. Paul calls them 'ear worms'. One of the chaos things he likes to do at his office is sing a few lines of something annoying just as the lad from the post room goes by with the trolley. Then he'll pick up a clipboard, just to look like he's actually doing some work, and saunter around the building to see how many people he's got singing, humming or whistling his annoying tune. 'The Teddy Bears' Picnic' is one of his favourites and he particularly loves it when the stuffed shirts from Accounts wander past the director's office going 'Picnic time for teddy bears . . .'

My current show-stopping number goes like this.
Verse:

> *'I can't believe they want you to work.*
> *For God's sake, how stupid are they?*
> *You know the whole Y2K bug thing is bollocks.*
> *It's not like it's really going to happen.'*

Chorus:

> *'It's New Year's Eve. Our first one together;*
> *or at least it ought to be.'*

And the video goes a bit like this:
Ellie tells me to call in sick. I say there's no way they'd believe me. And it's not just about work anyway. I try to explain about Adelaide, about the temperature in the tanks and what could happen if the computers really did go down. But then she puts both hands on my waist, pulls me towards her; waits a few seconds before she lets her lips brush against mine.

I'm about to tell her that I want to be at work, that I'd

rather be there than in the pub surrounded by people I don't know and don't care about. It's only her I'm bothered about seeing the New Year in with. Maybe Paul and Mark too, but that's it. I'm about to ask her to come and meet me at the back door of the aquarium at midnight. I could cut the alarm and sneak her in through the fire exit. But then she does that thing she sometimes does when she kisses me: pushes her tongue deep into my mouth. Almost too hard. If it was anyone else, I wouldn't like it. It's just her, the way she does it – and what it makes me think about . . . It takes all the tension out of my knees like someone's cut the strings off a puppet. Drives me nuts. She knows that's all she needs to do if she ever wants to get her own way. About anything. But, for some reason, this time it just pisses me off. I push her away.

Almost too hard?

Chorus:

> '*It's New Year's Eve. Our first one together;*
> *or at least it ought to be.*'

I blow across the surface of my gift shop mug, take a sip and scald my tongue. I'd forgotten that I'd used the boss's Coffee-mate instead of the staff milk and that my coffee wouldn't be cool enough to drink yet. I go over the argument again and again in my head. Take it to the bridge. I think about her, out in our pub with her friends. Our friends. I wonder if she's thinking about me, if she's having too much of a good time, getting carried away in the moment that I'm not there to celebrate with her. I wonder if she'll kiss someone else at midnight and whether it'll somehow end up being my fault if she does. For not standing up for myself more at work. For caring about animals more than I care about most people.

I glance back and notice that Adelaide's started favouring one side of the tank. Apparently, she's supposed to do that. Her time must be close. She's swirling around in small circles, propelled by a couple of aggravated flicks of her tail, like a cat you've taken a still softly pulsing mouse away from. I don't know if sharks have labour pains. It'd be pretty hard to tell if they did. I try to catch her eye as she circles in her corner of the tank. Her eyes are nothing like Bob's. I could look into them for hours, maybe even days, and see everything. She flips her tail and comes close to the glass, like she knows I'm studying her, trying to read her. She looks right at me. It's as if she's been alive for thousands of years and has the pain of all those years stored up in her fire-coloured eyes. Oil spills. Atlantis. Shipwrecks and tsunamis. Militant Japanese fishing boats and the plundering of the Great Barrier Reef for souvenir fragments of coral that'll sit gathering dust on the back of a shelf.

I hear Droopy splash in the feeding area again. And then in the distance is the familiar, muted rise and fall of yet another siren as it breathes its way through town.

I think I would like it if the millennium bug really did happen. If all the computers in the world went down, everyone would be in a right mess. Most people have forgotten how to fend for themselves these days. Where would everyone be without their gadgets and computers, their creature comforts? But I could go and claim an abandoned holiday home in the countryside and live out every post-apocalyptic fantasy or desert island daydream anyone like me has ever had. Meanwhile, people in cities would be panicking, looting and pillaging before trying to put things back just the way they were. Maybe I could climb through the boarded up windows back at my grandparents' farm and start a commune, just like

Paul and Mark say they've always wanted to. But better still, it could just be Ellie and me. No pubs and payday friends and going out every Friday night just because 'Everyone's going to be there'. No jobs and no bosses who deliberately make you work the shifts they know you don't want to work, just because they're the boss and they're on some middle-aged, middle-manager power trip.

We could shut the world out, what's left of it. We'd have nothing to argue about then. No reason to hurt each other.

Yeah, I would like that . . . Just not tonight. Not until Adelaide's given birth to her pups, the first new generation of large wobbegong sharks that's ever been bred in captivity. Not until I know whether they'll get the chance to be reintroduced to the oceans of the world. So the species doesn't die out. So they don't end up like Droopy.

I look at my watch. It's five to twelve. I guess I'm about to find out.

In town, I can picture drinks lined up on crowded pub tables. The giant countdown clocks that appeared in every single pub half a year ago and started to build up a weird, edgy tension. The people with glazed eyes, too desperate for this, of all nights, to be the best night of their lives. Their clumsy hands peeling the string from party poppers and wrapping it around their fingers, tips turning brackish blue, ready for the countdown to begin.

Ellie, Paul and Mark leave it late, staying at the flat drinking so they can afford the ridiculous entrance fees that everywhere is charging tonight. Maybe as they queue to get into our local, the bouncer herds out a group of lads in checked shirts, that would never normally be allowed inside the student bar. One of them has a cut lip and blood smeared across his teeth. He catches Paul looking at him and he grins. He's not done with fighting yet.

'What you looking at, eh?' His pupils are dilated, dead black eyes. Soulless.

Paul says nothing, looks away from him.

'And what's with that shirt? Just get out of nick, did ya?'

Paul looks down at his bright orange shirt, the death row one he ordered off the internet. He steps back to let the bloke pass. Pretends he can't hear him.

'Think yer 'ard, do ya? You're takin' the piss wearin' that.'

And one of his mates chimes in. 'Bet he's a fucking faggot an' all. He looks like one. This your boyfriend here, this your fag hag?' Ellie wouldn't stand for that. People talking about us like that.

By this point, it doesn't matter what Paul says or does. He could argue with the bloke, tell him he doesn't want a fight, walk away. None of it will make any difference. The bloke's mind is made up. If he can't ring in his New Year inside the pub then he's going to count it down on someone else's ribs and teeth.

Ellie tries to grab Paul by the arm. The bloke's mates all step in and slowly but powerfully shoulder Ellie, Mark and the bouncers out of the way. Inside the pub the music stops. The countdown starts.

Splash.

Outside, police sirens are joined by another, and then another. The sounds echo in the gloom, reverberating off the damp walls and bubbling tanks. I picture squad cars and ambulances winding their way through the streets of the town centre, having to negotiate groups of men and women decorated in tinsel, glitter, party hats, spilled drinks and other grim stains, oblivious to the difference between road and pavement. I run the tip of my tongue across the scalded ridges on the roof of my mouth. I like the fact that it hurts; at least it's something real. Something that's not just going on inside my brain.

The first set of twin sharks is born just as my watch beeps to tell me it's midnight. I wait for the lights and filters to clunk and rattle and sigh as some imagined super-computer deprives them of their power source by dying because no one thought to include in its design a clock that would carry on counting into the new millennium. It doesn't happen. It was never going to happen. I check the computers in the server room anyway, every few minutes, just in case my watch was wrong. And there's no change to the thermometers on the tanks. Everything carries on. I switch on the underwater video camera that's hooked up inside the tank. At least I get to keep the birth of the first two to myself.

Another set of twins is born right after one o'clock. I keep looking at my phone. No message from Ellie. Network busy. Anything could've happened.

Another beep, and another set of twin pups is born every hour on the hour, until six o'clock, which is when Mark comes in for the day shift. He says hello twice. I thought I'd answered him the first time, but maybe he didn't hear me. He leans in next to me, peering into the tank. It's hard to see the new ones now; the water's full of cloudy blood and fibrous, floating white stuff. But every so often we catch a tiny tail flick, a shadowy circle. I tell him there's twelve so far and I'm not sure but I think the male and female ones are different colours. The males are plain, dark. The female ones tiger-striped in brown and orange, like their mother. I tell him they look strong and lively, like they've got a chance.

He says, 'Yeah, just a shame about the rest of us.' Then he says, 'Has anyone called you yet?'

I yawn, stretch and feel my work T-shirt unstick from my tattoo. I say, 'No. Network's all jammed. You know. Same thing happened last New Year.'

He says, 'Yeah.' And then he takes a deep breath. Like he's about to tell me something I don't want to hear. I'm still staring into the tank. He's still breathing in. And it sounds like he's in there, moving through the murk with Adelaide and all her babies, and that he's somehow breathing under water.

A Float for Shez
Kavita Bhanot

It was one of those moments that hits a classroom every now and then. A wave of silence starts at the back, usually the noisiest part, and laps so suddenly across the room that it catches those at the front unawares. It was Shez, sitting in the front, who was caught by the silence. And once the words were out, we both knew she'd never hear the end of it.

It wasn't *what* she said. The words, if someone else had said them, would have produced a few laughs, a bit of teasing, but that was all. They would have been forgotten in minutes. But coming from Shez's mouth, they must have sounded really strange, especially to anyone who didn't know her. Because someone like Shez wasn't supposed to say something like that. She was 'trying to be who she wasn't' and that, as far as 9C was concerned, was unforgivable.

The first time little Shez told me that she fancied my brother Shakeel, even I asked her if she was feeling all right. Then I just found Shez's purely theoretical obsession with the male species funny, assuming it was because she spent too much time with her boy-crazy cousins, who all lived on the same street as her, and were bigger, louder, better-looking versions of her. She copied them in everything, wore their clothes, a hijab, straightened her hair. She'd recently started to put on black eyeliner, smudged and wonky.

But that day, in the maths lesson, when everyone heard her, I felt myself growing red with embarrassment. 'What did you say that for?' I whispered, dipping my head to join hers, as the girls around us echoed Shez's words, 'Ali's got a nice bum, Ali's got a nice bum.'

Some girls ask to be bullied. Girls like Mavis, who had an old lady's name and a stutter, but who still wouldn't stay quiet; always trying to make jokes that weren't funny, tagging along with girls who didn't want her, buying them Brain Lickers, telling them her secrets. And then, when they made fun of her, when they imitated her stutter, she got so splutteringly angry she stuttered even more. But from the first day of Year 7, when we had found each other, Shez and I had managed to make ourselves invisible. Apart from the odd comment about Shez's headscarf, nobody really noticed us. Until now.

Shez's words followed us around for weeks. And for the first time, I saw Shez as the other girls probably saw her. She was tiny, the second smallest girl in our class, and the smallest, Louise, was virtually a dwarf. Her school uniform, passed down from her cousins, was too big for her. The long blue skirt swept the ground as she walked and she was always tripping on the rippling waves of material. She wore a baggy blue jumper that came almost to her knees; the sleeves were too long and she was constantly pulling them up to free her hands. And then, to make matters worse, there was the thin black scarf with silver CKs stamped all over it, burying her in even more fabric as she gathered it around her small face.

So when Meena told me I was 'all right' and asked me why I was Shez's friend, I was ripe for the question.

It was a science lesson. A teacher stood in front of the

whiteboard, clutching a piece of paper, holding it up close to his face as if he'd forgotten to wear his glasses. As we walked in, he looked up every now and then to say, 'Hello, girls,' or, 'Good afternoon,' in a foreign accent.

'We got supply again,' called Jan as she walked in.

'Doss lesson,' sang Sam, behind her.

He waited several minutes for silence, for everyone to look at him. When this didn't happen, he looked embarrassed, focusing intently on his piece of paper, as if he was too busy to notice us. Smarter than some of the other supplies, he didn't try to shout over everyone, but turned his back on us and introduced himself on the whiteboard, writing his name and the date in scrawly letters, and underneath, 'Copy pages 128–135 of *Biology 7*.'

'What do you think of him?' Shez asked me. 'What do you think of Mr, Mr . . .' She narrowed her eyes, trying to read his name.

'Mr Balthusier.' I screwed up my nose. 'Shez, leave the teachers alone at least.'

'What? Teachers are men, too. Anyway, he's not a real teacher. He's supply.'

'But he's French or German or something. And he's got a beard.'

'Ali's got a beard,' Shez pointed out, 'and he's cute.'

I rolled my eyes. I couldn't comment, because I'd never seen the famous Ali. Shez had tried to arrange a viewing, but I refused to take the 7.33 a.m. bus that she'd been catching for the past three months, ever since she'd discovered Ali driving it. Just for the pleasure of seeing him – she'd never even said hello to him – she came to school forty-five minutes early every day.

'He's coming over,' Shez whispered, putting her head down. We both picked up our pens.

'Good. Good girls,' said Mr Balthusier, even though our pages were blank. 'The other girls, they don't want to learn, that is their problem, but you, you are good girls.'

I looked around. Apart from Saira, the refugee girl who had no friends and was scribbling away as if her life depended on it, no one else had bothered to pick up a pen, or to open a textbook to even pretend they were working. Hannah was brushing her hair, Jan was brushing her eyelashes and Meena was playing with her phone. Everyone else was talking. He leaned over and I could smell his aftershave, something fruity, mixed with nervous sweat, as he flipped the covers of our exercise books. 'Shezma Masood and Mariah Ahmed. I will leave a note for your science teacher to say how good you two have been.'

'Sir, it's *Maariah*,' I said. I hated it when teachers used flattery to divide and rule. And there was no point him leaving a note for our science teacher. Mr Miller had disappeared almost a month before; there were rumours that he'd had a nervous breakdown after some Year 10 girls locked him in the science cupboard for a whole day. We'd been copying pages from *Biology 7* ever since, with a different supply taking us for every lesson.

'Sir,' said Meena, standing behind Mr Balthusier, a hand on her hip, her open mouth going round and round like a washing machine as she chewed gum.

Meena was beautiful. She'd recently dyed her hair a strange maroon colour and her eyes, that day, were green. Sometimes they were an unexpected blue or a cat-like hazel, depending on the contacts she was wearing, but they were always under the shade of her extra-long, extra-thick, mascara-coated eyelashes. Meena was different from the other Asian girls in our school. Most of us kept our heads down and our mouths shut, but not Meena. She was friends with the white girls. Shez's cousins called her a coconut and said she pretended to be like them so as to fit in, but it seemed to me they were just jealous.

'Sir, I need to go now.'

He turned. 'Go? Go where?'

'Go and pray,' she said, as if this was the most obvious thing in the world.

Mr Balthusier looked the gum-chewing, maroon-haired, short-skirted girl in front of him up and down. 'Can you throw out the chewing gum?' he said, irrelevantly.

'No.' This confused him. His eyes darted round the room, before settling on Meena again. 'Only joking,' she said. 'I'll get rid of it. In a bit, though. I only just put it in my mouth. I don't want to waste it, do I?' Mr Balthusier blinked. 'Oh, do that again, sir.'

'Do what?'

'Blink like that. Oh, you've got such lovely eyes.' She turned to me. 'Hasn't he got lovely eyes?' I nodded shyly. 'What colour are they, sir? Ah, he's all embarrassed now. Look how pink he's gone. So, is it all right if I go now, sir?'

'Go . . . to pray?' he asked. Meena nodded slowly, with exaggerated patience. 'Are you the Muslim?' She nodded again. 'What is your name?'

She didn't even pause. 'Saira Salim.' The real Saira Salim looked up, opened her mouth as if she was about to say something, but then closed it again.

'Do you have a note, perhaps, to say that you go to pray at this time?'

Meena sighed. 'Sir! I didn't know you would be here instead of our normal teacher, did I? And Mr Miller knows I have to go and pray, so why would I bring a note?'

The logic of her argument seemed to stump him. With his big blinking eyes, magnified by glasses, he looked like a trapped rabbit, caught between the natural scepticism of a teacher and the political correctness of a multiculturalist. His eyes fell on Shez and me. 'Is it true?'

He looked at Shez, at her hijab. 'So why are you not going also?'

'We are, sir,' I said. 'We have to go too.' I stood up. 'Can we go now, please?'

'What did you do that for?' said Shez, when all three of us were outside the classroom. 'We're going to get into trouble now.'

'What did you do that for? We're going to get into trouble now,' parodied Meena. She set off down the corridor, her narrow hips swaying in her tight skirt, which she had rolled up a few times, making her legs, in their black tights and platform shoes, even longer.

'Can't we go back in?' Shez muttered, as we followed. We were supposed to be praying, I reminded her. We couldn't go back straight away.

Meena turned suddenly. 'So who's Ali?'

Shez blushed. 'Just a guy I know.'

'Does he have nice bum then? Does he? Have you felt it?'

When Shez didn't reply, Meena shrugged and walked off. She stopped a few minutes later to knock on a classroom door. 'Is Kate there?' she asked Miss Rai. 'Mr Garner wants to talk to her.'

'Yes, I'm sure he does,' said Miss Rai. 'Why aren't you in class, Meena?'

Miss Rai had taken us for science last year. She was a nice teacher, but she did her best to hide it, especially in front of girls like Meena. When she saw Shez and me her attitude suddenly changed. 'Oh, you two are with Meena. So she's not making it up. Right, Kate, Mr Garner wants to speak to you. Yes, now. No, leave your things. Come back here straight afterwards or I'll send out a search party for you.'

'You two are useful to have around,' said Meena, putting an arm through Kate's and walking on.

It was a whole new world, being out of lessons. There

was a different, hushed atmosphere in the school. It seemed as though only we were free, and everybody else was imprisoned in classrooms. We met other fugitives along the way and, whether they were in Year 7 or Year 10, for once it didn't matter: we were all playing the same game. There were exchanged looks, smiles and warnings. 'Watch out, Mr Henley's round that corner,' and 'I wouldn't go that way if I was you.' We picked some of them up on the way, so by the time we got to the bike sheds, there were eight of us.

'Can we go back now?' Shez whispered to me, as some of the girls started pulling out cigarettes.

Irritated, I told her that she had no sense of adventure. She could go back if she wanted to, but I was staying. She looked at me, lips pouting, a hurt expression on her face. As I watched her walk away, tripping over the folds of her skirt, I had an urge to follow her. I was no longer sure why I was staying behind.

'Where's your friend gone?' asked Meena, looking up from the phone she was playing with.

'She's gone back,' I told her.

Meena looked at me, blinking a few times, her eye-lashes sweeping the air, her green eyes almost hypnotic. 'I don't know why you hang out with her, you know.'

'She's not that bad. If you get to know her. Anyway,' I said, implying that I was bound to her out of some sense of loyalty, 'we've been friends for ages.'

Meena smiled and put her arm through mine. 'Well, *you're* all right.'

I tried not to show the pleasure that was reddening my face. 'So are you,' I said.

I carried Meena's words with me for weeks. Later, I wrapped them up and put them away, taking them out for reassurance every now and then. Sometimes, but not too often in case she caught me staring and thought I was weird, I glanced at Meena and if she caught my eye, she smiled. At other times, as she walked past, she called out, 'Wassup, Mariah.'

'Am I invisible or something?' Shez asked me on one of these occasions, as we sat in the dining hall. 'Why does she always ignore me?'

I shrugged. 'Maybe she doesn't like you.'

'That's so mean. Why would you say that?'

It was mean. Maybe that was why I carried on, in a twisted kind of self-defence. 'Because she said so. Kind of.'

'When?'

'That day we walked out of science.'

Was I referring, asked Shez, to the day she'd had to go back to the lesson on her own?

'I didn't make you, you wanted –' I stopped. 'Anyway, after you left, Meena told me I was all right.' The words that I had treasured, that I had replayed in my head, sounded petty now, even to my ears. Shez didn't seem suitably impressed either.

I pushed a chip round my plate. Maybe it was a way of making the fading words real again; maybe I wanted Shez to be grateful that I was her friend. 'She said,' I continued, 'that she didn't know why I hang out with you.'

'She said that?'

I nodded.

'What did you say?'

'I stuck up for you, of course. But she said, if I wanted to, I could be friends with her, with them, instead.' It might have been the next thing she said, I told myself, if Mr Mann hadn't come out at that moment and dragged us all back into class.

Something changed in Shez's eyes at that moment. There was respect perhaps, and something else: fear. 'So, what are you going to do?'

'What can I do? I'm not going to leave you on your own, am I?'

Shez never left her pencil case at home. Every night, she packed her bag carefully, then did a check in the morning to make sure she had everything. But that day, somehow, she'd forgotten it.

'Can I borrow a pen?' she asked. Normally, I would have given it to her without a thought. But now, for some reason, it felt like a big deal. I rolled my eyes as I reached, in slow motion, for my pencil case and, with a sigh, held out a biro for her.

At the end of the lesson, I asked for it back. 'I'll just keep it for the rest of the day,' she said, 'so I don't have to keep asking.'

'No, I want my pen back,' I said, holding out my hand.

She asked to borrow it again in maths, in French, in English. Each time, she was more apologetic, and each time it was with a greater show of reluctance that I gave it to her, demanding it back at the end of every lesson. In history, I said no.

She kept her hand out, thinking I was joking. 'What do you want me to do, beg?' It wouldn't make any difference, I told her. She smiled. 'Very funny. Just give it, na.' She reached for my pencil case.

I clamped my hand over hers. 'No, I won't. You can't always expect me to sort you out, Shez. What would you do if I wasn't around?' Her smile faded. She took her hand back. But she still waited, still expecting me to give in, to say, 'Here you are then.' As she waited, I watched her crumple, watched her sink deeper into her layers, losing her arms in her jumper, her head in her hijab. I watched and felt secretly thrilled.

Several minutes later, a deflated Shez put her hand up to ask Mr Thomas for a pen.

The next day I told her to buy me some chips. She didn't have enough money, she told me, she only had a pound, barely enough for her own lunch. I shrugged. She could use that. If she had said something then, if she'd put her chin up, looked me in the eye and said, 'Get lost,' like the old Shez would have done, I might have stopped there. But she didn't. She bought me chips and, after that, was buying lunch for me every day.

Over the next few weeks, I discovered parts of myself I hadn't known existed. I found that the box I'd always lived in, assuming that I had no choice, because that was me, was not made of metal or wood, but of something softer; clay or Plasticine. I surprised even myself as I found I could push at the walls, making the box bigger, changing its shape to create new corners, edges and angles, poking a finger out here, an elbow out there.

I didn't feel anything when, after telling her that she stank and needed to use a deodorant, I saw a tear spill from her eye and fall onto her page, causing the blue ink to spread out and create a watery black eye on her paper. I actually smiled when, after telling her that she looked like a furry little mouse and no boy, including Ali or my brother, was ever going to be interested in her, she lay her head into her folded arms on the table and refused to lift it until the end of the French lesson, emerging only when the bell went, with bloodshot eyes and her eyeliner smudged all over her swollen face. When we went swimming, I grabbed her float while she was in the deep end, telling her it was ridiculous that she still couldn't swim without it. And I watched her panic for a while; smashing the water with her arms and legs, swallowing water and sinking, before I gave it back to her.

I didn't let her speak, cutting her off when she tried to tell me about the Mela she'd gone to with her cousins at the weekend, or about the argument between her dad and her uncle. I even told her to shut up because she was giving me a headache, when she went on and on about Shahrukh Khan in a film she'd just seen.

Day by day, I watched Shez dissolve. She seemed to be drowning in real life as her small frame shrank into her clothes, her face peeking out from all the material like a distant head bobbing in the ocean, crying for help.

'I don't know why you wear your hijab,' I said one day.

'What do you mean? It's part of our religion.'

'What, it says in the Koran, "Thou shalt wear a fake Calvin Klein hijab"?'

I didn't really know about these things, had never thought about them properly. I'd just felt bad for Shez when Jan asked her if she always wore her headscarf, if she slept with it on as well, if there was mould growing in her hair. Or when Mr Thomas said, in front of everyone, looking directly at Shez, that it was a pity that some women couldn't fight for the basic right to wear what they wanted, after all the suffragettes had done to get women the vote. Afterwards, we'd both made little drawings of Mr Thomas, exaggerating the hair that poked out from his ears and over his shirt collar.

But now, encouraged by Shez's silence, by her wide-open eyes, the words just poured out. 'You don't know anything about Islam or why you're supposed to wear it. You're just doing it to be like your cousins. It looks silly, everyone makes fun of you. My dad says that it doesn't even say anywhere in the Koran that women have to wear the hijab, so I don't know why you feel so holy, so proud, as if it makes you a better Muslim or something.'

'There's nothing wrong with feeling proud of your religion,' said Shez, quietly.

But the next day, she came to school wearing her long black hair in a plait, with nothing covering it. Her eyes searched mine for approval, but found none. Instead, my lips curled into a mocking smile. She had taken off her hijab because of me.

When I told her that she was too hairy, that she should get her arms and legs waxed, her eyebrows and moustache threaded, she asked her cousin to take her to Shiraz Beauty Parlour. When I told that she needed to change her uniform, to buy a new skirt and a jumper that fitted her properly, she went shopping. She looked better as a result, but the more she changed herself to please me, the more pathetic she became in my eyes.

In the middle of the spring term, I got appendicitis. For weeks there had been a dull ache in my stomach, but Dr Gupta kept sending me home, telling me it was constipation. Then the pain got worse and I could hardly breathe. In the end, I was taken to hospital in an ambulance, almost screaming, and even though the violence in my stomach was filling my brain, I enjoyed the drama of it all. When I arrived, the doctor told me that if I'd got there an hour later, my appendix might've burst.

Shez came to visit me in hospital, bringing me a box of Quality Street and a poster of Shahrukh Khan. I sat up, leaning weakly against the pillow, and told her again and again about my almost-encounter with death. She seemed suitably impressed, although by then she was impressed with everything I said. She looked depressed when I told her that I wouldn't be back at school for at least another two weeks since I had to have full bedrest at home.

Every day, I expected her to come, but after that first time, Shez didn't visit me again. Not even to catch a glimpse of my brother. In the past she'd often made excuses to come round, just to see him, although he hardly noticed her.

Each day of those weeks at home dragged on, with

nothing to do but watch daytime television, programmes about redecorating houses, cooking and makeovers, or repeats of serials on Zee TV and PrimeTime. I lay all day on the settee downstairs, while everyone carried on their lives around me. Shakeel was always busy with his boxing or his friends. Abu came home in the morning after his taxi shift, watched television with me for a few hours, then went upstairs to sleep. Ammi was always attached to her Singer sewing machine, which sat in the living room and sang out its tune every day from eight o'clock in the morning to ten o'clock at night. Sometimes she gave me piles of belts to turn the right way round and then stuff, or skirts and trousers that had gone wrong, to unpick the stitches on. With no one to talk to, I found myself having imaginary conversations with Shez, collecting thoughts and stories to share with her when I next saw her.

On my first day back, as I walked into the history class, I saw Shez sitting with Saira, the refugee girl, in the second row. I noticed that she was wearing her hijab. Both she and Saira were laughing about something. I had never seen Saira laugh, or even smile before. She usually wore a blank expression on her face, looking perpetually lost, as if she didn't know where she was or how she had got there. I remembered how Shez and I had often imitated and laughed at the 'Saira Face'.

'Hi, Shez,' I said. She didn't reply. I sat in my usual seat in the front row, waiting for her to join me, and when she didn't come, I turned towards her. She was still talking to Saira as if I wasn't back at school after three weeks away. 'Shez!' I hissed, patting the chair next to me, but she didn't even look at me. She was ignoring me. I glanced at Meena, sitting a few rows behind her. She was looking in my direction, but right through me, as if I was invisible.

I had been gone for less than a month, and everything had changed. I turned to the front, stared straight ahead as if I didn't care, but found myself blinking away the tears that were filling my eyes.

'Mariah,' said Mr Thomas loudly as he walked in. 'Welcome back!' He froze in mock horror as he stood in front of me and looked at Shez, then at me, then at Shez again.

'Sitting alone?' he said. 'Have the two of you had a fight?'

For the rest of the lesson I burned with the embarrassment, highlighted so crushingly by Mr Thomas, of sitting alone. I refused to look behind me, using my back as a shield against Shez and the rest of the class, but I could hear Shez and Saira talking away in Urdu about the latest Hindi film *Jab We Met*, how they didn't like Kareena Kapoor but thought Shahid Kapoor was *so* cute and couldn't believe Kareena had left him for Saif Ali Khan.

She doesn't care at all, I thought, as I heard her giggle. Even if she wants me to, I'll never talk to her again.

But when a piece of lined paper, torn from an exercise book, folded and folded and folded again, until it was the size of the tip of my thumb, with *Mariah Ahmed* written in curls on the front, landed on my table, I was glad of the acknowledgement that I existed.

Each word was written with a different colour gel pen, in the same curly handwriting.

I know that you would rather be friends with Meena and I was stopping you before, but now I have Saira, and I like her, so you don't need to worry about me.

I read it several times. Then I tore the paper up into smaller and smaller pieces, until it was a pile of confetti in front of me. Picking up my bag and my books, I went to take the empty seat next to Shez and Saira.

I Know My Team and I Shall Not Be Moved

Rodge Glass

He was in the downstairs lounge again. As I parked the car, I could just about make him out through the front window – thinner now but still distinctive, even from a distance. Shoulders hunched. Back bent. Wiry frame. He was sitting with four or five others, dwarfed by one of those high-backed pink seats that reach halfway to the ceiling. Probably bought on the cheap years ago, in bulk. You shouldn't skimp on chairs. Especially in a place like that where you have to sit in them all day, looking at other people sitting in them all day. I turned off the engine and sat in the dark, hands tight around the wheel, just watching: my father was leaning forward, talking intently to the man next to him. Then he smiled. I made myself get out of the car, locked it and approached the buzzer, giving my name and the reason for my visit when the voice asked for it.

The automatic doors parted slowly and I walked through, trying to be confident, act relaxed, as if I came to see him every day or every week, not once or twice a year. As if I'd been there all morning and just popped out to do an errand, maybe stopping on the way back to buy something for his sweet tooth I just knew would make his day. But I was too selfish to think ahead, and didn't know what he liked. The doors whirred shut behind me and the strong smell of antiseptic hit hard. I'd forgotten about that. Also, how the layout of the lounge reminded me of a school corridor. A week-to-week timetable of events and day trips was written in large print, attached to a notice board on one wall, next to a Hebrew calendar peppered with festival dates and posters advertising future group activities. Today was Shabbat, so that explained the decorations.

'Hi, Dad,' I said brightly, leaning over to give him a kiss. 'Shall we have a drink?'

'Oh there you are . . . Thanks, but I don't drink any more . . . I used to be an alcoholic, you know.'

'I was thinking of something hot.'

'Tea then. Milk, no sugar. Sweet enough already, eh?'

I'd never heard his voice so soft or broken before. He had to keep pausing for breath and he looked really pale, really gaunt. David had warned me, last week, when he phoned from his surgery. He told me to be prepared. He said I was going to be shocked. I said he was obviously just trying to upset me and put the phone down on him.

'I'll see to it in a minute,' I replied, forcing a smile. 'Shall we sit over here?'

I gestured to a nearby empty table, which faced out onto the pretty, perfectly ordered gardens by the road. My father eyed the table carefully, considered whether there was any reason he should avoid this step into the unknown, then nodded in reluctant agreement, pulling me near so I could help him up.

'My daughter,' he said to the circle, wobbling slightly as he rose, swaying between the walking stick on his left side and me on his right. 'Good girl . . . Most of the time.'

The circle gave a murmur of weak approval. One of them was asleep, and at least one other was slumped in her chair, half awake.

'What do you do?' said one man. 'Are you the doctor?'

'That's my brother,' I replied. 'I . . . well . . . I haven't done much recently. But that's all about to change.'

A different man, who might have been asleep when I arrived, abruptly sat up and said, 'I know which one you are. You married yet?'

'No. Still happily unmarried, thank you.'

Another murmur started up.

'Don't blame me for that,' said Dad, his voice rising in anger, gathering in strength. 'I did my best. The world is full of wonder, I told her. Get out there! Live! Love! Dance! Roll around in the grass!' He shook his head slowly. 'But look at her. Forty-two and still lost. No job, no man, no fucking future. Her mother, God rest her soul, she was so ashamed.'

'Don't swear, Albert,' said the other man, nodding in the direction of a sleeping woman to his left. 'There are ladies present.'

Dad ignored him and turned to me, looking hard now. Gripping my forearm tight with his bony hand. It was so thin, it looked more like a vulture's claw.

'I do love you, though,' he said, tired again, having exhausted himself with his last speech. 'You big fat bugger. I don't know why, but I love you. Let Hashem strike me down dead if I don't . . .'

'Well, nice to meet you all,' I said to the circle, directing Dad towards the other table as fast as I could. I helped him into his new seat, just yards from the old one, then sat down next to him.

'Come here. Come closer,' he whispered. 'I want to tell you something.'

I leaned in and he jabbed a finger towards one of the men who'd been talking to us. 'That's Bert Silverman. A real *alter cocker*, that one.'

'Be nice, Dad. He's your cousin.'

'*Your* cousin. Distant. On your mother's side. After she

died I thought I'd never have to see him again. Such a *khazer* he was when the business was falling apart. He owed me a thousand pounds. That was a lot of money in those days! I had to chase him for months to get it back. And did I get an apology? You must be joking! They say he left his wife for some *shikseh*. Moved to Birmingham. Or was it Manchester?'

'*This* is Manchester, Dad . . . right here. This is where you grew up. See that street opposite?' I pointed out of the window. 'We used to live on the other side of that street. By the park.'

He ignored me and carried on thinking aloud.

'They always come back home to die. You noticed that? Half the kids at my fucking bar mitzvah are in this place.' He waved a hand weakly in the direction of the others. 'Not that any of us chose it. Thrown in together. Emptied out into this stinking dustbin full of miserable faces by the children we raised. I survived the Holocaust, you know. I used to be strong. But look at me now. Pathetic. My children *shit* on me.' He looked up, remembering who he was talking to. 'No offence. You understand.'

'I thought you liked Bert Silverman,' I answered, clasping my hands tight between my legs. 'Remember, I told you he was here? You were pleased. We talked about it. We chose this place because we thought you'd have friends.'

Dad folded his arms like a sulky child. 'And enemies,' he said.

I smiled and stood up. 'I'll get the tea now,' I said lightly. 'Back soon.'

As I walked away, I couldn't help but feel proud of myself. I didn't even tell him off for swearing. I was going to be fine. And this wasn't going to go on for much longer.

I ran into the Sister in the corridor. I smiled and went

to move past her but she ushered me into her office, closed the door and asked me to sit down. She spoke in a kind, steady voice about what she called 'your father's case', but I was bad at pretending to be interested in her opinions.

While I sat there, trying not to listen, she talked about why she believed people chose Lieberman Homes for their loved ones, what the homes offered, how elderly people often liked things they knew well, how they were most comfortable in their own communities, and how that was fine really. How maybe it was difficult for some people to understand, but those different generations saw the world in a different way and that really that was OK, wasn't it? We might think they're silly, but we should try to understand, shouldn't we? Especially after what my father had been through. One day, she said, our children would probably laugh at our stuffy old opinions. The way we dress. How we behave. That was something to look forward to, wasn't it? She laughed but I didn't know why. She was asking too many questions. Her voice was a faraway noise. All I could think of was what I was going to say to Dad, and how I didn't trust myself to get the drinks to the table without spilling hot liquid all over my hands.

'Would you carry them please?' I said.

'I'm sorry?'

'I mean, would you carry the drinks to the table for us?'

The Sister didn't understand. 'You don't have any drinks,' she said.

'Two teas. Milk, no sugar. Sweet enough already. That's what I'm here for. I'd really appreciate it because my hands shake and . . . and . . . and I can't help it.'

My voice faded to nothing. The Sister put her hand gently over mine.

'Do you understand? Your father's condition has

deteriorated greatly since you were last here. He had another fall two days ago. Now, I know you find this difficult, but you really must try not to repeat the kind of incidents we've had with your previous visits. Please try to make allowances, for your father's sake. Be patient with him. Don't take anything he says too seriously. He does have occasional lucid moments, but mostly he doesn't know what he's doing or saying any more. He may be grumpy, but that's a side effect of the condition – any of us would be the same. Speak to your brother about this. He's here most days. He knows.'

She removed her hand from mine and smiled, back to her standard professional voice – cheerful, understanding, but firm too. 'We have a great deal of experience in this kind of thing and, I assure you, the best we can do is make him as comfortable as possible. There are a few simple rules that will help. Do you think you can remember them?'

'Yes,' I said, straightening my skirt, then looking at the floor. Then looking out of the window. Then back down at the floor again.

'The first and most important rule is never to correct him. If he says it's 1974, it's 1974. OK? Sometimes he's happier in the past – though any talk of war upsets him, naturally. He still gets occasional flashbacks. Also, if he repeats something, don't tell him he's said it before. If he's forgotten something, don't remind him. You wouldn't know it from how he is today, naughty thing, but your father is actually perfectly content much of the time. He enjoys celebrating the festivals and retains a strong religious belief, which is usually good for the health of patients in this situation. He's kind to others. He can be very good socially too. But he's only happy when he forgets that the world he lives in is his own. If he's reminded of his condition, or made to feel foolish, then he's likely to get confused. And perhaps aggressive. Right?'

'Yes.'

'The second thing is, try not to show him you're distressed. He will sense the reason for this, and he'll react. Remember: this is not his fault.'

'I see.'

'And thirdly, try not to give him any demanding news. Well-meaning relatives often come in here to tell people in your father's situation . . . I don't know – let's see. That so-and-so is dead, or that they're having money problems. It's understandable, yet totally selfish. They do it to make *themselves* feel better, but it only causes further trauma. And besides, their loved ones forget it all a moment later anyway, and all that remains is a lingering sense that something is wrong, but no knowledge of what that something is. We want to avoid that. We must not judge your father by the same system we judge ourselves. OK?'

I dabbed my eyes with a tissue, stood up and said, more harshly than I meant to, 'Yes. Right. I've heard all of that. Can you help us with the tea now, please?'

But the Sister didn't get annoyed. She continued just the same. As if she'd seen thousands of people like me before, desperate to leave her office. Not really listening. Not coping.

'Someone will see to it,' she said. 'They'll probably be waiting for you when you get back to the table. The kettle is constantly on here.'

And they did arrive before me. Two piping hot teas, safe and secure on the table, in white plastic cups. It was beautiful. I could have cried.

Dad was deep in thought when I returned, and it took him some time to notice me. But eventually he looked up and said, 'Oh there you are. You left me on my own! You took me away from my friends and then left. You know I can't move without help! It's all *fercockt* around here. Nobody cares about me.'

'That's not true, Dad. I'm so sorry – it was the nurse's fault. She wouldn't let me go. And I'm here now, isn't that something?'

He thought for a moment, then his expression softened. 'Yes. Yes it is . . .'

'Good. Well, I have something to tell you.'

'That's fine. Don't worry about your old dad, I'm OK. Good Jewish people here.' Another, more troubling thought occurred to him. 'Half the staff are bloody foreigners, though. From Poland, Nigeria, God knows where else – *alle schwarze yorren* basically – but I'm OK. I survived the war, I can survive this nuthouse! And you're here now. Which is more than I can say for your sister.'

'What?'

'You've always been a good boychik, I know that. But that sister of yours . . .' He shook his head slowly, as if he could hardly bring himself to speak. 'Don't tell her I said this, she'd be devastated, but what a waste of space she is!'

I felt hot and clammy. I wondered if anyone would notice if I just got up and ran away. I thought about reminding him gently, lovingly; saying *I am Deborah, Dad* – sparing both of us whatever he was about to say. But before I could do it he was speaking again.

'Did you hear she's running away to Israel now, to fight in the war? On the other side! Jews are fighting Jews now! She's killing her own family! She hasn't come to tell me, but I know. I have my sources.'

'I think you're talking about your own sister, Dad. Elly. Remember? She worked in a hospital in the West Bank for a long time – it was a good thing she did – she puts the rest of us to shame. People were dying. They still are.'

'People are *always* dying! Your grandfather must be spinning in his grave, God rest his soul . . . They'll never accept her over there you know – she'll be hated by both sides. Is that what she wants? To be hated by everybody? Ducking for cover as the bombs fall? She could get herself killed!'

She had, but I couldn't remind him of that.

'Please, Dad, listen. I, er, *Deborah* . . . she's not gone anywhere. But she will be, soon. She's moving. You won't be seeing her for a while. She's finally happy – isn't that what you always wanted? She's very much in love with a man who –'

'Is he black?'

'Why? Does it matter?'

'If he's not black it doesn't matter at all!'

'Well, he's not. He's a good man, and he loves her. He's definitely leaving his wife soon and *Deborah* is moving to be with him. They're going to live in a little town on the south coast. It's very attractive.'

'I'll never see her again if she goes there. Never has been peace between us and the goys. Especially in that place. There never will be. What arrogance to imagine you can just make it burst out of your *pupik*. Poof! Magic! Peace! She doesn't understand what she's doing. She's going because she's got no children of her own so her heart bleeds for everyone else's.'

And then I said what I came to say.

'Sorry, Dad, but I just can't come back. Will you forgive me?'

I began to cry, but he was so far away in his own thoughts that I might as well have been somewhere else already. He was warming to his favourite old themes now.

'All that time we fought for a homeland, all that time

wandering in the desert,' he wailed, his face contorting as if he was transported back sixty-five years, standing at the entrance of the camp again, dreaming of freedom. 'And she wants to give it away! She spits on six million dead! My own child! But you're a good boy. Speak to her for me. She listens to you . . . Oh, when I think of all the friends I lost. The worst crime in history! Oh, oh . . .'

He began to weep too now, but I couldn't console him. Though I'd promised myself that, whatever happened, I wouldn't get angry today, I stood up and shouted as loud as I could.

'You have to forget your war! You never let anyone forget it! Look – I'm trying to tell you something about *me* – just *shut up* for a second –'

Tired once again, my father wiped away his tears with a damp palm and composed himself. He would gain a sudden burst of energy, then lose it, then regain it again.

'Sit down and behave,' he told me. 'Have some respect. Who do you think you are? Those bastards would push us all into the sea if they could and you know it.'

'Who? Who are you talking about?'

'I tell you, when Martin Luther King was killed, do you know what I did? I bought a round of drinks! Another one bites the dust. Boom! Do you see what I'm saying?'

'No, Dad, I don't see at all. What's that got to do with anything?'

'They say he's President of the United States now. Doesn't matter! Nothing will change! It never does! Filthy niggers . . . they *hate* us. Everyone does. They pretend that they don't but they do. They'd drive us into the sea if they could –'

'DAD! STOP!'

A few of the other patients turned round to see what was happening as the Sister arrived and put an arm around my shoulder.

'That's enough now I think,' she said without looking at me, then smiling at Dad as if she was talking to a child. 'Isn't it nice for your *daughter* to come and see you? Your daughter *Deborah*? It's good to talk over old times. I'm glad you've had a lovely afternoon together. But say goodbye now. It's time for Deborah to go.'

This seemed to jolt him out of previous worlds and into a new one. He looked into the middle distance for a moment, processing the information, then looked at me as if for the first time. Finally he recognized me.

'Ah yes,' he said. 'My daughter – little Debbie. Good of you to come and see your pa. Good girl. I remember when you were born . . . such tiny hands. But strong. You held my little finger so tight! I love you, dear. I love you so much. You know, David is getting married today. Isn't that nice?'

I felt a strong pain in my gut. I wanted to tell him David had got married twenty years ago, divorced ten years ago, and that I was leaving. But instead I just gave him a kiss and said, 'Yes, Dad. That's lovely.'

I nodded at the Sister then walked away, noticing that both cups of tea remained untouched. That detail upset me more than anything. I hadn't even managed to stay with him, be good, be brave, for long enough for us to enjoy a single sip together. As I reached the automatic doors I heard Dad say to the Sister, 'What's for dinner then?'

She politely explained the menu in full, like a waitress in an exclusive restaurant, and he told her he was going to make a complaint. Standards had been slipping recently, he said. There was no excuse for it. Did she know he survived the war? Did she have no respect? Why wasn't he being treated properly? When was he going home?

I left the building. He was her problem now. Not mine.

Staying Together
Sarah Butler

'Do you remember this, Simon?' his mum asks, as they pull off the road onto the gravel driveway. He listens for a hint of apology in her voice but there's nothing, and so he glares out of the window, keeps himself stiff and straight as the car bumps and wheezes between two rows of trees; they are winter skeletons still, though bluebells throw up lush blue-green lines beneath them.

'Simon?' She twists her neck towards him and he sees the side of her face, foundation-caked, familiar.

'I remember,' Jack says, and Mum laughs and shakes her head.

'Stupid,' Simon mutters, and re-crosses his arms. Last time, they had all been there, Jack trussed up in the baby seat, Mum and Dad arguing about which way to go. Simon can remember the stuffy smell of car upholstery and his mum's perfume, the buttery sweet taste of the mints his dad always kept in the glove compartment. The mints had disappeared after his dad left. They reappeared in another, better car, doled out by his dad's new girlfriend with her big breasts and simpering smile; Simon always said no.

The house comes into view; the top of the roof cut out like a picture of a castle. Jack punches Simon's arm in excitement.

'Look, look,' he squeals. 'It's gigant-ee-normous.'

'That's not a word.' Simon stares at the house: three layers of windows, fancy carvings of twisted leaves above the doorway. He remembers wooden floors, a stone stairway twisting upwards, a girl who looked like a doll. 'I'm making magic stew,' she'd declared. 'We need more stuff.' He'd obediently sneaked into the kitchen to hunt for ingredients. She had examined each one solemnly before adding it to the bowl, stirring them into sickly brown over a pretend fire. They had to find one last ingredient, she'd said, for the magic to work properly. So you could argue that the whole thing – the fight, the long, silent drive home, the eight years of not visiting – was her fault.

'Why couldn't I stay at home?' Simon asks.

'You know exactly why.' His mum parks their car – a crappy Nova – next to a sleek black Lexus.

Mum's sister answers the door. There is a fraction of a pause before she opens pudgy white arms that jut from a dark blue dress Mum wouldn't be seen dead in. She and Mum hug for a long time, then step apart and turn towards him and Jack.

'Aren't you boys grown?' she says. 'Practically a man, Simon, aren't you? Not too old to give your Auntie Stephanie a hug I hope.'

Simon lets her embrace him. Where his mum is angular and bony, she is soft as marshmallow. She holds him at arm's length and shakes her head. 'Just like your father,' she says. 'It's remarkable.'

Simon bites down into his lip until it hurts, pushes Jack forward for his turn.

To the right of the thick wooden door, Simon glimpses a large windowless room, painted white. Washing hangs from a wooden rack – limp white shirts suspended from plastic coat hangers; a kid's T-shirt; pale pink pants too small for Auntie Stephanie to wear. Simon looks away, follows his mum up the stone stairway.

'You remember what we talked about,' she hisses at him.

Best behaviour. No swearing. Simon grinds his knuckles into the rough stone wall. Jack's up ahead with Auntie Stephanie, chattering away, sucking up. As they reach the top of the stairs, Simon catches a slice of conversation, his brother saying, 'They say I can't remember being here, but I can too.'

'Is that so?' Auntie Stephanie half glances back towards her sister, but she's walking with her shoulders hunched forward, and she doesn't see.

Auntie Stephanie ushers them into a huge kitchen. Its shining steel surfaces make Simon think of the morgues in TV detective programmes. Four people sit around a white table in the middle of the room. He recognizes Frances, the girl he had stolen for – food colouring, blackcurrant squash, cocoa powder. She's plain: mouse-brown hair parted down the middle; a pale face scattered with freckles, no makeup. She wears a pink cardigan and a thin silver chain without any kind of pendant. He thinks of the pants hanging up downstairs, and feels the tops of his ears turn red. To her right sit two boys, about Jack's age, blond mirror images of each other. And here, turning in his chair, wide blue eyes and tanned skin straight out of a bottle: Uncle Paul.

'Simon!' He takes Simon's hand before he can do anything about it and pumps it up and down and up again. 'You've grown up.'

Simon says nothing. His uncle's palms are sweaty. Dark hairs protrude from his nostrils.

'And Moira.' Uncle Paul stands and walks towards Mum, who looks nervous, like a year seven cornered by a gang of year elevens. He pulls her into a hug. Simon stares at Uncle Paul's hand just above Mum's arse and he curls his fingers into fists. He watches him hold her at arm's length, as though she's something he's thinking about buying. 'You look well.'

She glances at her sister, then looks at the floor.

'Lunch will be in ten.' Auntie Stephanie hovers at her husband's side. She reminds Simon of a video he saw at school – about hummingbirds that stay still by moving their wings so fast the movement becomes invisible. 'Frances, would you show the boys their room? I'm afraid you're in together, boys.'

'They're used to that,' his mum says and Auntie Stephanie blushes, blotchy red shapes reaching up from her neck.

Jack trails after Frances, chatting happily. Simon follows. The corridor is lined with gold-framed pictures of pale, ugly people. Underneath one there's a huge wooden chest, the colour of burnt chocolate, with an ornate brass lock. Frances stops at the doorway to their room and smiles at Simon.

'You've got exams too?' she says.

'Yeah.'

'Maybe we could revise together?'

The laugh escapes before he realizes it is there. She steps backwards. Her face makes him think of the porcelain dolls his granny used to collect: paper-white skin and painted red cheeks.

'I don't mean –'

'It's fine. We're probably doing different subjects anyway. There are towels on the bed. You're to use the bathroom next door. The adults use the other one. I'll go and help Mummy with lunch.'

Simon watches her walk back towards the stairs, tries to think of something to say, but she's gone before he can get the words in any kind of order. He catches Jack staring at him. 'Piss off.'

'Piss off yourself.' Jack runs out of the room and Simon hears him sliding along the polished floorboards outside.

The room has a chest of drawers, a window, and two single beds separated by an old wooden table. The walls are so thick the window is an arm's stretch away; the windowsill a seat. Simon pulls himself onto it and sits, knees pressed to his chest, staring at the murky breadth of garden. The rain, that had started as Mum handed over money for the ferry ticket, still falls, dense and light as silk; turns the world into a black and white film strip. They're all liars, and he hates them. Some things are best left, Simon. That was all his mum had ever said about it. Even when Dad left, and he asked if it was because of Uncle Paul, she'd shaken her head and patted his hair like he was too young, or too stupid to understand. He'd tried to tell her about the magic stew: how the final ingredient was a drop of Auntie Stephanie's perfume, which she kept in a delicate green bottle on her dressing table – how the magic wouldn't work without it – but she hadn't listened to him.

He shouldn't have laughed at Frances, but she reminds him of the girls at school who always put their hands up to answer, who always have their homework done. Swots. Virgins. He's sure she's never let anyone so much as kiss her. He thinks about the pants downstairs – wet pink silk – and, without deciding to, swings his legs down from the windowsill.

He finds her room behind the second door. The air smells of girl deodorant and some kind of hippy incense. He had expected neatness and pastel colours. Instead, there's a huge poster of a black man playing a trumpet, and one wall is covered with curling photographs. The bed – double, he notices – has a purple cover and Indian-style cushions strewn across it. There are clothes everywhere: a turquoise bra hanging from the desk chair; disfigured tops and trousers in heaps on the floor. He picks up a soft pile of green T-shirt, and drops it immediately. He can feel his heart thump against his ribs; a warmth in the pit of his stomach. The desk is stacked with open textbooks and pieces of paper. He looks at the bra. It's one of those underwired ones that keep the shape of breasts even when it has no contact with skin. He touches it with one finger.

'Simon?'

He looks at his hand on the turquoise satin.

'Simon, lunch is on the table.'

He bolts out of the room, half slips on the rug outside.

Lunch is brown sludge.

'Lentil soup.' Auntie Stephanie grins at him across the table.

Simon tries to catch his mum's eye, but she won't look at him. He takes tiny spoonfuls, and swallows quickly so he won't taste it. Frances sits next to her mother, opposite Simon. Faint red circles still stain her cheeks. She holds herself ruler straight as she eats.

'So, how is your father?' Auntie Stephanie asks him.

There's a ripple along the table. Simon senses his mum listening.

'He's fine.' Simon takes a thick slice of bread, concentrates on buttering it.

'I hear wedding bells are round the corner?'

Simon looks at her. There's a light in her eyes that the girls at school get sometimes, when they're pretending to be nice but really they're setting you up, laughing at you. He lifts his chin into a half-nod.

'Jack's a page boy,' he says.

'And you?'

Simon shrugs. He doesn't want to have anything to do with it. He doesn't even want to go.

Auntie Stephanie takes another ladleful of sludge from the huge steel pan on the table. 'And is there any love on the horizon for you?'

Simon lowers his head to his soup. He feels like he's eaten more than a man should be asked to eat, but the bowl's still over half full. When he glances up he sees his mum looking at him.

The day after Aisha had dumped him he'd cried at the dinner table. It had taken the three of them by surprise; even Jack looked shocked instead of gleeful at such a display of weakness. Simon had fled to the room he shared with his brother, and wedged a chair under the door handle. His mum had whispered wheedling words from the hallway, but what was he supposed to tell her? That the fact the packet of condoms in his jacket pocket was still sealed in plastic proved he was a failure? That the expression on Aisha's face made him feel like a criminal just for asking? That he didn't understand girls, and he was so angry it frightened him?

Simon shakes his head. Auntie Stephanie makes one of those patronizing adult noises, says something about everything happening in its own good time, but Simon doesn't let himself listen, because he can still feel the anger, bitter hot inside his stomach, and he can't afford to let it out.

The next morning Mum stands at the bedroom door and badgers until Simon gets up. He makes her pass him a T-shirt so he doesn't have to get out of bed in just his boxers.

'Have a shower,' she says. 'It'll wake you up.'

'Saying I smell?'

'Simon.'

The bathroom handle turns but the door doesn't

budge. He listens and hears the noise of water running, then a soft rustle of towel and skin. He leans against the corridor wall and waits.

It's her. She comes out with a green towel wrapped around her head. Her face is flushed with heat. She wears a thick white dressing gown and her feet are bare. Simon stares at her legs and imagines her shaving them, the glide of a razor across her skin. She glances up; passes him in a breath of shower gel and shampoo. He tries to say hello, but it comes out as a grunt. She doesn't even blink.

The bathroom's warm and smells of vanilla or lavender, something girly. He stares at the blurred shape of himself in the fogged up mirror and thinks about Aisha: their hushed explorations on his bed while Mum and Jack watched TV next door. He'd never seen her naked, not the whole way, just snatches of flesh. Now she glowers at him in science lessons, tosses her black hair and presses her coloured-in lips together when they pass in the corridor.

He writes his name – Simon Hayden – on the mirror, revealing letter-shaped glimpses of himself. Water gathers at the bottom of each loop and seeps downwards, distorting the words. He steps under too-hot water; feels better once the smell of his shower gel – sharp, breathtaking mint – displaces that of hers.

When he gets downstairs, everyone else has finished breakfast. A lone bowl sits on the far corner of the kitchen table. There are five different breakfast cereals, none of which he likes. He jams a slice of bread into the toaster. Frances and Auntie Stephanie are stacking the dishwasher. Frances is wearing a blue and white checked dress that stops just above her knees, and huge slippers shaped like dogs' faces. She is humming under her breath.

'Chop, chop,' Auntie Stephanie says. 'We're leaving at nine-thirty.'

Simon looks up from his toast.

'Church,' she says. 'The service starts at ten sharp.'

'We don't go to church,' he says.

'Well, we do,' Auntie Stephanie says, as if that changes things.

In the end he has to agree to go. His mum uses the voice she reserves for absolutely non-negotiable situations, so at nine-thirty he follows the rest of them down the sweep of the driveway. The twins wear matching suits, and even Jack's put his best trousers on. Simon wears his jeans, trainers and his favourite top – Nike, pale blue with large letters across the back – a too-small victory.

They take the road round the edge of the island. Simon feels the wind lash up from the sea and notices seagulls, almost invisible amid whipped white and grey, bobbing in time with the waves. He finds himself next to Frances. He takes a breath; there's nothing to lose.

'Do you remember when I was here before?' he asks. 'You made me steal stuff out of the kitchen, for your magic stew.'

Frances half turns towards him and a frown flickers across her face before she shakes her head. 'No, I don't remember.'

They end up in a small stone church with old lady flower decorations in the windows. The vicar, or rector, or priest, or whoever the hell he is, drones on from behind a dark wooden lectern. In front of him is a crap model of a cave, stuck over with green tissue paper, with cotton-wool rabbits and wonky figures made from bits of wire and material. Simon sits behind Frances. He can see her bra strap, peeping out from the shoulder of her dress. He squeezes his hands into fists until he can feel the curve of his fingernails in his palm.

When they pile out of church, it has stopped raining. The sky is a patchwork of charcoal clouds, slashed with bright cold light. Simon concentrates on the crunch of his shoes on the loose stones at the edge of the pavement.

'It's perfect,' Auntie Stephanie says, wringing her hands. 'Perfect weather for an Easter egg hunt, eh, boys?'

Simon watches Jack scuttling along beside the twins, and wishes, briefly, that he was ten years old again.

Back at the house, Simon sulks, knotted up by the bedroom window with a book in his hand, pretending to work. His eyes skim across chemical equations, taking in nothing. He watches a squirrel skitter up a tree trunk and stop, stock still, like a caught criminal. He listens to the clattering of feet up and down stairs, Jack's voice shouting: 'I've found one, I've found one.' He has a sudden craving for chocolate – sweet, cloying brown inside his mouth. He imagines gold-wrapped eggs nestled in their hiding places. Before he knows it, he's standing up, walking down worn stone stairs to the front door.

Jack and the twins run in wide zigzags across the lawn, calling to each other, holding up their tiny foil prizes. Frances is at it too, sedately scanning the flower beds at the side of the house. She flicks a glance at him, then returns to her search. At school, Simon thinks, she'd be sneered at for her pathetic clothes and her boring face, but here she looks at ease, and he feels a prickle of jealousy. He'll look further afield, he decides; see if Auntie Stephanie could bear to hide anything out of sight of the house. He follows the drive down towards the road, and takes one of the thin paths that curl into the trees. It's wet underfoot; he can feel the soft spring of the earth as he walks, has to step around puddles to keep his trainers clean. He keeps his eyes fixed on the floor, looking for a flash of coloured foil. The absence of noise starts to make him feel unstable. He picks up a stick, its loose bark coated in damp moss, and bangs it against tree trunks as he goes.

The path broadens out into a clearing. Simon looks up and sees a slice of sky, pigeon-feather grey. He glances around, knowing there'll be no chocolate, but looking all the same. It's only then that he sees her. She sits on a fallen trunk to his right, her fingers fidgeting against the wet bark. She must be eighty, older even. Simon feels liquid fear run through his body. He wants to turn and run back to the house. He makes wild promises inside his head: he'll join in with their stupid games; he'll read that Shakespeare play; he'll help with the washing-up.

But he can't move. He stands, like the squirrel caught in freeze-frame at the top of the tree, and stares. The old woman, who has just lifted her head towards him, is completely naked. Her body is like nothing he's seen. He thinks of Aisha's breasts, Frances's neck, the glossy smoothness of magazine pages. This is sunken flesh. The woman's breasts hang like half-full shopping bags made from skin. Her stomach, too, is an empty envelope of flesh. Blue veins score lines across wrinkled, stick-like legs, and where her thighs meet is a mass of pale, unkempt hair.

'You came,' she says. 'I knew you'd come. I've been out looking for you and it's terrible cold.' Her voice sounds like glass – bright and fragile. She struggles to stand; he stares at her feet as they walk towards him, the skin is faintly blue, the toenails curled yellow.

'I don't know you, I'm sorry,' he mumbles, and manages to turn round. She grips his sleeve and he can't shake her off. He can smell her – a sharp, animal smell like his trainers after football if he puts his nose right up to the material and breathes in hard.

'John, you remember me, don't you?'

She tugs at him and he turns. She has pink-rimmed eyes, the irises canal-water grey.

'I don't know you,' he says again. 'I think you're lost.'

'But you must remember. John?'

Simon looks at her. He remembers his granny's funeral: sitting in the front row looking at the closed coffin at the front of the church and wondering if her toes reached all the way to the end; whether they'd dressed her up and done her makeup, like on the TV; or whether they'd just left her in her hospital gown.

'I'm not John,' he says. He wants to unpeel her fingers and run away.

'Not. John.' She says the words as though they're unconnected. Tears pool at the edges of her eyes. Her hand drops from his arm.

Turn and run, he tells himself. No need to get involved; she's some loony from the hospital across the other side of the island, she must be. Simon takes a step backwards, then another.

Wind hustles through the tree branches and snatches at the woman's hair. She lifts her hand to smooth it and Simon suddenly imagines her as a young woman, standing in front of a mirror, brushing her hair like his mother does every morning, long dark strands looping themselves into the brush.

The rain starts like someone's turned the shower on, fat warm drops tumbling from heavy clouds. The woman looks up as though surprised. She's shivering, Simon sees; her muscles jerking against the cold. He pulls his jumper over his head and holds it out to her. She doesn't move. Simon steps forward and wraps the jumper around her shoulders. Her skin is chilled, like raw meat from the fridge.

'Come on. I'll take you home. I'll find John for you.'

He takes her hand in his. The rain seeps through his

T-shirt, sticks his hair against his scalp, seeps muddy brown through the silver-blue aerated sections of his trainers. As they walk, he finds himself talking to her, a crooning string of half-words that come from nowhere. She says nothing, just shivers. She doesn't seem to notice the rain, or the change from the wood's soft ground to the hard edges of the gravel drive beneath her feet.

'Simon, what on earth?'

He looks up to see his mother standing by the doorway, mouth open.

'Mum, I don't know. I just went for a walk. She –'

Feet thunder down the stairs. Auntie Stephanie, goldfish like; Uncle Paul looking flustered.

'John?' The woman turns to Simon, her hand tightening in his. 'John, who are these people?'

Simon casts a desperate look at the trio of adults in the doorway. 'She's really cold, Mum. I didn't know what to do.'

Mum and Auntie Stephanie bundle the woman away from him, half carry her upstairs. She works herself into a state, shouting for him – for John. Simon waits a while, but no one comes downstairs. He steps outside with his T-shirt still clinging to his skin.

'Can I come too?' Frances appears from the room where he'd seen the washing.

Simon shrugs and starts to walk. He hears Frances's steps just behind him. By the time they're halfway along the drive, they are walking side by side. The rain has slowed to a light drizzle, which feels somehow disappointing.

'She's got Alzheimer's, I bet,' Frances says.

Simon spies something white at the base of a tree and slows his pace.

'My gran had it,' Frances continues. 'My granddad

looked after her for years, even when she didn't know who he was. And the weirdest thing is, as soon as she died, he just gave up and died too, a week later. They'd been married for sixty years.'

Simon picks up the white bundle. It unravels into an old woman's nightdress, scratchy lace around the neckline. Earth and moss have drawn brown fingers across it, like dried blood.

'I guess your family's pretty good at staying together.' He tucks the nightdress under his arm and turns back towards the house.

'I guess my mother puts up with more than most.'

Simon looks at her then; her hair is damp from the rain.

'I get angry with her sometimes,' she says.

'Not with your dad?'

Frances lowers her head and drags her heels against the gravel as she walks.

They are almost at the front door when Simon notices a glint of gold paper. An Easter egg sits in the shadow of a stone by the side of the path. He bends and picks it up. The gold paper comes off in reluctant fragments. He offers it to Frances. She takes a bite, and hands the rest back to him.

'I do remember the magic stew,' she says.

Simon bites the chocolate between his back teeth, tastes the sweetness on his tongue.

'I threw it away after you'd left,' she says. 'I didn't want to know what it tasted like after all that.' She takes the scraps of gold foil from him and scrunches them into a ball between her fingers.

The chocolate melts and fades in Simon's mouth. 'It would have tasted disgusting,' he says.

For a moment, he thinks Frances is going to cry, or turn on her heel and walk away. Instead, her face breaks into a smile, and after a while he finds that he is laughing too.

Fatima
Mehran Waheed

'Here we go again,' Mum said, switching off the radio and Paul Young's soothing voice telling me that wherever he lays his hat, that's his home. That summer, 1983, he was number one in the UK charts for three glorious weeks.

The wheels of our car crunched against the gravel driveway as it crept up to the grand Victorian house. 'It's like Beverley Hill-Brummies,' I said. There was a red Porsche, silver Mercedes and black BMW parked near the front door.

'Well, that's Westfield Road for you,' Dad said, as he parked our BMW next to the black one.

'And it looks like we're one of the first again,' Mum continued. 'Always late, aren't they?'

Dad removed his glasses, reached across Mum and placed them in the glove compartment, slamming it shut. He pinched the bridge of his nose as Mum struggled to get out of the car. She was testing out another sari, a dark blue one embroidered with gold this time, and she was still coming to terms with the material that snaked up and draped over her shoulder before pooling like curtains at her feet. Her bangles jangled erratically as she made some final adjustments.

'Pfff . . . fiddly things,' she said.

'You look fine, Eva,' Dad said as he closed his door. He turned to me and spoke through the window. 'You coming or not?'

I stepped out of the car reluctantly. I'd been force-dressed into a georgette churidar kurta: a flared black blouse dotted with red sequins like pomegranate seeds, and red trousers. The churidar was really baggy at the top and had to be tightened with the drawstring, while the bottom parts of the legs were so tight that they were clamped around my calves and ankles, like the hands of little monsters. The trousers matched the red dupatta scarf that I was wearing across my shoulders and I couldn't help but scratch at the itchy V-neck where the designer had gone nuts with the sequins. In short, I felt like an idiot.

'And don't fidget with your clothes once you're inside,' Dad added, giving me the look. You just don't mess with Dad when he gives you the *look*: his brown eyes widen like an owl's in the dark, his lips become taut and his face totally expressionless. I stopped in my tracks, bit my lip and nodded, trying to suppress the butterflies in my stomach.

As the front door opened I could almost see the spices in the air wafting towards me: garam masala, chillies, cinnamon, cloves, coriander and saffron – all wanting to escape. With the pungent smell came a barrage of greetings: overfed and wrapped in insincere saris and salwar-kameezes, boasting colours of emerald, topaz, ruby, sapphire and gold. And this was just one family.

'*Assalamu alaikum*,' they all said, smiling with brown teeth, like they'd sucked on teabags and coffee granules instead of lollipops as children. Dad, making out like he was a dentist rather than a GP, told me later that it was the fluorine in the Kenyan water that stained their enamel like that. Deceptively healthy teeth, though, he'd say with pride; it's gum disease that you need to watch out for.

'*Wa alaikum assalam,*' Mum said quietly. I tried not to giggle. She sounded so funny when she said it.

'Salaam little one.'

'*Salum lek . . . umm . . .*' I said, looking at the floor. God – Allah! – I hated saying it, too. It felt so false bestowing such a greeting – *Peace be upon you* – on complete strangers.

My cheeks were sloppily kissed, leaving wet patches. I wanted to rub the spittle away, but I didn't want to appear rude and I feared Dad's *look*. Some of the kissers had the audacity to squeeze my cheeks hard, biting their lower lips in sadistic pleasure, while I winced in polite, respectful pain.

'So cute! Look at those cheeks!'

Then there was the stroking of my long hair, which made me shiver, as always. I wanted to tell them that I wasn't a dog to be petted.

One exceptionally beautiful woman was taking a disturbing interest in me; I didn't know who she was either. 'Hasn't she grown? She's shot up since I saw her last time. So pretty! How old are you now, Aisha?'

'Umm. I'm elev–'

'You must visit us more often, OK? Why don't you come and stay with us, huh?'

I smiled briefly. *I hope not.*

'Haa! So shy! Just like you, Omar, when you were a boy in Nairobi. That dark hair, those big brown eyes, the same dark skin. And she even has the nose, too!' she said, laughing menacingly. 'But of course she has her mother's face. The shape I mean, Eva. Those high cheekbones! Oh, how I wish I had her blue eyes!'

I looked up at Dad, at his nose and his greying hair,

thinking I didn't resemble him at all. I glanced at Mum, who was looking rather embarrassed. Unfortunately, I didn't look like her either; with her cascade of blond, wavy hair, her slender white figure, and long legs, she was like a Barbie doll dressed in a sari. Pakistani Barbie.

Maybe I was adopted. Yes, that's it! I must be adopted.

Next we toured the rooms for more formal introductions. I find it difficult to pronounce Asian names at the best of times and the din from the Bhangra music made it even trickier to hear them properly. Apparently I'd met most of my father's friends before, but Asian society feels a bit like the universe to me: it's infinitely big and impossible to fathom. Each family is a galaxy, and every family member a planet. Then each member, in turn, has their own friends, like their own moons, each with their own relations. And at the centre of the universe is food; which is why being a good guest and a good host is so important.

I was pleased to realize that the Tour de Pakistan was almost over, ending quite aptly in the hustle and bustle of the kitchen. Somebody said, 'And this is Fatima.'

She wasn't dressed up like me at all, which made me immediately angry with Mum and Dad. Her long hair appeared to be blond yet, next to Mum's, it looked almost white like an old woman's but still healthy and lively. Her eyebrows were as light and feathery as goose down. Her skin was the palest pink. She was wearing a lot of purple: purple cardigan, dark purple pleated skirt, purple Alice band; even the tint in her thick glasses appeared to be purple. The only things that weren't purple were her white blouse and socks, and her patent black sandals.

Fatima stepped forward and shook my hand. 'Hi!'

'Hello,' I said.

'How old are you?' she asked in a soft, unusual voice. She had a Birmingham accent, but it wasn't laced with loud Asian intonations.

'Eleven. You?'

'Same.'

Her father was busy speaking to someone else, but her mother was beaming at us. It suddenly dawned on me that they were both Asian, but Fatima wasn't.

Was she adopted too?

Then I noticed her eyes. It made me dizzy just to look at them. Through her glasses I could see them flicking left and right in a frenzy, as if someone had rattled her brain and her eyes were still recovering from the shock. Her light blue irises were semi-translucent, but they sometimes flashed red, depending on how lit-up the room was. She reminded me of those white mice, and white rabbits with red eyes I'd seen on the telly. That's when I realized she must have been an albino too, though I'd never really thought that human albinos actually existed, until then. But I didn't say anything about it. I was just glad there was someone my own age that I could talk to.

'You know, Aisha, not many girls talk to me,' Fatima said as we played Monopoly on the living-room rug. Her vision wasn't very good and she needed a lot of help with the board. 'Or if they do it's only cos they feel sorry for me.' She looked up, waiting for a response.

I didn't know what to say. I wasn't particularly interested, and I didn't think to question her as to why. I was more concerned with acquiring Mayfair. My pewter Scottish terrier was only a few squares away on Regent Street, and Scottie and I had already attained Park Lane. It was my throw. I started to shake the dice in my hand.

'Dyed my hair black once, but that just made things

worse. Bet you have loads of friends, don't you?' I could feel the sting in her tone.

'Well . . . a few . . .'

'Which school do you go to?'

'Umm –' *I need an eight. Give me an eight. Eight, eight, eight!*

'It's an English school, isn't it? I mean, private an' all?'

'Well, yeah. I guess.' I threw the dice.

Fatima snapped her head back in laughter. 'Ha! Knew it! All your friends are white, aren't they?'

I felt my cheeks flush, as if I'd been winded. I forgot about the dice. Fatima was keeping her chin raised so she could peer at me through the bottom of her glasses.

'Aren't they?' she pressed. Her eyes seemed to stop moving in this position; they drilled into me as if she was looking through me with X-ray specs. Strangely afraid that lasers were going to beam out of her head and melt me, I looked down at the board and pretended to focus on the dice.

'What if they are?' I said. 'What's so funny about that?'

'Now I understand.'

'Understand what?'

'Why you'll talk to me when no one else will.'

'Why?'

'You're a coconut, Aisha!' Fatima said triumphantly.

I didn't reply. I had no idea what she meant, to be honest.

'You know? Brown on the outside, white on the inside!' she said with such smug satisfaction in her voice.

I glared at her, suddenly angry. 'No I'm not! I'm not white on the inside!'

The smile vanished from her face. Perhaps I'd given her the look. 'It's OK, Aisha. There's nothing wrong in . . . in being a coconut.'

Scottie trudged to Old Kent Road.

I really wanted to say that if *I* was a coconut, what was *she*? But I didn't. I was nearly a teenager, after all, and was learning to be mature about such things. So we carried on for a while in an uncomfortable silence. I fixed all my attention on beating her, but each square, each instruction spelled out the same name: Coconut. Go To Coconut. Do Not Pass Coconut. Collect Coconut.

Fatima broke the silence. 'I *was* in an Asian school, but got transferred.' She paused, before saying, lackadaisically, 'You have the best of both worlds. You're part of what Dad calls the Asian equation. You'll probably be a doctor, or a dentist, or a pharmacist or something like that.'

'Hmm,' I said. Was she trying to make me feel better?

By the time dinner was ready everyone had arrived – in periodic bursts, naturally – so we had to postpone the game, which was fine by me. But we stayed together – with me still thinking about what she had said – and proceeded to fight our way to the buffet. Fatima kept her head down, though I noticed the other guests glancing curiously at her.

None of the sizzling mush on offer looked appetizing, but we orbited the table dutifully, squashed together like pilgrims in Mecca with our paper plates. As we did so, a very old man, who was standing next to me, whispered in my ear with a sharp, thick accent, 'Is she your *friend*?' His white-ringed eyes bored into me. 'Be careful! White *shaitan*.'

I froze. I knew the word, but I would never have associated it with Fatima, until then. *Shaitan: Devil.* The man squinted at me and his wispy white eyebrows joined together. The wrinkles around his face buckled even more, like a concertina. He was waiting for an answer.

I wanted to tell him that she wasn't my friend, but my mouth appeared to have sewn itself up out of fright. He grabbed a plateful of food and hobbled away. I breathed out, in relief.

Fatima asked, casually, what the old man had said. I stared at her: the pale pink devil, whose flesh now reminded me of pigskin.

'Umm,' I said. 'I dunno. Something in Punjabi, I think.' I felt a prickly heat radiating from my face.

Fatima tilted her head, her eyes scanning me back and forth. 'Really?' she said.

I looked down at my plate. I had torn it to smithereens. Fatima followed my gaze and leaned forward to get a better look.

'Whoops,' she said, giggling.

I darted out of the circling crowd and threw the remains of the plate into the bin. Fatima watched me find a fresh plate from a pile on the kitchen counter, then beckoned me back next to her. I returned, reluctantly.

'What?' I said, bracing myself.

'You don't know how to speak Punjabi?'

'No. I don't.' I huffed. 'My dad never taught me, OK?' That was the end of that conversation and I set about randomly choosing food that I would later regret.

After dinner Fatima asked if I wanted to finish our game of Monopoly. I said no. I let her pack the board away by herself, on her hands and knees; watching her made me feel a little odd, I must say. I then stayed with Mum and Dad for the rest of the evening, carefully avoiding her – and the old man.

I was even more relieved than normal when they told me it was time to go. I put up with the last round of pseudo-sad goodbyes and then I was out the door, walking away with my parents. The lights from the house were casting long golden rectangles into the darkness. I heard someone running down the driveway. I turned around and Fatima pounced. I flinched. She wrapped her arms around me and held me tight; the cold metal of her glasses pressing against the side of my head. I heard my parents say *Aah*, as they got into the car. This was embarrassing enough without them watching.

'*Khudaa Hafiz*,' Fatima said and she let me go. The words turned into vapour. Her face was in shadow, but there was enough light for me to see that she was smiling, a wincing kind of smile.

I sighed. I may have even rolled my eyes.

'It means *May God be your guardian* in Urdu. Goodbye.'

'*Khudaa Hafiz*,' I said, surprised I could pronounce it first time.

She kissed me gently on the cheek. Her skin felt soft and warm, like a baby's. She walked away, turning back as she went. At the doorway, she stood motionless, like a porcelain statue: hands clasped in front, feet together, her flaxen hair illuminated like a halo from the hallway light behind her. I stayed where I was, surrounded by the night, paralysed by confusion. She didn't look like a devil at all.

'Aisha.' Fatima seemed to be calling my name, but her lips weren't moving and her voice sounded distant, an echo on the wind, like a siren. 'Aisha.' The call was growing louder.

We held each other's gaze. Fatima waved. I waved back.

'Aisha!' Mum shouted.

I jolted back to life and got into the car. Fatima waved again as we reversed out of the drive. I mirrored her action, not sure whether she could see me in the backseat. The tarmac river took us away.

*

We were on the Hagley Road, heading towards Birmingham city centre, when I realized I had been wrong about her, about Fatima. She'd tried to befriend me and I had pushed her away. I had behaved like that stupid, ignorant old man. I felt bad; guilty even.

'Aah,' Mum said again. 'It's just so sweet. I think you've made a friend for life there, Aisha.'

I tried to smile, but couldn't think what to say. How could Fatima still want to be friends with me after the way I'd ignored her at the end of the party?

Mum turned around to face me. 'Are you OK, babs? You're very quiet.'

'Uh-huh . . . yeah, fine.'

'Fatima really liked you, didn't she?'

I shrugged. *But she did call you a coconut, Aisha!*

'I feel sorry for her,' Dad said.

I wanted to tell them that Fatima didn't want people feeling sorry for her. Maybe that's why she liked me, because I'd treated her just the same as anyone else. But, then again, had I? I wasn't convinced.

Mum stared at me with her blue eyes for a moment longer, gave me a puzzled look and turned back to face the road. 'Yes. It's a shame. Poor thing. So unlucky.'

I kept quiet for the rest of the journey, feigning fatigue. Mum switched the radio on – I think she knew it was best to let me be.

'Oh no, not again!' she said.

It was Paul Young, still wondering where to put his hat.

As we drove onto the Aston Expressway back towards Sutton Coldfield, I noticed how the streetlights were making my shadow loom up across the back of Dad's seat. It disturbed me to see it build up, fade away and build up again.

Then I caught Dad's big brown eyes – intermittently

obscured by the oncoming headlights reflected in his glasses – analysing me from his rearview mirror.

I moved my head to escape his gaze. Looking out of the window and into my own reflection, I realized how dark I appeared at night, my face illuminated by orange. My big brown eyes stared back at me, unblinking, completely still. Without looking away I leaned my forehead against the cold glass and sighed deeply. Warm mist steamed up the window, fogging my vision, turning everything ghostly white.

Ball Pool

Chris Killen

'It was a strange year,' Charlotte says to herself about the year she is in, not the previous one. It becomes a private catchphrase. It appears at bus stops and in shop doorways. It causes children to turn round and look up at her. She starts saying it just four days into January. 'It was a strange year.'

To reach a point of objective distance: this is what she needs. To see herself as someone else, a query on a problem page, something 'fixable'.

So:

She breaks up with Gareth for the third and final time.

She sits him down in a bar and buys him a drink and tells him it isn't working. There is inappropriate music, piped in, and someone, somewhere is laughing.

'This has happened before,' Gareth says. 'You'll change your mind.'

But Charlotte is very definite. She tilts her chin to prove it.

And then Gareth begins to look very small and sad, and doesn't get angry or leave, just sits there at the table, looking down, fiddling with a napkin, all bottom lip and eyebrows, until Charlotte feels confused again, and says (and thinks she means), 'I still feel the same about you, you know. I don't know what I'm doing.'

'Done,' Gareth says. 'What you've done.'

*

In February, she tries to get hit by a car.

It's late and cold and dark and she is coming home from work, standing, waiting to cross the street. The road becomes clear, and still she waits. When the car comes, she grits her teeth and walks out into the middle, very slowly.

She's imagining a teary, shocked answerphone message to Gareth from a mutual friend, even though Gareth doesn't own an answerphone, even though no one owns an answerphone any more: 'Did you hear about Charlotte?'

She is walking very very slowly, half knowing that the car will see her; that it will swerve to avoid her or else pull to a stop.

The car is headlights and engine noise and screeching brakes.

Charlotte is a wobbling traffic cone.

It is dark and raining and the car is just a silly black box with headlights and something else inside that she can't see.

Now a horn is beeping, and another car is pulling up behind the first one. Charlotte waves and mouths 'Sorry', running for the kerb with her head ducked.

Charlotte gets a 'verbal warning' for continued lateness and apathy. The bookshop operates a 'three strikes and you're out' policy. She's not sure if this is her first or second strike.

It's March.

She is asked about twice a day, by members of staff, and occasionally by the public (usually old women) if she's OK.

Charlotte's not sure how to reply. When she thinks

hard about the question, she feels weird, like something in her life has shifted, changed tense. She's begun to see human beings not as individual things, but as one large group of sad, doomed creatures, and she's not sure if this is 'OK'. So she tries to imagine a new scheme, a kind of playgroup maybe: like a giant ball pool where all the human beings could go and just hug each other and not have to feel so alone and ridiculous any more.

Charlotte buys about three hundred ping-pong balls over the internet, from a specialist sports supplier. They arrive in a big plastic bag, which she has to sign for. She tears open the bag and tips all the ping-pong balls into the bath.

It's her day off, a Wednesday.

It isn't enough; there's just a three- or four-inch layer of ping-pong balls in the bath, but she takes off her clothes anyway and gets in. The ping-pong balls are uncomfortable. They squeak and crack against each other and don't even start to cover her. She gets out of the bath again and runs in lukewarm water. Turning on the immersion heater is impossible. She gets in again. Now the balls float around her body and touch her chin and her knees. They're like little planets. She is out of scale. She should be smaller than them. The water is the galaxy. She should be living on one of the ping-pong balls. She should be small enough to pinch between her own fingers, to put herself out like a candle.

The ping-pong balls look sad and confused, so she takes out two, holding one in each hand, and kisses them.

'This one's me,' she says. 'And this one's Gareth.'

Then she starts to cry, knowing that her metaphors are tangled and ridiculous, like a pair of knickers or her hair in the morning or her and Gareth, or just her, by herself, probably getting fired from her job some time in the week.

*

Maybe she will cut off her mouth, or sew it up, like that man she read about in the paper. Maybe she'll visit the doctor's.

In April, she calls Gareth. He sounds wary on the phone, and a little too quiet, like he's doing something else at the same time; looking at the internet or playing that tennis game on his Xbox. They arrange to meet at a bar, the same one she broke up with him in.

Charlotte arrives first.

She sits at a table in the corner. When Gareth arrives, he doesn't see her at first and she doesn't wave, she waits for him to notice her. He looks somehow longer than she remembers, and bent over like a bit of corn in the wind or someone searching for a contact lens. He is clean-shaven and looks well fed and healthy, but his eyes are just two black holes, trying to contract small enough to disappear into his face. He goes to the bar, then turns and looks around and notices her and comes over. She doesn't remember him being this awkward. It's as if he's been dismantled.

'How are you?' she asks, once he's sat down.

'Oh,' he says. 'You know.'

He doesn't look her in the eyes. He is wiping his finger up and down his glass, and then picking at a bit of thumbnail.

'I got sacked from my job,' she says.

'That's nice,' he says.

They don't say anything else for a while. He keeps picking at the thumbnail and touching the glass and not looking her in the eye.

'Listen,' she says. 'I'm really sorry about what happened. I think I've made a big mistake. I miss you. I think I want to be with you again.'

He looks up from the glass and his thumbnail. His eyes

are so small they are like little black animal eyes. There is no expression in them.

'What the fuck?' he says. 'What the fuck?'

As Gareth launches into a loud, shaky-voiced attack, Charlotte floats upwards towards the ceiling. She perches on the dusty light fittings. She can see herself down there, not saying anything, keeping her mouth closed because she deserves this – yes, she is a horrible person and she should be told – and even though she can't really hear what Gareth is saying from up here, she doesn't really mind because she can feel the sentences sinking into her, and knows that they will pop up again, complete, later on: on the bus, in bed tonight, halfway through a sandwich, etc, etc.

Once Gareth is finished – once he's said his piece and downed his drink and stormed out of the bar – Charlotte goes downstairs. She sits on one of the toilets and puts her head in her hands and makes a dry hissing sound, her eyes screwed shut and her tongue extended.

Charlotte spends a month inside her house with the curtains drawn. The only light comes from the computer screen. There is a duvet near by. She looks at: yoga, reiki, ear candling, sensory deprivation tanks, hypnotherapy, adult education, gym memberships, book groups, life drawing classes, photography clubs, swimming, archery, creative writing.

She hovers her mouse pointer over electronic payment buttons, but doesn't click.

She never gets past the 'about us' page.

In June, she receives three 'winks' from men in her area. A wink, she thinks, means they are probably a bit interested, but not enough to send her a private message. She looks at their profiles.

One is in his late forties, divorced, and likes going out, staying in, food, cinema, and music.

One is in his early twenties, single, and likes going out, staying in, food, cinema, and music.

One is just a question mark (no profile uploaded for this member yet).

She likes the look of the question mark best.

She likes the mystery. She lies in her bed, not in her pyjamas, and imagines making love to him. He curls around her like a giant black snake: he rubs his dot softly between her legs until she comes.

Two days later, she sends him a private message:

> HI THERE
> TELL ME A BIT MORE ABOUT YOURSELF.
> LUV
> CHARLIE-CAT X

Charlie-Cat is her screen name. The 'X' is just a kiss. She doesn't know why she's chosen the name, something to do with alliteration, probably.

While waiting, she does shopping and laundry and online banking, transferring £500 chunks from the savings account her parents, for some reason, still pay into monthly.

Then the question mark sends a reply.

Why am I so excited about this? she thinks, clicking on the email, waiting for it to open up.

The question mark is called Dean. He is thirty, and he likes going out, staying in, food, cinema, and music.

He sounds sweet, she thinks.

When Dean arrives at the bar, wearing a red shirt, and is a human man and not a long black question mark, Charlotte feels disappointed.

*

July. She sleeps with Dean twice and then he stops answering her calls, stops sending her private messages, and stops winking at her. She wasn't really that into him, anyway, so the whole thing doesn't feel too upsetting.

She's started drinking in the afternoons now, mostly Lambrini. It makes her dizzy and hyperactive, then later sluggish and irritable. There is no one around to be dizzy with or sluggish with, so she starts phoning her parents, dropping hints; she is thinking of going back to university, she's sick of Manchester. So what if they turned her room into a study when she moved out? Surely it wouldn't be too hard to turn it back into a bedroom? Surely their only daughter is more important than a computer and a desk to put it on? Computers are small these days, anyway. If you really want to, you can just put one on your knees in the living room.

In August, the months get mixed up and somehow, impossibly, it is January again. Or maybe it's September. Has October been and gone? She's thrown her calendar away. She's also thrown some of her other things away and given some to Oxfam. Birthday presents, paper plates, half a box of teabags. She divided her things indiscriminately between Oxfam and the bin, no longer able to discern between 'useful' and 'not useful', unable to see the difference between 'expensive' and 'worthless'. So, some days Oxfam get the teabags, and some days the bin men get all her Laura Ashley dresses.

Where are her friends? Does she have any?

Charlotte can't remember.

And sometimes she wakes up and it's September of the previous year, and she is trying to call Gareth and feeling confused when he doesn't pick up the phone.

'I'm not making much sense right now,' she says out loud to herself, forgetting to turn the lights on in the evenings, all the new toilet rolls thrown away. 'It was a strange year.'

Nothing happens in November. Absolutely nothing. There are no people on the streets or animals in the trees. Crisp packets don't fall out of bins and get blown down the street because there are no crisp packets in the bins or wind to blow them around. November is the black part at the back of someone's throat. November is a joke, and she is waiting for the punchline.

Just one more month, she thinks. Just one more month to get through, and then something is going to happen, surely. Because if nothing happens, if it's just the same as every other month . . .

Her lips are almost always moving.

Her hands are making strange shapes in her pockets.

Everything is directed towards her; when she is on a bus or in a supermarket, it is no longer just a suspicion – everyone really is looking at her.

She is waiting for a crash or an explosion or even just a peck on the cheek. She is waiting to be nine years old again, physically sick with excitement at the appearance of a plastic teaset.

And when her parents open the door in December, grey-eyed and a lot older-looking than she remembers, they say they have something to tell her, that they didn't want to say it over the phone, that it might not be anything yet, that she really shouldn't worry, but.

The Mermaid and
the Music Box
Megan Dunn

'Is she blond?'

'No.'

'What colour's her hair?'

'Black.'

'She might like to dye her hair later.' Raymond smiles. 'Does she speak English?'

'As far as we're aware she doesn't speak at all.'

'Oh.' Raymond crosses out the goldfish he has doodled in his diary. 'But can she sing?'

'Our scientists haven't examined her vocal chords yet.'

'I told you: I don't want any scientists involved,' Raymond says, the pen falling from his hand.

'Yes, yes. That's fine. No scientists.'

'Is she friendly?'

'It's hard to tell. She's been heavily sedated since her capture off the coast of the Caribbean.'

'So, she's from a warm climate?' Raymond says.

The voice at the other end of the line coughs. 'I must warn you: she's been known to bite.'

'To bite?' Raymond runs one hand through his long ponytail, then reaches down and adjusts his lavender codpiece.

'Yes. She is still extremely distressed. We think it's the shock.'

'I suppose that's only natural,' he says. 'I'm sure she'll feel better when she has a new home. How old is she?'

'We don't know.'

'What do you mean? She'd better be young – I haven't paid to have the Ancient Mariner delivered to the estate.'

'Don't panic, Mr Lavender. She's definitely very young.'

Dusk descends upon the lawn. Dew licks the grass with a wet tongue. Downstairs, the pool filter purrs, effortlessly sifting chlorine. Raymond paces the tiled floor, unable to rest. Upstairs, the Dream Dates are having their afternoon nap. Earlier he passed by the door of the communal bedroom and saw them sleeping naked on top of the silk sheets. Their blond hair tangled across the lavender pillows, a row of silicone breasts, nuzzling arched backs. He has told them to go clubbing tonight without him. He doesn't want anyone else to see the truck when it arrives at midnight.

Outside, the sky deepens to dark blue, bruises itself with clouds, then turns black.

She wakes. Her brain fights its way through an army of memories. Rope digging into scales, chafing. The sharp bite of oxygen slipping in and out of her gills. Fish writhing beneath her, their mouths opening and closing in surprise; the prickle of their tails against her flesh; their fins flickering. One by one, the fish lying still.

Odourless night. A snatch of ocean. The lap of waves.

A creature in white inches towards her. Large fingers of coral wiggle in front of her face. The creature holds something, a barb that punctures her skin. She shrieks. Pain pierces her limbs and the putrid scent of simmering flesh fills her nostrils. Water scratches her scales; bubbles rise around her waist, popping and fizzing. She is hot. Too hot. Her tail writhes and twists in shallow water

until, finally, the mermaid opens her mouth and screams:
the high-pitched scream of an animal being cooked alive.

His hands tremble at the heart-shaped lock. With sweat
on his brow, Raymond turns the key; he hasn't used the
attic in a long time and the lock is stiff. He pauses, runs
his hands through his long hair. Then tries again. The
door clicks open dutifully this time, like a lover accepting
a kiss.

Inside the attic, warm water rises between his bare toes.
The floor is swamped. The mermaid is lying next to the
Jacuzzi, shivering. The carpet squelches as he rushes
towards her.

'What is it? What's wrong?'

She screams at the sight of his face. The interior of her
throat is alarmingly opaque. She has a set of baby teeth,
small and slightly pointed.

The Jacuzzi bubbles like a cauldron in the background.

'Is the water too hot?'

Her tail hammers through the air towards him and he
is knocked sideways onto the floor. The mermaid
clutches at his legs. His lavender codpiece splays open
and his penis flops out like a parsnip. Raymond is
dazzled by how fast she can move. She lunges at him like
a crocodile. Her hands are slightly webbed, her talons
long and white with a sheen of blue. She scratches four
lines into his face. He raises his hand to his cheek,
stunned. The wound stings of salt. Her eyes stare at him.
She has no pupils. Just the blackened eyes of a shark.

'There, there, good girl.' He fumbles in his dressing-
gown pocket. 'I've got something for you.' He holds up a
shiny shell, stabs it into the parched flesh of her tail. The
mermaid wails. Then the morphine rushes into her blood
and she is out cold.

Raymond turns off the Jacuzzi. He picks her up and

rocks her against his chest. 'I'm sorry. I didn't mean to hurt you.'

He kisses her head. Her hair is still wet. She smells of the deepest part of the ocean. Of places human eyes will never see. The dark shifting carpet of sand, the never-ceasing darkness from which all life has grown. He imagines the quivering souls of amoebas clustering on the bottom of the ocean like abandoned silicone implants.

As he rocks the mermaid against his chest, time seems to run backwards. Human flesh grows coarse brown hair, faces shrivel, eyes blink and open: they are the raisin eyes of apes. The apes get smaller, their backs hunch until they are the smooth hairless backs of Mexican walking fish, sitting in the white heat of the sun, their amphibious skin still glazed with seawater. The earth turns and the Mexican walking fish walk backwards into the ocean. A pterodactyl flies overhead, searching the waves for shoals of fish.

The next day Raymond fills the gold-plated Jacuzzi with oxygen weed.

The mermaid sleeps; her face underneath the water. The tip of her tail hangs over the Jacuzzi and drips onto the carpet.

Raymond sits on a nearby chair and watches her. The scratches across his face still sting of salt. His hands ache to touch her tail. Bubbles float up from her nose and cling to the skin around her mouth. Her lips are mauve and a bit more rubbery than Raymond would have liked, but she is barely a teenager.

At night, the mermaid cries. Her eyes gaze at the sea of stars through the skylight. He hears her calling for her kind. He plays her a CD of whale and dolphin sounds. This makes her crying worse. In desperation, he sings her the same lullabies his mother sang to him as a child.

Twinkle, twinkle little star, how I wonder what you are.
He brings her toys. She bites the head off his favourite Barbie, tries to eat it. He hangs a mobile over her Jacuzzi as though it's a cot. He brings her a music box and sets it up on a table out of the range of her tail. He winds the box up and opens the lid. A plastic ballerina springs up and turns around to the tune, 'Raindrops keep falling on my head'.

Every evening the Dream Dates listen to Raymond's footsteps climbing the stairs to the attic.

'Can you hear music?' they ask. They stop buffing their nails and sit still. They have started wearing pyjamas to bed.

'Why doesn't Raymond come and visit us any more?'

'He's old,' says the wisest Dream Date. 'He'll probably die soon.'

The Dream Dates gasp in horror, but each girl longs for a slice of the Lavender Estate. The faint tinkle of the music box seeps into their sleep. They dream of fresh fish and shell-shaped combs and wake up hungry with knots in their hair.

In the attic, the mermaid's eyes dart towards the box. She listens. Her luminous hands grip the side of the Jacuzzi. Her black eyes drink in the music. Every time the tune winds to a close, she slams her tail against the surface of the water. Waves fly over the shagpile carpet. Raymond spends all night winding up the music box. In the morning, he stumbles downstairs with heavy bags beneath his eyes.

The cook looks up from her bowl and gasps. She drops her spatula.

'Señor Lavender!'

She hands him a fresh shrimp cocktail and he returns to the attic. The sight of the mermaid sucking and chewing on the small pink ringlets of shrimp fills his heart with pride.

He sleeps during the day. Strange dreams flicker behind his eyelids. A bevy of mermaids dances towards him under the ocean; he hears their voices, rich and deep; the sound vibrates in his ears. Just as he is about to reply, the mermaids move in and strip the flesh from his bones like a pack of piranhas. He wakes with a dry throat and reaches down to squeeze his balls. Inside the right sac, he finds a hard lump the size of a pea.

'Ray?'
  'Are you all right?'
  'What's the matter?'
  'He's burning up, feel his forehead.'
  'Oh my God.'
The Dream Dates loom over his bed. Their blond faces mime concern. Raymond tries to swing his legs out of bed. He can't sit up. His balls throb. The Dream Dates dress in nurses' uniforms and escort him to a black limousine. A fine layer of sweat breaks out over his forehead. He stumbles on the pebbled drive. The Dream Dates hold him steady; their tanned arms are strong. They open the door onto the large back seat. Beige leather: the palm of an embalmer's hand. Raymond pauses. He looks up at the attic window, glazed with sunlight.

The doctor admires the X-rays with the zeal of an artist exhibiting his latest set of paintings. Raymond stares at his balls in black and white. The smell of sterilized needles and surgical gloves peppers the air.

  'The tumour is extremely advanced. The growth is surprisingly aggressive.'

'Do you think it's a side effect of the Viagra?'

'No, no, there's no proof of that.' The doctor snaps the projection off. The X-rays disappear.

'How much will it cost?'

'Excuse me?' The doctor slides his glasses down onto the tip of his nose.

'To cut it out.'

The doctor frowns. 'I'm afraid it's not quite that simple, Mr Lavender. The tumour has already spread. There's no easy way to say this –' The doctor squares his shoulders. 'We need to remove both your testicles.'

Raymond swallows. 'That's out of the question.' He manages a little laugh, but there's no one to share the joke.

'I understand.' The doctor nods. 'But we must act quickly. Think of your family.'

Raymond thinks only of the mermaid.

Death hovers in the room like a moth, flapping its wings at him.

His shoulders collapse. He feels older than Rip Van Winkle. 'OK. But I want to keep them.'

'Keep what?' The doctor's mind has flown away already, projecting into the future, the surgery he will have to perform . . .

'My balls,' Raymond says.

Clouds smother the lights of Los Angeles. A veil of mist shrouds the gates when Raymond returns to the estate, still groggy from the operation. His head lolls against the back seat. Clutching a sealed plastic bag, he gazes out the window as the limousine penetrates smog as smooth as cream. Worms shuttle through the ground. The petals of roses close. Dripping leaves hang from the trees. The chauffeur helps Raymond to the door. He shuffles across the marble foyer, the bag carefully concealed in his dressing-gown pocket. Outside, lightning lacerates the sky and the Dream Dates scream.

The mermaid is waiting. Her head turns towards the door as it opens. She howls. Her face is streaked with tears and her cheeks are hollow. It has only been one night, yet she is thinner, her skin almost translucent. He can see the river of veins beneath her flesh. She reaches out for him and Raymond smothers her webbed hands with wet kisses.

'Ssshhh. I'm here now, I'm here now,' he croons.

He has brought her a lobster and a pickled eel. She tears the lobster apart in her mouth. Flakes of orange shell crackle between her teeth. The lobster's white flesh disappears. Raymond watches her throat expand. She sucks on the eel and gives a satisfied slurp as it travels towards her stomach. He winds up the music box and she falls asleep with her head resting on his lap. Her damp hair seeps through his dressing gown and soothes his wounds.

Above the skylight is a full moon. Unblinking. Cold. The mermaid's tail twitches as she dreams. Raymond hears her mew in the night, like a kitten calling out for its mother. Across the world the tide is rushing into estuaries and inlets. Waves smother sandy beaches and rivers overflow . . .

The mermaid can sense the change in Raymond. She touches his face for the first time. He feeds her fruit in shades of pastel lingerie: pineapple, mango, watermelon and guava. She tastes the sunshine in bananas, swallows the earth in a mouthful of roast beef. Her tongue leaps out of her mouth and chases the juice. Raymond feeds her his mother's favourite recipes. The mermaid eats fried chicken and her face is stained with wonder. Raymond dangles tender marinated strips of porterhouse steak above the Jacuzzi. Tiny bites adorn his fingers. The sheen of blueness disappears from the mermaid's skin. Her breasts swell and an apricot glow assaults her cheeks.

Raymond sits on the edge of the Jacuzzi. A sliver of moonlight illuminates the room. The mermaid cocks her head like a dog and regards him with intelligent eyes. He holds his hands behind his back. She watches his lips closely and tries to imitate the sounds.

'Raymond.'

'Ay – ungh.'

'Good, good!'

He holds out a pineapple ring and she grabs it, stuffs the fruit inside her mouth. Juice races down her chin and drips onto her chest. She reaches out for another.

Raymond shakes his finger. 'Not yet. One more time. Ray-*mond*.'

'Ay – ay.'

His shoulders sag. He sighs; rests his head in his hands. The mermaid slaps her tail against the side of the Jacuzzi. A spray of water wets his lap. He passes her the tin of pineapple and she fishes the slices out with her fingers.

The drugs the doctor prescribes percolate inside his veins. Chemotherapy teases the beautiful long hair from his scalp. Raymond cries. The Dream Dates buy him a platinum-grey wig. 'You're looking better,' they assure him. 'The wig is so natural.' His penis shrivels to the size of a baby's finger.

When Raymond emerges from the attic, he finds one of the Dream Dates standing guard outside his room. He phones his lawyer, redrafts his will. Celebrities appear at the door: friends, lovers, journalists. His ex-wife brings him a bunch of green Californian grapes. 'Oh my God,' she says, her blue eyes bulging at the sight of his face. The cancer has whittled away his skeleton, hollowed him out. Raymond grabs the grapes and slams the gates of the estate shut. He refuses to see any more visitors, except for a naturopath.

The naturopath waits for Raymond in the oak-panelled library. Her sensitive hands caress the erotic statues on the mantelpiece. She strokes a woman's naked torso, admiring each marble breast. Raymond enters: a cadaver smoking a pipe. Two Dream Dates flank him like Shetland ponies. A bright blue aura radiates from his skin. The naturopath is overcome by the stench of seaweed. Raymond sinks into a comfortable chair. 'Can you help me?' he asks.

The naturopath unwraps a quartz pendulum from a soft leather pouch around her neck. The pendulum quivers above Raymond's forehead. She smiles. 'How much seafood do you include in your diet?'

Raymond licks his lips. Saliva coats the roof of his mouth. For the first time he wonders what the mermaid herself might taste like. Is she pink and tender like corned beef, or grey and salty like canned tuna?

Light ebbs and flows like water. The mermaid's nostrils fill with new smells. Baked bread. The tang of the cocoa bean. Meat braised and seared and sautéed. Her stomach inflates. She salivates at the sound of Raymond's footsteps on the stairs. Her tail plumps up like a cushion. The scales flake off to reveal flesh as pink as Spam.

She forgets what the ocean smells like. Only when she dreams can she glimpse the greenness of the sea. Her fins quiver, her spine aches. She smells him on her hands: the stink of dry land. Weeks of stagnant water, the scratch and drag of oxygen weed. A tune plays in her head. Her throat stings as, alone, she tries to make his sounds. Ay. Ungh. Ay-unnngh.

The mermaid submerges. She cries for the ocean. Her tears blend with the Jacuzzi water. Movements echo below her: the gallop of legs. Tentacles of white light drift down through the skylight. His key clicks in the lock.

Raymond bundles the mermaid in his arms like a bride and carries her down the oak staircase into the grand hall. Her tail drips onto the stairs. Outside, the lawn wets his bare feet. The mermaid shivers in his embrace. She opens her mouth and drinks in fresh air. Raymond stumbles under the weight of her. He walks slowly through the sprinklers, water raining on them like confetti.

The mermaid sees the pool. Its blueness lit up by a funnel of yellow light. She mews for the water. Her tail begins to tremble. She twists in his arms. His dressing gown falls open and the night air shrivels his flesh.

'Be patient, darling,' Raymond says, lowering her into the pool. The mermaid breaks free of his embrace and slips beneath the surface with a splash. She moves with the stealth of a shark. She laps the pool several times as though searching for a channel back into the sea. Her head pops up in the distance, her face in shadow. Below the pool's surface, her tail hangs like an anchor. She stares down at it, as though it has surprised her – with its usefulness, its strength and speed. Raymond is surprised, too. He claps as though she has won a race, then fears a Dream Date will have heard him. He glances back towards the estate, but its windows are dark and expressionless.

Sprinklers fan out on the lawn behind him, the soft patter of drops hitting the grass. A dog barks. The mermaid's head jerks round.

'It's OK.' Raymond smiles. He forgets there is so much of the world she has not seen or heard.

'Shall I join you?' he asks.

The water feels cool and indifferent on his skin as he swims towards her. The mermaid bares her razor-like teeth, arches her back and growls.

He holds his arms out to greet her. 'There, there, it's only me.'

A lash of water breaks over his face. Her tail rolls him under. They turn together as though twisting through silk sheets. Raymond claws at her. Her black eyes are large and calm. He thrashes through the turquoise water; bubbles explode from his nostrils. Finally his mouth breaks the surface. He lurches towards the side of the pool, kicks off her hands and heaves himself onto the grass. Blood runs down his leg and splashes onto his feet. His breath pours out in staccato bursts, fogging the air. The mermaid submerges with a chunk of his flesh between her teeth. He limps back towards the estate, the night heavy with the spice of blood and cologne.

Midnight. Raymond removes a plastic bag from the freezer. He opens the microwave door, places the pouch of flesh inside and pushes the defrost button. He dices an onion, hears the oil in the pan hiss. The microwave beeps. He lathers the meat in octopus ink. The bite on his leg fizzes. Blood pools on the black marble floor. He hadn't wanted to use the syringe to sedate her, but he'd had no choice.

In the great hall, the Koi carp carved into the staircase's oak balustrades gleam in the dark. Raymond's leg clenches on the stairs and he grips the banister. His slippers slide back and forth on the soles of his feet. At the attic door, he fishes into the pocket of his dressing gown and pulls out the key. He can hear her voice through the lock. A lonely, high-pitched sound that brings him out in a rash of goosebumps. She is singing. His ears string together the broken sounds. He recognizes the tune. 'Raindrops keep falling on my head.'

Inside the attic, the mermaid's dark eyes turn towards him: the echo of the moon behind a cloud. As Raymond holds her last supper, light plays on the silver platter.

She regards the meal cautiously. The morphine has made her docile; she fumbles for the pale, beige flesh. The moon sinks below the cloud and the skylight is smothered in blackness. Raymond listens to her slurp and crunch. He imagines her eyes widening as she breaks into the soft centre of his right ball. A river of salt splashes onto her tongue. Sperm mingles with saliva. When she has finished eating, she licks the platter clean. Nothing is left. Not even the sprig of parsley.

The embalmer and his daughter take special care with the penis: a wilted flower.

'It's smaller than I imagined,' the embalmer's daughter says.

Her father nods.

She lifts the penis gently and dusts underneath. She sees the scars from where his balls were removed. Two pink smiles.

Together the pair drain the fluids from the corpse. The body still smells of cologne. The blood is thick and lusty. In the contents of his stomach they find the half-digested fin of a strange fish.

She holds it up. 'A shark?'

'No.' The embalmer shakes his head. 'Something else . . .'

The day of the funeral approaches. The smog above Los Angeles is whisked away, revealing a garter-blue sky. The Dream Dates attend the open coffin at the funeral parlour. They have taken special care in choosing the white casket with its lavender satin interior. 'It was his favourite colour,' they say. A large white candle burns in each corner of the room. Their tears rain on his skin. Their fingers skim the surface of his face. They leave after ten minutes.

The embalmer's daughter sneaks back into the room for one last look. She lifts the corpse's legs up one at a time and eases the codpiece from beneath his bum. Lavender silk ripples beneath her fingers. The tumour has whittled each leg to a twig. She holds up the bizarre garment and shakes her head, smiling. She will sell it on eBay, fetch a handsome price. She blows out the candles and clamps the coffin lid shut.

A helicopter scissors through the Los Angeles sky. A fleet of Dream Dates haul a white coffin out of the back of a hearse, their black satin mini-skirts shimmering in the sun. A thousand cameras flash like diamonds.

The gates to the Lavender Estate close. Without a gardener, the grounds revert to their natural state. Vines grow up around the driveway and thread through the iron gates.

The pool filter utters its last sigh. The air conditioning breaks. Mould spreads green tentacles across the belly of the grotto. Dead leaves fall through broken glass and settle like a film over the water.

The polar icecaps melt. Mountains cascade into the sea. Seaweed towers above skyscrapers. Schools of fish travel freely through the underwater world; their scales flare in the dark like car headlights.

Mermaids surface above the waves and gaze at what remains of the earth. They dive down to hunt for treasure in desecrated cities. A fishbone from a rubbish bin. A pair of leather trousers. The mermaids sniff and stare.

They find a solitary stiletto, the instep bloated and strange, hanging out like a tongue.

The coral reef restores itself: a white, breathing world laced with fish.

A throng of mermaids rests on the roof of the Empire State Building. They dip their tails into the sea and scoop out funnels of saltwater. They wash their faces, then comb the knots from one another's hair. The carcase of a cat drifts by, its fur straggled, its eyes eaten out by the birds that circle overhead. A young mermaid plucks the cat's body from the waves and nurses it in her arms. A sense of déjà vu glitters behind her black eyes. She looks up at the gathering storm clouds and hums an ancient tune. Raindrops keep falling on her head.

To the Bridge
Amy Mason

I am out of practice speaking.

'Help me up,' I try to say, but all that comes out is 'hrrrrrrrrp' and spit.

I want to open the window. It's too dark in here and it smells of pee, but my legs are stuck to the plastic chair and I'm struggling to stand. An old man sits right next to me, his hand almost touching my skirt. There's a crusty white stain on the knee of his trousers and his face seems to be melting, his bottom lip wet and drooping like it's going to fall off. He's watching television.

'I ask you now, my brothers, and my countrymen, revoke Islam and embrace Jesus Christ,' says a dark-skinned gentleman from the screen.

'What the fuck is this? The terrorist channel?' says someone behind me, a girl.

'She's one of them, mind, Jodi,' says a big fat woman with thick legs who's standing to my left, nodding towards me.

'Shit,' says the first girl.

Me? One of whom?

It goes to the break – a book about the devil for just £9.99.

Thick Legs says to Melting Man, 'It's about the devil now, chicken, do you want to watch about the devil?'

He doesn't answer, but she switches over anyway, her big white behind filling the screen.

And then there's Bette Davis staring at the stars and smoking. Where are my cigarettes? I reach to touch my long hair but it's gone.

'They loves this old stuff,' someone says and hands me a cup of tea that looks like gone-off milk.

My Hebrew isn't good enough.

I want to ask them, How long do you think for the bus to Tel Aviv? Enough time to buy falafel from the stand?

I think I make a noise because a girl laughs. She is wearing a white dress, but she isn't a nurse; her tights are ripped and she smells of sweat.

Michal? No. Dinah?

Dinah. In fancy dress.

I hold out my hand and she kneels down. She is looking me in the eye now. Our father would have a fit – all that stuff on her face! I won't tell. I want to touch her cheek but she pushes my hand back at me, annoyed.

'Sweetheart, your daughter is here to see you – to take you out.'

I laugh. This girl is mad.

She stands up and walks away. Dinah! Don't go, please!

'Rega!' I say. Wait!

But then my mother takes her place. She is plump, with black makeup round her eyes, and a few lines round her mouth. She lets me touch her face.

'Mummy . . . your hair!' she says and cries quietly. 'What have they done to your hair?'

I wince. I am not her mother – she's mine.

'I don't know what you mean, Mama. I'm not sure,' I say.

'OK,' she says quietly. 'OK . . . Mummy – Miri, my dear one, let's go to Brunel's to eat.'

I smile. That's right – almost right. She puts her head on my lap and I rest mine on hers. Her hair is a mass of curls, so tight and sharp, like the wire wool I use to scrub the sinks. She smells clean, of sweet lemons, and her face is soft and warm, an almond in its skin.

'Delicious,' I say and she makes a small sound.

'I want to go to the bridge,' I say.

'My God, I'm so sorry that you went there, that we went away and left you. It's horrible, truly horrible. I could bloody kill Abe. What in God's name was he thinking?'

I nod. I don't know what she's saying but I like this girl. I'll humour her. I smile over the mirrored counter at the man in the apron – he looks like the owner, Jimmy, but he's old. He blows me a kiss and I laugh. This soup is good – it's all over my fingers.

'So I've decided, for now at least, you're going to come to live with me and Emily and Clem. I know you don't approve of us, Mu–Miri, and I feel bad because if you were totally yourself you wouldn't even come round for tea, but I think it's for the best, OK . . .'

I try to smile but it's hard. Live with this girl? Jimmy, or Jimmy's father, looks at me and laughs. He understands.

She holds my hand and her fingers are long and thin – just like mine. I lift one to my mouth and kiss its tip.

'Sir,' I say, as clearly as I can, to the man who looks like Jimmy, 'do you know where Simon is?'

'Oh Mummy,' the girl says, and she starts to cry into her soup. Poor thing. I push at her hair and it springs back, fighting me. I laugh.

We are in a restaurant, in Tiberius I think. Simon is in the bathroom; he's always had trouble that way. There are rugs on the walls, beautiful rugs, but dusty and torn. I'm drinking black tea from a small cup and it tastes of tobacco and spice. There are books piled up all over the place.

A Chinese child is staring up at me. 'Nee How,' I say. I learned that from my father. The child wrinkles up her nose and runs across the room.

'Clementine, Clem, sweetie, it's your grandma, don't be scared.'

It's a curly-haired girl speaking. I know her face. Against the pink-brown walls she's a picture. Why is she here?

The child looks round. She is a sweet little thing.

'Hello, Grandma,' she says in a perfect English accent.

'Very good!' I say, and then, 'Nee How!'

'She speaks funny, Ma,' the little girl whispers to Curly Hair, half hidden behind her leg.

'You'll get used to her,' Curly Hair says back. And then, to me, 'She doesn't speak Chinese, Mum—Miri. Can I just call you Mi? How would that be?'

Mi is what Mama calls me. What Simon called me at the start.

'That would be fine,' I say.

The men aren't home yet, God knows why, so I'm saying the prayers tonight. I watch the door carefully as I speak. There is a blond girl here and she's whispering. I put my finger to my lips.

'Are we going to have to do this every Friday, Sara, every single week?'

She is speaking to a Jewish girl with curly brown hair, a good girl, who also puts her fingers to her lips. The goy sighs but doesn't speak again. There's a small Chinese girl staring up at me through the two flames.

The chicken is good but I want harimi and am nearly in tears. I need to taste the sharp sweet sauce, feel the fish collapse on the back of my tongue. The Jewish girl says,

'I'm sorry there's no harimi, Mi. I didn't have time to make it.' How does she know what I want? How does she know my name?

A blond girl is taking me upstairs, leading me by the hand, and I hold on.

'I know we haven't always seen eye to eye, but I want you to be happy, I really do. I hope you like what I've done to your room. I know it's not much. Sara wasn't sure, but I thought it might help. A colleague suggested it.'

Somehow I know that she's a doctor.

'Clever girl,' I say, and I kiss her and she smiles.

On the door is a photograph of me and Dinah in swimsuits blowing raspberries. We have thick, dark hair, the curls slicked into gentle waves by the water. I don't know which of us is which.

'We put it there so you know which room is yours, Miriam. We know you sometimes find it hard to read these days.'

In the room there is a small single bed made up with pink flowery sheets, and a side lamp with an orange shade – my mother's orange velvet shade. I walk over and touch it.

'If you look on the bed – Mi – there are some things we thought . . .'

I look at the bed and begin to sink to my knees. The girl says, 'Umm,' but helps me down.

A brown button shoe of Mama's – a tiny shoe for her little foot – my daddy's medals and Sara's babygro, Abe's hat with all the dropped stitches and a photograph of me on my wedding day, me and Simon with Mama and Daddy and Dinah and all the cousins. And Simon's fabric shears. I close my eyes and snip at invisible lace. That noise!

I am crying and someone touches my hair.

'You're going to be all right, Miriam. You're going to be OK.'

But I'm not all right. There's something wrong. I want the cat. Where's Boots? I want to cry into the cat. Someone lifts me to my feet.

They have told me to go to sleep and put out my light, but it's morning time. I need to get ready for work, and I can't find my skirt. I leave my room and stand in the cool, dark hallway listening to my breath and wondering if I've died.

A door to my left is ajar and I tiptoe in.

There's a little girl in bed on the right, breathing gently, the moon hitting the blue-black sheet of her hair, and next to her a baby in a small cot. I gently pick her up, supporting her cold, hard head. Sara! My darling girl.

I take her back to the hall, clutching her to my breasts, and back through the open door. Her babygro is on the chest of drawers and I put her in it. She is too small and the legs and arms hang off her. She's worryingly cold. But she'll be fine. I'll feed her up.

I get into bed and begin to sing, 'Lula lula bye bye.'

Where's Si? Come back to me, Simon. Please.

A Chinese child is standing next to me holding a baby in her arms. I am lying in bed.

'Is she your daughter? What's her name? Do you speak English?' I say slowly.

'It's not a baby, Grandma. It's a loaf of bread,' she says. She giggles but looks confused. She shows me and she's right – granary.

'You've got my baby doll, in bed with you,' she says.

I don't know what she means and I don't want to find out. I don't know where I am or why I'm here. I look down at my bare arm and nearly scream. The skin is gathered into waves along its length. I look at the girl, my mouth open with fear, but she doesn't see and carries on.

'Mummy and Ma and me went and got this bread for breakfast,' she says. 'Would you come and have breakfast with us?'

'How lovely of you to ask me. I'll get dressed,' I say.

I sit up. My wedding photograph is on the chest of drawers next to me, along with Simon's favourite shears. I kiss them both.

Next to me my baby is sleeping. I will be quiet. I don't want to wake her.

There's a knock at the door.

'Mi, it's Sara . . . do you want to go to Shul?'

'Do I have to?'

'No. Of course not. I just thought . . .'

'No,' I say.

'OK. That's fine. Abe is downstairs.'

'Tremendous,' I say, but I don't know which Abe she means.

'If you could give us a minute, we need to talk.'

'Fine,' I say.

I can hear them downstairs. A girl sounds cross.

'We *had* to leave that place, Abe. I know the nurse said she's got very difficult, but first of all that's bollocks; second of all, you could have found her somewhere better to stay than there. Don't you give a shit?'

A man's voice.

'That place was fine, Sara. You're just a bloody snob. You hardly went near her yourself, not for years.'

'She wouldn't go near us, Abe! She wouldn't have anything to do with us; you know how stubborn she can be. Daddy was her world and when he stopped speaking to me, well, that was that. But all that's in the past now. What matters is that she needs us, she really needs us now. She's very confused, but I think she'll be OK here, or better at least. They hadn't got a clue about her medication at that place. She can live here with us. Emily has said it's OK, and we'll get a nurse again if it gets too bad.'

'Yes. Of course. I'm sorry. Sshhh now.'

Someone is crying.

I wrap Sara in a towel and carry her downstairs.

There's a smell of coffee and I know that in the kitchen there'll be watermelon and pickles and eggs and fresh bread. I want to hurry, but I'm careful because of the baby.

At the bottom of the stairs I hope they'll all be waiting for me, all of them together – Dinah and Mama, even little Michal. And standing next to them, strong and handsome in a beautiful suit, will be my Si. I will rest my head on his chest and smell him as he hugs me tight.

As I turn the corner into the sitting room I see three girls. They are sitting listening to music, all together on the sofa. The room is warm. A man comes out of the kitchen. He is tall and thin; he is beautiful. He's not Simon.

The doll in my arms drops to the floor.

'I want to go to the bridge,' I say.

The blond girl parks on the Leigh Woods side and I'm out before they can help me. The little girl runs after me and I take her hand. She's wearing a red coat and a matching woollen hat.

The air is wonderfully sharp against my face. I feel like I'm being cleaned.

'Do you like it up here?' I ask her.

'I don't know. I don't think I've ever been before.'

I begin to walk as fast as I can, pulling her along and off her feet as she squeals with glee and I laugh.

I hear my name behind me, shouted by three voices. I ignore them and breathe in. We are in the sky. The world is below us, boats and cars and homes. I struggle to lift her up to look.

'Do they tease you at school because you're different?' I ask.

'Mummy! Don't say that . . . don't be ridiculous.' It's the Jewish girl behind me, panting at the cold.

'Sometimes, not often, but sometimes,' the little girl says quietly.

'Clem, you poor thi–' the Jewish girl begins.

'I understand,' I whisper to the child. 'I was the only Jewish girl at school, the only one. You'll grow to love it, I promise.'

'You know I'm funny about heights, Mummy. Let me take her, please, you'll fall,' says the woman.

I let her take the child and I walk ahead. They follow, murmuring.

In the middle of the bridge I stop and stand, my arms out, one towards Clifton, one towards the woods, and I fill my rusty lungs.

I feel an arm around my waist and I close my eyes.

His English isn't good yet, his face is still dark and thin with the things he has seen. All of them are gone.

He's brought me here by the hand, as excited as if he's discovered it. I'm prepared to smile politely. I've lived in Bristol nearly my whole life; I've been over this bridge hundreds of times. Bristol is boring. It's not my home. I don't know why my parents brought us here. I want to be in Tel Aviv with my cousins, I want to be in America; even London would be better than here.

'We go over the Clifton Bridge, yes?' he says. 'The famous suspension bridge.'

I think he's weird. It's chilly and I wish I'd brought my

scarf. 'Look,' he says and I look, towards the old tobacco factory and the little houses and the hills.

'Wow,' I say.

He takes my arms from behind.

'Now look this way.' He turns me away from the view, towards the toll house, along the bridge towards Clifton. Then round again, the other way.

'Ha!' He seems pleased. 'This is our home! Right here, right in the middle. I belong nowhere, Mi. I have no one and nothing. I would like to stay here for ever with you, in the land of no man. Would you like that?'

And for some reason, accidentally almost, I say, 'Yes. Yes. Me too. I'd like that too.'

'It's getting cold, Mummy.' A man is speaking now. 'Sara and Clem and Emily want to get back to get lunch ready.'

I lean on him and we stand for a while. I don't want to leave.

'Come on, Ma. There are pickles at home and Sara's made harimi. Come home with us.'

I stand and think.

I am too frail to climb the barrier; they'd pull me down before I got to the top. I am too old to run away or refuse. They would say I had lost my mind.

I turn and roar into his chest. Every inch of me is stretched and hard and alive.

He doesn't say sshhh sshhh. He doesn't speak at all and I am grateful.

When I am out of sound, we link arms and walk back towards a car. Two women are looking at us, and a small Chinese girl is jumping and whooping and waving her red hat.

Venus in Firs

Richard Milward

'Ahdfjskdhfgsisgkdjvbasdkviwa8yefgqweguhpas9ufhaie!'
I squealed, just before my flesh turned to flames.

Eighty-eight minutes earlier, I wasn't papping it quite so
much, although it was always nerve-racking going on a
blind date, alone in the car and stone-cold sober. I mean,
first dates are bad enough – half the time you're sitting
there desperately thinking up things to say, the other half
wondering who's going to get lucky or phoned or blown
off. You wish it was date four or five; still getting off with
each other like wide-eyed feral animals, but not having to
make up pitiful, painful jokes or laugh at your partner's
pitiful, painful jokes. You know you're in love when you
can sit with someone in utter silence, ignore each other's
eye contact, not buy each other any drinks, and not feel
completely terrible about it. But, as it happened, Colin
turned out to be a prick anyhow.

I sulked over the washbasin, feeling sick to death and a
bit wobbly. I had on the new lipgloss off Gina, but Colin
didn't really deserve it – he certainly wouldn't be waking
up with it all round his collar and bed-sheets and knob-
shaft, anyhow. I pushed my hot cheeks against the cool
mirrors, sighing a layer of condensation. I was roasting

for some reason, but all I had on was the baseball top from America, the long scarlet skirt, and four measly drinks inside me. I wasn't pissed; just pissed off. I sighed again, and fluffed my sweaty hairdo.

It was Gina who'd set me up on the date. Colin was her creepy loner mate from university (the type with good cheekbones, but who spends too much time with them in the middle of books), and I hadn't been out with anyone since coming back from the US, and she thought there was something wrong with me. I blamed it on the hamlet – as soon as I moved out to the sticks six months ago, it became clear I wasn't going to meet many cute suitors. The best the hamlet had to offer was the moustache and the bald head and the flat cap in the pub supping Tetley's Imperial and making lewd comments at you. It was soul-destroying doing the shifts at the Cleveland, tied to the live-in, lonely lifestyle, but that didn't mean I was desperate to go with a load of weird boys all of a sudden. Boys only ever seemed to want one thing, or they didn't want it and I did. In the pub, all they ever wanted was their Tetley's.

I splashed a little water on my face, then tried to breathe deeply but my lungs were getting tighter and tighter, like balling two paper bags up in a pair of giant fists.

When Colin walked into Barracuda, he had very awkward hermit-boy body language; the type that makes you wonder if he's about to kiss you or beat you over the head with a mallet. Nevertheless, Colin kicked off the night with a passionate peck to my left cheek, his hands lingering dangerously close to my left bum cheek. I gave him a withering look instead of returning the kiss.

Oh, Colin. His delectable face was wasted on such hunched shoulders. I kept my distance for the rest of the night, sweating out a force field. Gina and her new volleyball hunk were meant to be there for moral support, but neither had shown and I was ever so edgy. No doubt they were getting into the two-for-one drinks down the Union, or getting into each other down the back of Gina's sofa. The bastards.

Me and Colin spent an agonizing fifteen minutes trying to find somewhere to sit, Barracuda being rammed every Friday with Lacoste jumpers and Ben Sherman shirts and half-naked lasses sipping from half-empty glasses. Colin seemed intent on sitting away from the crowds but, when we finally got stationed at a table-for-two up up up up high on the balcony, we quickly realized we had nothing to say to each other. Colin kept tugging at the cuffs of his suit, as if he was stressing the fact that he was better dressed than me. I sniffed and sat there the whole night with my arms crossed, making sure I was giving him lots of defensive body language.

I felt comfortable in my baggy Chicago Cubs top, despite Colin staring at it all night through narrowed eyelids as he shifted in his chair. Either he was disgusted by my dress sense; or he was a St Louis Cardinals fan; or he was just trying to sneak a cheeky peek at my knockers. To be fair, I didn't actually like Chicago all that much – it was far too windy for my liking – but the letter C on the baseball top matched the letter C at the start of my first name, and I enjoyed parading it around. Deep down, I wished I'd grown up as a popular cheerleader in America, and got all those treats like prom nights and homecoming and jocular jock boyfriends. I'd been almost tempted to stay in the US after the work experience but, as far as prom nights were concerned, I felt miles past my sell-by date. It got annoying after a while, anyway, serving boisterous businessmen coffee in a short skirt; a skirt conveniently short enough to flash my knickers every time Lake Michigan coughed across Illinois. Needless to say, I came home with lots and lots of tips.

Sighing, I crossed my legs in my long skirt; a skirt conveniently long enough to keep Colin's prying eyes out from under its hemline. I watched him sipping his pint with two hands, his sweat mixing in with the condensation. In a way, his awkwardness was slightly endearing, although endearing is more the quality you look for in kittens, not boyfriends. I sat back and squinted, trying to find the gentleman in him.

I was at least enjoying the cocktails he kept bringing over. The first was a creamy, dreamy White Russian; the second was more of a poor man's Cosmopolitan, since the bar was fresh out of Cointreau; the third was a perfect Moscow Mule; the fourth was a kind of Sex on the Beach, with a gritty aftertaste, like supping the inside of a beautiful oyster. I picked a bit of powder out of my teeth, waiting patiently for the aphrodisiac effect, but it didn't come. I sighed.

'What do you do again?' I asked him, solemnly.

'Er, I'm in my third year, er . . . doing Medicine,' Colin replied, in a monotone which matched the robot chanting 'COME OUT AND PARTY COME OUT AND PARTY' over and over again, over the sound system.

Soon, my heart began to thump in time with the music, at about three hundred beats per minute. I scratched my chin, feeling weird. Perhaps I was getting drunk, after all. Colin's grin grew into a large, Halloween half-moon.

'Do you like this sort of music? I've got an absolute shitload of it at home, you know,' Colin asked, leaning forwards.

'Not really,' I replied, touching my belly.

'So, er, what are you into then?'

'Oh, anything really.'

Colin grimaced. I could see I was paining him, but

likewise a pain was conveniently beginning to surface in the pit of my stomach. All I wanted to do was make my excuses, get back to the pub and curl up in bed with a hot water bottle, or have Gina and her hunk turn up with a packet of Rennies. I yawned and burped, internally.

'Come back to mine, if you want. I've got shitloads of records,' Colin continued, his face all twisted. He really was a desperate, sorry soul.

I glared at my empty Sex on the Beach glass until he offered to buy me a full one. On his way back downstairs, he made all my neck hairs shiver, leaning over my shoulder and whispering through his best wily smile, 'Stay hot, darling.'

Ironically, as soon as I made a run for the Ladies, I was completely burning up. My cheeks were like two hotplates, hiding beneath the foundation. I ran my hands under the cold tap again and splashed my neck, wondering if I always got this annoyed when it came to boys.

I think the problem stemmed from the first love of my life dumping me in such a long-winded, pathetic manner, six and a half months before. His excuses ranged from 'acute boredom', to 'extreme mental anguish', despite not going to the doctor's about either. I think he just wanted to shag around a bit. Nevertheless, I had to move out of his super flat in Redcar with the fake wood floors and pirates wallpaper I liked, and I felt so depressed and detached, all I could think to do was detach myself entirely from England and go in search of work – and a new man – in the United States.

Unfortunately, I came home empty-handed, having managed only one semi-successful sexual encounter with an impotent office worker named Glenn. Having said that, it was Glenn's tips that helped fund my flight back to Britain – I told him I owed him a hand shank if he ever happened to get his strength back and found himself in the Cleveland Inn in a one-horse hamlet in the North East.

Sighing, I felt my heart flutter again as somebody burst into the Ladies. Fortunately it wasn't Colin. A girl with braided blond hair caught my eye in the mirror, and suddenly I felt embarrassed having such an upset face on a Friday night. I quickly dried it with my baggy left sleeve and then, trying to be inconspicuous and keep my heels quiet, I scuttled back out of the toilet, making a speedy beeline for the EXIT.

The cool breeze felt nice on my cheeks, charging at me from all corners of the car park. I skidded over to where I'd parked the Corsa, and ducked inside. I wasn't a girl racer or nowt, but being out in the hamlet meant I had to drink-drive quite a bit if I wanted a social life, or any happiness. I'd be all right – the main thing was getting away from Colin. I did feel bad standing him up and making him buy me a Sex on the Beach I wasn't even going to drink, but that's what you get for being a seedy hunchback on my night off, I'm afraid.

I decided I'd better drive myself home, before he drove me up the fucking wall. Sniffing, I stuck the headlights on, put it into first and zoomed off, still feeling a little dazed though I could only be two or three cocktails over the limit.

Back when I was with the first love of my life, we used to drink bottles of Protocol vodka deep in the valley and knock ourselves out with this stinky skunk stuff he always had, and I still drove him back every time. That's the beauty of living in a county where no one seems to leave their houses after one in the morning. Every single night, we reclaimed the tarmac of Redcar and Cleveland.

Trying to keep focused, I sped up slightly and started counting the cat's eyes. When I first moved to the hamlet, each journey was a picturesque mystery tour through wet, epic woodland, my eyes wide with joy at the sight and smell of the wild garlic woods and frosty fir trees. Now, though, all I wanted was for the scenery to disappear and for the pub to swallow me up. I had a feeling *Friends* was on the telly, and there was bound to be some hot chocolate or Nesquik left in the kitchens. I gurgled with glee.

Past the overgrown bungalows, it started getting tricky pushing the pedals down in heels, so I kicked them under the passenger seat and drove on in bare feet. Following a long daisy chain of electricity pylons up the valley side, I breathed in and out slowly, feeling light-headed. Perhaps it was the altitude. I sat back and watched the green scenery unfold, like a Swiss Alpine pop-up book with all the firs jumping to attention as I zoomed past.

I burped again. There was a chance I was getting travel sick off all those cocktails and the sixty-miles-per-hour speed limit, but I didn't feel as drunk as I might've hoped, compared to what the sickness was telling me.

Taking it easy round the crash barriers, all of a sudden I began to feel very dreamy and detached, as if I was merely a passenger watching all the foliage whizz past. I felt my skull sinking against the headrest. I panicked, then blinked and got drowsy, panicked, blinked and got drowsy, panicked, blinked and got drowsy. I couldn't think what was up with me. My brain was knacking inside and out, and I dug my nails into my palms, desperate not to fall asleep at the wheel. Why did the upholstery have to be so comfortable, though?

THE HAMLET 6M, said the white road sign, goading me. All I could think to do was put my foot down further, charging ever closer to safety, ever closer to Nesquik. My sweaty hands turned the steering wheel into a salty lifebelt. I clung to it for dear life.

Blinking heavily, I got within five miles of the hamlet, then four miles, all the while getting further and further out of reach of consciousness. What was wrong with me? I couldn't imagine four cocktails could knock me for six. I bit my lip, trying my hardest not to start hallucinating. As the car moved forwards, the trees kept moving backwards, creating a sinister corridor of navy blue sky and greenery. I licked my dry, crusted lips, pinching myself.

Sniffing the Christmas tree smell, I wafted my loose baseball top to get some air flowing round there. The big C trembled, fretting about me. Nevertheless, the hamlet was now a mere three miles away, and my bare right foot was still pressed firmly to the accelerator. If I'd stopped the car I would've dozed off for sure, and God knows who'd get their hands on me then. I shivered, sweating, imagining Colin hot on my heels, on a Harley Davidson with fire spewing out the exhaust. I checked the rearview mirror, then checked the dashboard for a tape to keep my mind on the road, and off Colin. Even that tiny movement felt like a massive struggle, though, and my poor head span as the wheels span.

I couldn't find a tape.

I couldn't even remember what was so bad about Colin any more.

I coughed, both knees trembling.

My eyes just couldn't stay open, as if each eyelash was carrying its own ton-weight or grand piano. I was vaguely aware of the sharp bend coming up before the WELCOME TO THE HAMLET sign, but when I reached it I panicked, pulling up the handbrake instead of casually nudging the gear stick to number two. The car made an almighty shriek, skidding between the gap in the crash barriers, then hurtling sideways across the grass. I tried to slam my bare feet on all three pedals, but before I knew it, we were sliding along the slope like one hefty metal ice skate. The Corsa went squealing over the valley edge, kissing the fir trees at first, then fully crashing into them. I was aware of the car roof splitting open like the shell of a giant oyster, but then the Corsa's main beam met the main beam of someone's luxurious Alpine bungalow, and all three of us exploded.

One o'Clock Special
James Hannah

'Look,' the waitress mutters as she returns to the bar. Putting down her tray, she gestures to the chef. 'Table 2. See it?'

Table 2: man and woman, both in work clothes. Smart, but hardly stylish. Blandly sort of formal.

The chef doesn't see it. She sees pre-wrapped Christmas presents gathered in bags and bundled around the woman's legs. She sees an umbrella. She sees a couple looking around for a menu that isn't a wine list. 'What?' she says.

'He's got a wedding ring. She hasn't. It's usually the man who opts not to, isn't it? What do you reckon?'

The chef weighs it up with a shrug and resumes blowtorching a crème-brûlée for Table 9.

The waitress is decided: no woman would ever pass up the opportunity of a new ring, would she? No. The woman lets out one or two truly happy laughs at something the man says. It's reckless of them, wouldn't you say? Bringing this performance out into a public space. They could be caught. Any one of their work colleagues might see them – a lot of them come in at lunchtimes.

'Perhaps he's a widower?'

The chef puts down her torch and squints over at them again. 'No,' she says. 'Too well dressed.' This as if she's made studying and cataloguing potential widowers her life's work.

The waitress picks up her tray and brings them over a glass of red and a glass of white and a basket of bread and butter. She sets the glasses and basket down, the man looks up to her in silent thanks, and she moves away from the table, withdraws to a nearby one to pretend to clean it.

'I don't want to pry,' says Elizabeth, letting her silly laughing face fade and taking up her glass of white, 'and tell me to mind my own business, but something seems to have been bothering you lately. You're not your usual sparky self.' She doesn't want to be more explicit, but he's hinted at fractiousness at home. For ages, actually. Whenever the subject of his wife comes up in conversation he slips too easily into a cynical tone, and sometimes Elizabeth's felt a little – what, disapproving? – of the savagery of his humour about her.

'Hm!' he snuffs into his glass. 'You could say that. Yeah, not very sparky at all, really.'

Elizabeth says nothing, simply lifts her glass, leaving him a bit of space. She's dying to know. But she knows: never let it be seen that you're dying to know something.

'Choppy waters,' she suggests, looking casually across the room and accidentally catching the waitress's eye. They both dart their eyes away. 'Never very pleasant.'

'Ha! Choppy waters, yeah. It's just – I don't know. You start talking about these things and you can never stop. Let's not get into it; otherwise I'll go through the whole lot again.'

'Well, I haven't got any pressing plans,' Elizabeth says with a chuckle.

Paul laughs, somewhat ruefully. 'Ah, well, I don't really want to unload it all on you. It's really none of your business. None of your concern, I mean. But as soon as I start on it, I just talk and talk and talk, but I never seem to feel any better.'

She says she knows what he means, and leaves it at that.

The waitress deciphers the signals. Sure, sure, she thinks, just two friendly colleagues out together. But they are definitely attracted to one another. She sees it in the way they look at one another, and the way their eyes glitter and twinkle as they laugh. Oh, it's so *obvious*.

Springtime finds the waitress occupying herself with trying to avoid coleslaw thumb as she bears the plates steadily from the Cornhouse kitchen to the customers. More often than not, the delicate selections of leaves and tomato and onion are returned untouched to the kitchen. The chef takes it all in her stride. Each plate that is rejected or returned for some adjustment is dealt with caringly and without quibble. The waitress wishes she could look at things in the way the chef does, but however much she wishes she could be so committed, the complex mathematics of pros and cons in her mind invariably results in her railing against the customers.

They never seem to tire of pointing out that the tea isn't loose-leaf, that there are tea stains in the teacups, tea specks on the teaspoons. They grumble that the salad could be fresher, that the crème-brûlée isn't up to scratch. The one o'clock special is fish followed by lamb. I don't like fish *or* lamb. The steaks are too well done, too bloody. There are sullen murmurs about the quality of chicken under this sauce, that there is too much sauce. Could I have one with less sauce?

Taking away another plate for de-saucing, the waitress must negotiate the room without being asked –

'Could I have another glass of house white, please, darling? Don't worry, I'll keep my old glass.'

– anything else.

The waitress looks down and acknowledges the request from the regular at Table 4a, who resumes gesticulating to her husband with a breadstick. She passes the plate through the hatch to the chef – 'less saaauce' – before tracking back to 4a with the bottle of house white. Her shadow briefly deletes the sunbeams, blotting the love story couple as they sit at Table 3, mumbling beneath the kerfuffle.

Glug glug glug.

'Thank you, pet,' says the woman at 4a, taking up her recharged glass. 'How are you? How's college?'

'Oh, oh, not much good, actually. I haven't got time to, uh –' The waitress can feel her response drifting as she tries to take in what's with the love story couple over on 3. 'To, to, uh –' Things are rather more earnest across the coffees, this one o'clock. There's more touchy-feely going on between the two of them now, but they're not as careless as they once were. They're more intense, more urgent, less light-hearted. Less innocent, maybe.

'Well, you stick at it. It's precious time. You're a sharp girl – you just make sure they give you the help you need.'

'Yes, yeah. No. Would, um, can I get you the dessert menu?'

'Ooh. I'll take a look. And so will Ian, won't you, Ian?'

'Right, right.' The waitress drops away and makes a fuss of finding a spare dessert menu.

Paul chops his teaspoon into the sugar. 'I'm telling you, though,' he says, 'it's *every night*, it really is. Every night in the office I dread that clock on the wall edging round to five.' He looks up into the middle distance at an imaginary clock. 'That's the hardest part of it for me, really. It's the change. It's the switch from home to work or from work to home that seems to make things flare up. It makes me sick to my stomach, because when I'm at home she can be hanging off my arm, and so loving and so needy and so clingy, but in that hour before I leave for work everything will change. Her patterns will change, you know? She'll grow frosty. She'll go quiet, and it's like I can *feel* it coming over her. She'll start fussing, silently, organizing things with a real sort of mania. If I leave my bag somewhere for, like, thirty seconds, she'll manage to kick it over or trip over it, and she'll pick it up and throw it back in the cupboard. Or I'll put my cup of tea down while I put on my shoes, and I'll get this sense that she's *clocked* it, and I'll be waiting for her to snap and pick it up and put it in the kitchen. You know, it's enough to make you frightened to do anything in your own home. No one should be scared to do anything in their own home. But in that hour you can see it in her face. She goes *grey* – literally, her skin gets this colourless look about it. It's horrible to see. I hate it when I can see it creeping over her, and it creeps over me. It's like a creeping death. And when I get back home in the evenings it's just *worse*, you know? Because I know that for the hour before I walk through that front door she will have been prowling round the house, battening down the hatches, putting everything in its place, preparing it all for my arrival, and so I arrive and I take my shoes off or whatever, and wherever I put them they're already a mess. They don't fit in with this neat pattern she's made.'

He looks up from the sugar bowl. 'In fact, that's it, yeah. I – in my own house – I don't fit in.'

Elizabeth looks at him intently, but she says nothing. She likes that he's talking. It's important to her.

'So the hour after I come home is the worst hour of the day. I've got to force my way back into her pattern. Every day, reinvent the wheel. And it's been getting worse these past few months. We had it out, and she promised to try to allow me in, but now it's just this false *thing*, isn't it? I get home and we both act out an hour of this horrible performance, where we're both pretending everything's OK, and it's just this *farce*. I mean, what a *waste of time*. Isn't it? Our whole time together feels like a waste.'

Silence.

'I don't know,' he continues. 'You enter into these things.' He drifts off for a moment, squinting at the imaginary clock. 'It's hard, you know?'

'I think I do,' says Elizabeth. She stops herself launching into a tale about her own situation, keeps herself disciplined. It's coming, it's coming from him.

'I just don't know if this – this whole *marriage* – can go on. Not like it is, anyway. You know, you look at yourself, and you look at your situation, and you think, I'm at an age where I need to start making some decisions. I'm in this situation and it's going nowhere, it's going rapidly downhill, and I think, what can I do? Am I making things worse by being here? But there's nothing I can do. All I do is make everything worse. She doesn't want me, and I don't want her.' He seems to shock himself somewhat with this and half-heartedly back-pedals: 'I don't want what we've *become*.'

Now it seems Elizabeth has hit a rich seam of confession – just the loveliest way to become close with a new friend. Spine-tingling time, with him talking to her candidly, telling her things that he probably wouldn't tell anyone else. Not even his own wife. Certainly not her. The best, the *friendliest* thing she can do is to be silent and let him work it out. The two of them alone in the world, airing his problems. How lovely.

The waitress finally settles a dessert menu between the

regulars on Table 4a, and stands ready with her pad while they mull it over.

'Sorry,' says the love story man behind her, and then lowers his voice. 'Sorry. I said, didn't I? Once I start talking about it, I can't stop. I just bang on and on and on. Very boring.'

'Well, no,' says Elizabeth. 'The only bit you keep banging on about is that.'

He chuckles, emerges out of himself a little. 'It feels a bit strange, saying these things to you,' he says.

'It shouldn't feel strange,' says Elizabeth in an undertone. 'I understand, I really do. And I don't envy you what you're having to go through.' She picks up her own teaspoon, and joins him in excavating the sugar pit. 'And, you know, if things are that bad at home, then it makes me feel a lot better that you can say these things to me, because at least you're being heard. I know what it's like, when you feel you're not being heard. But I hear you.'

He looks up at her.

'So long as you know there's someone here to hear you. And – you know, I've –'

The waitress skips across the floor and over to the hatch with an order for 1 stck toff pud (2 spns), full of news. How many couples, she speculates, have ventured to confess over these tables that they have grown – how to put it – *very fond* of their time together, their one o'clocks in this restaurant, and that they dearly hope that such one o'clocks can continue for ever?

'Ah, they all say it,' says the chef, solemnly. 'All of them.'

'I feel so sorry for you,' says Elizabeth. 'Really, to go home to that every day. You're a saint. A sensitive man. I think she knows it, too, somewhere inside herself.'

Paul absently contours the sugar. 'I don't feel very sensitive,' he says.

'Oh, you *are*,' she says. 'How many men would even begin to show the understanding you've shown? How many men would keep returning every night to be faced with that from their wives? None, that's what I'm saying. Not many, anyway. You're *brilliant*. I think you're brilliant. You're one of the good ones, Paul. Worth loving. And she'd better buck up her ideas or she'll lose you to someone who appreciates you.'

'Well,' says Paul, and briefly fumbles the spoon, before shooting Elizabeth a coy glance.

The waitress breaks the moment of silence between them by screwing up a discarded cellophane wrapper on Table 5 and cramming it into her pocket.

'I'm sorry,' says Elizabeth, withdrawing. 'I don't mean to be embarrassing.'

'No, no,' he says. 'No, not at all. I was just, you know. It's lovely to hear. You're so nice to say those things.'

'Oh, people should say them. Best friends should be able to say those things, and be upfront about it because, well, no one else is going to do it, are they?'

'No.'

'And you'd do the same for me, I'm sure.'

'Oh yeah, definitely.'

'Well, here's to straight talking and no complication.'

'Straight talking and no complication.'

They raise glasses and clink.

'To best friends.'

'To the best of friends.'

Clink.

'You know that makes us worst enemies?'

'Does it?'

'Ha! Yeah. Best friends; worst enemies? Never mind.'

And they mean it, bless them, thinks the waitress, as

she looms up with the credit-card machine. They mean it platonically. *Anyone* can see that. But if you're saying things like the love story woman's saying, then, well, it's already happened, hasn't it? She's already given him clear signals. Take me. Take me I'm yours. No man's going to pass on that offer, is he? He's going to say thank you very much. They all do.

As the one o'clocks come and go, so the menu evolves to keep all the regulars on side and to keep pace with the year. Caramelized onion and goat's cheese crostinis, sun-dried tomato and avocado salads; such plating up and serving of the seasons only makes time pass more achingly for the waitress, making her ever more aware of being trapped, here, in this job, with these people.

The customers know it. The regulars wink and grin at the chef, and the chef looks heavenwards as the waitress stumps from customer to customer, bashing plates down on tables, standing on one haughty hip and sullenly thrusting out her jaw in anticipation of some addition to the order. The irregular customers sometimes offer a little resistance, loudly tutting and raising their eyebrows at her, straightening the plates to their own specifications, establishing the fact that they are the sole authority in this transaction. This doesn't help matters at all. Once again the chef will outline the basics of customer service to the waitress, drawing her attention to the onion skin fragility of the profit margin.

Table 8: one o'clock. They're slumped in a secretive huddle, no longer maintaining that respectable distance from one another, but replacing it with ever-deeper seclusion, screening themselves behind the iron spiral staircase, now that things seem so serious.

Tending to the table directly on the other side of the

stairs, the waitress gets it all. She hears him far more brassy, much less depressed, saying, 'Do you know, this is the part of the day I look forward to most, when I think of all the misery I have to contend with at home, the toys everywhere, the fact that we only ever talk about the one subject, and then I come to work and I have an inbox stacked with complaints and complications from the marketing department and human resources, and it's all – all of it – rubbish. It's just so-called professionals coming in to work every day and dreaming up diversions that they estimate will take them eight hours to deal with, and arguing points of principle that have no basis in actual fact, and that's all they do. When I think of all this, the only place I ever want to be is here, with you, where we can just be together.'

And they agree, he agrees, she agrees, that everything's so easy, so easy with you.

'You understand me so naturally. You understand me far better than I understand myself. Because when I get stuck and ramble on, you can make it all make sense.'

And the waitress is swept away with the feeling that, at Table 8, behind the iron spiral staircase, hearts are swelling with happiness, with desire and sorrow about how they were destined to be together, and yet how their togetherness seems destined not to happen.

'Oh, I just long for someone to come home to,' says Elizabeth. 'I go home to an *empty* house. Not even empty. A house with my teenage daughter in it.'

'Oh, God.' Paul dramatizes and grins at her as he sips his tea.

'You're dead right,' she says. 'Oh, God. I get home and all I get from her is a grunt – if I even see her at all. Maybe I hear a grunt coming down from her room, and then I make myself a cup of tea. Then I'm hungry, aren't I, so I make us both some tea. And she'll come down and collect hers and take it back up to her room. So I eat my tea on my own. Then if there's nothing on the telly, I read the paper and go to bed.'

Paul is silent.

'And the rest of my life,' she adds, 'is work.'

They both consider their cups.

Autumn draws in to the Cornhouse. There are hints of the winter service, with the reintroduction of warming broth in molten bowls, which slide around dangerously on their trays.

'Are you going to be doing your mulled wine again this year?'

The waitress shrugs. 'Yes?'

'Oh, right, right. Um, just, uh, two house whites to begin with, please.'

Table 12 is right beside the bar and at the back of the bistro, away from the prying eyes of pedestrians descending the Wyle Cop hill. Something is not well with the love story couple. Long silences sink between them.

'You can't come here,' she tells him, 'and talk to me like this, if you're not prepared to act. I can't sit here any more and listen to you because it's tearing me in two. I think of nothing else all day and all night. You think you can come here for your one o'clock special and that everything will always be the same, that you'll get tea and sympathy from me.'

'No, I don't. I –'

'But you can't. You can't do it all the time. I know things are hard for you, but you're making them hard for me, too. It's not easy for me to . . . I know it's none of my business –'

'No, it *is*. It *is* your business.'

'You've got a funny way of showing it because it seems that every time we come here, I find myself sitting here and wondering whether anything's progressed at all. And nothing's progressed. Nothing's ever progressed. Nothing ever seems to happen, because you don't *make* it happen. We sit here every day and we go through the same old thing every time.'

They sit in silence, embarrassed maybe. There's no doubt that the waitress is earwigging, but Elizabeth's beyond caring.

'It's up to you,' Elizabeth says, leaning back from the table. 'It's up to you to make things better or to make them worse, because if you don't decide either way, then this is just going to go on and on. And I'm not . . . I can't sit here every day and go through all this. It can't go on for ever.'

They both sit there and agree with one another that this has got to end. And he agrees that he's the one who must end it. He will, he will. She, for her part, agrees that he must be given time and space to do it in the way he chooses. The humane way. Because, after all, his wife has done nothing wrong, really, and though we agree it's for the best, this isn't going to be easy for her to hear.

He will have to pick his moment.

'Pff,' spits the chef to the waitress. 'I've heard it all before. All men are the same at the end of the day, aren't they? They just agree with the woman who's in front of them. Then, as soon as they're on their own, they do what they want. It's always been like that, and it always will be.'

'I don't know why she puts up with it,' says the waitress. 'I wouldn't put up with it if it was me. If it was me, I'd tell him straight away, you know, don't mess me around, or it's hit the road, Jack. That's what I'd say. I'd say, you sort yourself out or it's my way or the highway. Simple as that.'

*

November's frost doesn't thaw in time for the lunchtime rush, and vapour from collected conversations gathers on the windows, sealing off the Cornhouse from the translucent beyond. The waitress lingers at the back of the bistro for warmth, only reluctantly coming forward to take an order and to endure a fresh surge of wintry air when the front door is inevitably opened.

Elizabeth sits some way back at Table 9, nursing an uncertain stomach. No more appetite for this menu. The door opens, and she looks up as a wave of winter sweeps across her. A smart couple walks in and the waitress greets them and settles them at Table 2. The pair are quite giggly together, and the waitress waits impatiently as they peruse the menu.

'Two glasses of house white to begin with,' the man says. 'Um, could we just have a couple of minutes?'

The waitress manages a smile and heads back through the tables, avoiding eye contact all the way. The door onto the street opens and the November air once again fills the room.

'Shut the door, shut the *door*.'

Paul fixes the door shut behind him and approaches Elizabeth at Table 9. She has given him space, and she has given him time. So here we are again, lunch at one. This is when things happen. What's the verdict?

'Well,' he says, 'I –' His mouth open, he stops, looks down and irritates his empty wineglass on the table.

Elizabeth can feel the heat rising within her at the endless hesitation, but she knows she should say nothing. She can't force it.

'I –' Paul looks up at her as if willing her to say the words for him, but she can't. 'We talked,' he says. 'It got bad, and I walked out.'

'Right,' says Elizabeth, exhaling, unsure whether this is the conclusion of matters.

'But I went back. We talked some more.'

Elizabeth remains silent. The news, the conclusion is about to come. Best be prepared.

'And nothing. Nothing came about. This morning, I left.'

The waitress comes over and fusses around the table beside them, makes a deal out of adjusting a piece of cardboard wedged under one of the table legs to keep it on an even keel. They stay silent awhile until this intrusion passes.

Paul's last words hang static in the air between them and Elizabeth's mind fixes on them, repeats them over and over, but finds them hard to decode. Has he left, as in left her, or did he leave, as in just leaving the house for the day?

'You left?' she says as the waitress recedes once more.

'Mm.'

'Do you mean you've left her?'

He pauses. He should be nodding firmly and smiling guiltily, but he pauses. 'I . . . I really don't know.'

She looks at him, careful to shield her disbelief that he might be doing this to her deliberately.

'It's strange,' he says weakly. 'I always thought it would be a clear-cut thing, but now I'm not so sure.'

'You *make* it a clear-cut thing. You *have* to be sure,' Elizabeth hisses. 'Are you going back to the house tonight?'

'I don't . . . I don't know. I think I'll have to. Just for a visit, to explain things. We didn't finish it properly.'

As the waitress bears out two bowls of warming winter broth, she notices only the love story man now at Table 9, and the love story woman and her coat both gone. He hasn't ordered anything, and she weighs up whether she should go over.

Forget it. He can call her if he wants her.

God Damn You, Patsy Cline
Katy Darby

The trail down from the casita is pale sand with lumps of bark and whatnot in it. My hair's up off my neck in a clip, and the sun beats on the tender nape, but this time of morning the air's cool like the inside of a haunted house, and the sky's soft and pink through a black scribble of twigs and tree branches. Dead quiet. I like these chill dawns, when it feels like you're the only person awake in the whole world. Like everybody died overnight and it's just you and the birds and horses, for ever. The ground'll start steaming soon, as the sun burns off the dew and mist. Seen it a thousand times. Been here a while now.

The courtyard between the cookhouse, the lounge and the gift shop is laid out real pretty, the borders marked by white rocks Jesse and Elaine found out in the scrub somewhere. There's a big old hunched-over tree in the middle of the yard, circled with stones. Don't know what type it is and don't much care, but Jesse planted it way back when him and Elaine bought this place. It was still a working farm then, just. Now it's a ranch-style guest destination. I know 'cause the website says so.

The cowboys still ride the range, rope cattle, brand steers and all, but it's more for the tourists these days than for its own sake. They come from all over; from New York and Los Angeles, from London and Paris and Stockholm and God knows where, just to taste that desert air, that Marlboro-flavoured freedom. And, of course, my famous refried beans and hamburger.

That's how I came here first, with a few girlfriends, as a guest. Lost my head over it, like men do over a pretty woman. The riding, the trails, the sky full of nothing, the guys down at the barn rolling their own cigarettes, casual and quick in their movements, like animals. I grew up in town and I was amazed by the rainbow dawn and the quiet stars. Oh, I fell for it all right. Came back three times, even helped out in the cookhouse that summer season to pay my way. Then, when Martha retired, I jacked in my secretary job in Nevada and took over as cook. Never wanted to leave, that first year; I was so happy just being out here. Still don't, but I got a different reason now.

Breakfast's at seven every morning. I start at six and fire up the range, get bacon and sausages out of the refrigerator, start chopping tomatoes and mushrooms and onions, crank open tins of beans, crack eggs for scrambling and whatever else. I can hear the horses whinnying from the barn across the ranch, but not the guys with them. Men's voices don't carry so much as women's. I can always hear women coming a mile off. Higher, more piercing. Our female guests are mostly a certain type: skinny, pretty gals, high-earning, low-carb women with jobs or husbands that buy them their luxury downtime in the desert. They soon learn to eat a real breakfast after they've been on a few morning rides; lunch, too. Three hours in the saddle works up their appetite for more than a side salad and a Diet Pepsi.

I put the sausages on to grill and the bacon to fry in the

big lead skillet. I'll do the eggs in it later. The grease makes them come out just perfect. I got fifteen mouths today. About average for off-season. Coming up to Thanksgiving soon, then I'll be worked to the bone. We all will, horses included. This week we got a family of five staying; parents, two sons and a girl, teenagers, skinny and pale. Indoor kids. It's only been three days and the girl's already crushing on Earl, I can tell. The other guests are two couples; one middle-aged, one pair of honeymooners. Then there's the four boys from the barn, and Jesse and Elaine.

Jesse smiles at me, teeth like fresh white bread in his old brown crust of a face.

'Well there, Claire,' he says as he slops beans onto his tin plate, 'you been cooking the books this morning?'

I do the accounting and book-keeping for the ranch as well, not to mention running the bar. No rest for the wicked. I smile at him, teeth behind my lips.

'That one never gets old, does it, Jesse?'

'Surely does not, Claire. Surely does not.' He ambles away, shaking his grizzled head and grinning. He's got no idea how sick to fuckin' Christ I am of that goddamn joke. Senile old asshole.

Elaine's different. She's old, but sharp. Been working here five years now but I still don't know if she trusts me. Leathery skin over good, strong bones. Norwegian blood. Behind her in the line is Earl, his eyes spacey like they always get when he's ridden out early. Like a cross between a daydream and a thousand-yard stare. He stands there patient as a horse waiting to be saddled, quiet and calm, while Elaine helps herself. She catches me looking at him and I catch her catching me. She smirks and walks over to join Jesse at their corner table. Bitch.

I hand Earl his platter. One of them is just that bit bigger and newer than the others. He don't know it, but that one's his. Only I can tell the difference. Just like only I know why we have ribs for dinner so much. They ain't cheap. But Earl likes them. He smiles at me and his eyes crinkle up, bright blue in his brown face. When he's not grinning you can see the fine smile lines white on his cheeks where there's no tan. But he's always grinning; that's how they got there. I drop my eyes and grin back. We're friends, Earl and me. I guess I'm friends with all the staff by now. I never got in a fight or a temper with none of them, anyhow. Not that I ain't got bad words to say about them – hell, they're human and so am I. Just I got no one to say 'em to.

Me and Earl stay up with a few beers in the bar most nights, shooting pool, shooting the breeze. He's had a few choice things to say in the past concerning this cowboy or that summertime maid, but I don't get involved, just smile and nod. He knows anything he tells me won't go no further.

'You're so damn nice, Claire,' is what he says to me. 'Too nice.' He grins when he says that. 'You make me look bad.'

How can I tell him all the shit on my mind when he says things like that? So I smile, drop my eyes and shrug.

'Good morning, Earl,' I say. 'You get stuck in there.' He nods. When the last guest is fed I'll get myself a cup o' joe, go over and join him. I don't generally eat in the morning; cooking puts me off. By the time you've fried bacon for fifteen the smell's already fed you twice over.

At breakfast, Earl usually sits alone, away from the other cowboys. He's comfortable in his own company. I like that in a man. He nods politely at the family of five as he passes, and the daughter's eyes follow him all the way across the room. Seems like he has that effect on pretty much every woman, me included. I know full well he'll never look at me the way that teenage girl looks at him, but so what? Friends is better, in a way. You don't marry your friends, but you don't divorce them neither. We're buddies, and I'm happy with that. Mostly. Except when Patsy Cline comes on the radio, singing some sad song like 'Crazy'. Then I'm not so happy for a spell. Country music, you can't get away from it out here, however hard you try. Fiddles and goddamn guitars and lost love and lorn love, fuckin' soundtrack to my life. God damn you, Patsy Cline.

Only one woman I can think of ever resisted Earl's charm, and she was married to him. Debbie was from Tombstone originally, just a couple dozen miles down the road. She'd trained as a stylist, done a few beauty pageants and then married Earl far too young, both of them teenagers. Debbie was a good-looking woman; tall, shapely, high maintenance, a born city chick who never got further than Phoenix. I did kind of pity her 'cause of that. But then she started screwing one of the summer hands, a kid from Boston, about a year after I began working here. Everybody knew about them but Earl. Then one day Earl got wise, and next day they were both gone. He found one of her stockings in the guy's saddle pouch after an overnight camping trip. She confessed. What else could she do? Better that way, he told me once. They weren't suited. What kind of dumb fuckin' woman wears stockings to camp anyhow?

On my day off I always go on Earl's rides with the guests. He taught me how to ride Western-style and how to handle the horses, and I got a favourite: Judy, a big sorrel mare, meek as a lamb and sweet as a kitten. On the days I don't ride her I always go down to the barn with a few lumps of sugar from the kitchen. I cast my eye over the cookhouse; everybody fed and happy. I got ten minutes. Time to go give Judy her morning treat.

I lift my hat off the hook and grab some sugar cubes. Outside, it's ten degrees hotter already. I'm damn glad I'm not riding today, and not just 'cause it's Gena's weekend to visit. On the path down to the barn there's a patch of shade with a juicy-leafed plant growing tall and lush. The horses go crazy for anything fresh and green. I grab a handful and pull a good bunch off. Judy'll love it. It's a long trek, so she'll need her strength. Got to be careful, though; some of the plants out here ain't good for cattle and horses. We can't let the guests feed 'em 'cause the wrong stuff can snarl up their guts, give 'em spasms and such, sometimes even kill the animal. Lost a few cows that way.

Judy tosses her head and shakes it when my cigarette smoke gets in her eyes, just like Earl does. But I know she's real pleased to see me. I stroke her nose and give her the greens and sugar.

'Good girl, Judy,' I say. 'Now you behave on the ride this morning, you hear? Don't do anything I wouldn't.'

This is our little joke. She's the calmest creature on four legs. That's why Earl always gives her to the kids and the novices. Same way a nervous person can unsettle a horse, a placid animal can quiet a scared rider.

I remember the first time Earl took me out on her, first week I was here. I was just a guest then, but we'd bonded somehow, already. Me and Judy, sure; but me and Earl, too. We discovered we were almost exactly the same age and we knew the same movies backward and inside-out. Dumb shit like that can mean a whole lot if you want it to. We're the same height, too, near enough; he's on the short side and I'm tall for a woman. Like a matching set of knick-knacks bought at different yard sales; the cowboy and the barmaid.

I got good at riding pretty soon. Better than Debbie, who never cared for horses. Earl's a wonderful teacher but some people don't got patience to learn, and that's dangerous. A few months back a guy over at Choctaw Ranch was crushed to death when his horse rolled on him. By all accounts, he rode it too hard, spooked it so it stumbled and tumbled. You got to treat them with respect, like real cowboys do.

I got a few minutes till I need to start on the dishes, so I head for the cookhouse by the back way, the shady path overlooking the shooting range Earl and Elaine built a few years back. It's a whole bunch of doors and wood and shit hammered together and painted to look like an Old West scene – a saloon and a bank and a jail, with cut-out cowboys and robbers and a sheriff for targets. They got nails on their heads and bodies you can tie balloons to, which bang when you hit 'em. Elaine thought the guests would get a kick out of that.

Now that was one thing I was good at straight off. I was raised by my mom and I never held a gun before nor wanted to, but I sort of took to it at once. Earl showed me how to use the air pistol and I just blasted away, hardly even aiming. *Bang bang bang bang bang.* And all the balloons were dead. He looked a little scared at that, but he laughed and called me One-Shot. I was declared that week's shooting champion and Earl printed me out a colour certificate and signed it, 'To One-Shot from Dead-Eye'. I've still got it; it's pinned above my bed. Earl's got a pennant hanging above his that says, 'Ropin' On Faith'. I asked if he won it one time and he said, no, they were giving them out at church. I never would have figured him for a churchgoer. But I guess most folks stick with the religion they're born to, for good or bad.

My mom raised me God-fearing, all right, but I stopped believing in Him ten years back, when Danny left me and I had to get rid of our baby. My whole life I'd been told it was a sin. Mortal. Mom always said that killing an unborn child is the worst kind of murder. That's why she had me. You'll be punished, she said, and I believed her. But I wasn't gonna be punished the way Mom was – always on her own, slaving for a kid, shitty jobs in dime stores, dead by fifty. I cried for weeks after I did it, but I wasn't punished, not then or anytime since. Not for that sin, nor any other. I've been siphoning off a few dollars here and there for my nest egg for three, four years now, which is technically theft I guess, but not on these wages it ain't. I know how much Jesse and Elaine make, and I know how much they can afford to lose. They don't even notice. And who else understands a damn thing about book-keeping? Nobody, that's who.

Coming up this way you approach the cookhouse from the rear, where the deck is. A few tables and chairs are scattered around for when the bar opens in the evenings. There's a slim, dark-haired girl leaning forward in a porch chair. Her back is to me and she's shrilling something into her cellphone. Gena. She's early. Her voice makes my head ache, like when you wear a tight hat for too long. She snaps her cell shut and stands up. She's wearing new jeans with rhinestones on 'em, from the outlet mall in Phoenix. They're tight-fitting; the wrong type for horse riding, with seams on the inside where they'll rub. Earl teaches everybody about the correct riding attire but, being his girl, I guess she thinks she's above all that. Her narrow thighs will be red-raw like hamburger meat inside an hour. She vanishes inside, her round, vacuum-packed ass winking in the sun like she's sat in broken glass.

He's had these little things since Debbie went. Don't take me wrong, I don't mind. Some of the girls are nice enough and, besides, a man's got needs. With me and

Earl, it's different. Friends last longer. For ever, if you're lucky. And you can't say that about love. None of his flirtations outlive the month. Gena's survived three, but that's 'cause they only see each other odd weekends. When she's not touring, he's working. Which is maybe how he's managed to stand her so long. Gena and her daddy, Rudy, are reliable standbys on the local country-music circuit, playing small-town bars and weddings in clapboard churches. A little country, a little gospel, a little blues; but mostly country, of course. Rudy plays the fiddle real well, and Gena sings in her high, piercing voice and plays guitar, not so well. Sometimes they duet, and that sounds better. Rudy's the real musician. She's just relying on T&A and her tiny talent to snag herself a husband from somewhere. Plenty of lonely cowboys in this county. Not so many cute girls.

There's a clatter of tin platters and coffee mugs as everybody scrapes and stacks their dishes. Must be quarter of eight now, near enough. They'll be moving down to the barn to saddle up for the morning ride; Jesse and Elaine leading, Earl gently herding the guests, Gena following behind like a sleek black stable cat. The other cowboys sauntering behind her, watching the diamanté twinkle on her ass. She'll be getting herself a real diamond soon, though she don't know it yet.

I remember just where I was when I heard about it. Down at the stables, a few days back, feeding Judy her sugar and some leftover salad. I was earlier than usual and the boys didn't notice me. Just a snatch of words in between the jangle of tack and the snort and thump of the horses restless in the barn. They all knew about it; the whole ranch knew, 'cept me. Just two words. *Engagement ring.* Earl never mentioned a syllable of it to me. We talk every night, maybe just a quick chat over a beer, sometimes two, three hours reminiscing and whatnot. Every night. And not a single word.

I slide open the glass door to the empty cookhouse, cross and pour myself a mug of tart, over-brewed coffee, topped up with half-and-half. Then I go back out on the deck. I rummage for my lighter, and my fingers touch on something silky and smooth. I draw it out of my jeans pocket, long and dark and light, like a magician's trick handkerchief. The other stocking. I'd almost forgotten it was there. I always keep it on me; it's my talisman, a reminder. My skin's rough from cooking and cleaning, and the delicate nylon snags easily, so I ball it up and cram it back down into my hip, pushing it deep.

They'll be heading for Hope Bluff by now. I know the trail like the lines around Earl's eyes. Earl on Sumo, the big black gelding. Elaine and Jesse on Bambi and Thumper. Gena . . . well, Gena's a little flighty, and she's not a strong rider, so Earl will probably put her on Judy. I'm pretty sure of that. In fact, I'm absolutely positive.

One thing I'm not so sure of is that the green leaves I gave Judy earlier weren't from one of them plants that give horses the spasms. Now that I come to think of it, I'm really not sure about that at all. But how the hell should I know what's poison and what's not? I'm nothing but a jumped-up guest who don't even know what kind of tree grows in the courtyard. Just a gal from the suburbs who does a little accounting and makes great ribs.

Out on the sun-striped porch, with my mug of cold coffee and a cigarette, I hear Judy whinny in the far distance. She sounds alarmed, like she's frightened, or in pain. Or is that a horse at all? It's hard to tell. Could be a coyote. Or a woman. A woman screaming.

I crush the cigarette under my boot-heel and step back

inside. The morning's warming up and the sun's strong on the stoop. But as I load the dishes in the sink and squirt the detergent in, I can't help thinking how much I'll miss Judy.

Ania's Wake
Dea Brovig

When Ania died, Lukasz knew it would take some time
to adjust to his new circumstances. True, it had been
many years since they had lived together as man and
wife, at least in the proper sense of the term. He could
hardly remember the last time they had shared a bed.
Even so, as her coffin crept along the conveyor belt, as
the crematorium flames licked their welcome and she was
gobbled up whole, he thought to himself, This is going to
take some getting used to.

After the funeral, Lukasz greeted their friends at home,
shaking their hands and kissing their wives and, at
appropriate intervals, moaning and clutching his
daughter Joana's arm. He saw that she was doing a good
job. Her face looked pale and strained as she accepted the
terracotta pots and platters of food – *pierogi* half-moons,
golabki parcels, three prettily iced cakes so far – and
placed them carefully on the table behind her. At one
point, Tomasz's wife Ewa leaned into her and whispered
for a long minute, holding her shoulders tight in her own
ham-hock hands. Lukasz saw Joana's lip tremble as she
bowed her head and the tears came and he thought, She
is a good girl.

It had been a wretched day and, now that the sad
business of laying Ania to rest was over with, Lukasz was

looking forward to having the whole ordeal of the funeral behind him. He was touched by the kindness of his friends and neighbours and he knew his poor wife would be grateful for their respects, but he longed to be alone with Joana. When they were through welcoming everyone to their home he excused himself and snuck out the back door, eyeing the table of food on his way out. He had been making a mental note of which wives had brought what as he stood and accepted their condolences – and now, as he lit his Silk Cut, he began to calculate how long he would be able to last on his own without Ania. Joana should manage to pack up her pokey flat in Newcastle and get settled home in a week or two at the most. Lukasz decided he could live on cake in the meantime.

With a sigh he stretched his back and cracked the ache out of his neck. It felt good to be outside in the cold air, although Lukasz wished he had thought to bring a jumper out with him. As he smoked, he studied the sky, grateful for a few moments to himself. The sun was skimming the top of Elland Road in the distance and already in places there was a wash of pink, like burst capillaries in a giant gold and blue eyeball. How many times had he sat out in this garden with Ania, admiring the sunset? When they had first moved to Beeston from Wroclaw thirty years earlier, they used to carry out a blanket and sit on their bench – the first and last piece of furniture he had ever built – and together they would count the stars. Even on cloudy nights, Ania would say she could see at least one. Lukasz would snort and tell her it was a satellite or an aeroplane.

'Look, it's moving! There's a big red light blinking right below it, woman!' He would nudge her underneath the blanket wrapped around their shoulders and she would smile and shake her head.

'It is what it is,' she would say. For a time, when they first got there, they had been happy together again. At least for a few months they had been able to make a go of starting afresh.

Lukasz rolled the cigarette between his thumb and middle finger and flicked it into the garden, noting with satisfaction the fizz as it landed in a murky puddle near by. Ania always used to grumble to him about the butts that littered her flower beds. Well, that was one thing he wouldn't have to worry about any more.

With one last look of longing towards the burgeoning sunset, Lukasz resigned himself to return to his guests. He was unprepared for the slap of heat as he stepped through the door – and so many people, where had they all come from? In the sitting room, he began to pick his way through the crowd of mourners, checking for signs that they were getting ready to go home. Lukasz imagined they would be anxious to put the day behind them and leave him and Joana in peace to grieve for their loss. Instead, it looked as if a party was starting.

He was annoyed to see several guests standing with plate and fork in hand chomping away on his food. Hopping up and down on the balls of his feet, he tried to signal to Joana over their heads to stop dishing it out – what was the idiot girl thinking? – but when she noticed him she just pursed her lips and turned back to piling up a plate for Mrs Healy. Greedy old goat. She always had been a hungry one. He had often come back from a long shift in his cab, tired and aching for a bath, to find her sitting with Ania in their kitchen being fed. She was thirsty, too. He would have to be sure no one started on the vodka or she was liable to stay here all night.

Lukasz realized that if he was to get through the rest of the evening, he would have to do so sitting down. He spotted Tomasz on the sofa, his lumpy body already settled in. Lukasz flinched when he noticed the shot glass in his friend's hand. Then he began once again to push his way through the crowd.

'Tomasz,' Lukasz hissed as he plonked himself down next to him. 'No to the vodka. What are you doing?'

'What are you talking about?' answered Tomasz, who had evidently helped himself to more than just one drink.

'This is not a party, it's a goddamn funeral. It's time to go home now; you can drink yourself stupid there.'

'But it *is* a party, Lukasz. For Ania,' Tomasz said, as if Lukasz had forgotten who had just died. 'It's only right that her friends want to drink to her. If not tonight, then when?'

As if on cue, Lukasz heard the clinking of glass on glass and all heads turned towards the doorway. He couldn't see what they were looking at from where he was sitting, but then he heard Joana's voice above the sudden hush.

'I'd like everybody to raise their glasses to my mother. She didn't have the life she deserved and she was taken from us too soon. May she finally now find peace in death. To Ania.'

'To Ania!'

Lukasz sat gazing around the room at his friends toasting Ania's undeserving life. He felt as if Joana had just thrown a drink in his face. She didn't have the life she deserved? What was that supposed to mean? Granted, the end was terrible. She definitely didn't deserve *that*, no one did. But her life, even though cut short, had been spent mostly with him and he had always done his best for her. Didn't Joana appreciate that? Did everyone here think otherwise? Where had they all got their glasses from anyway?

Lukasz felt sure that, despite what they all seemed to think, this gathering was not what Ania would have wanted. She would have wanted him and Joana to sit together and reminisce, and then she would have wanted them to watch an episode of *Midsomer Murders* before bed. Just like they had always done when she was alive. Lukasz knew she would not have wanted this hubbub, and he knew her better than anyone. Even so, a drink was starting to sound like a good idea.

As Lukasz heaved himself off the sofa, Tomasz tried to pat him on the back but instead managed to slosh a fresh helping of vodka down Lukasz's now wrinkled shirt. Furious, he stalked off towards the kitchen, leaving Tomasz peering mournfully into his glass.

He found Joana sitting alone at the kitchen table. Two lines of tears slipped unchecked down her cheeks. She wiped her face when she saw Lukasz in the doorway, as if she had something to hide from him, and again he felt the slight of her earlier comment.

'You've been drinking,' he said, pouring himself a large measure of brandy. She didn't answer, so he sat down next to her and tried again. 'Joana.'

A pause, and then, 'I'm going to miss her, Papa.'

'I know you will,' he said as gently as he could manage. 'It will be all right. As soon as we get you moved in here so I can take care of you, everything will be fine.'

Joana looked blank for a moment, then confused. 'Move in here?'

'Of course.'

'What are you talking about, Papa?'

'Why do people keep asking me that tonight? Of course you'll be moving in here. It's what your mother would have wanted.'

'What? No! Papa, I can't do that. I'm in the middle of my university degree! You want me to drop out?'

'Come, Joana. A university degree in business or medicine, OK, but your media rubbish – what is it again?'

'You've got to be joking. For the two hundredth time, it's Media, Communication and Cultural Studies.'

'Media, Communication and Cultural Studies.' Lukasz smiled and shook his head. 'This is not a degree. When your mother was alive you could do your funny things, but now we can't afford this luxury.'

'Luxury? I'm on my third loan so far and I'm hardly living in the lap of luxury. Jesus, Papa,' she said, rubbing her forehead wearily, 'your timing is perfect. You really expect me to feel differently about this now that Mama's gone? Why? I don't suddenly *not* want to be a journalist.'

'I know, I know. The British Bloody Broadcasting Corporation. Your big fancy dream.' He flapped a hand in dismissal. 'It's time to be a grown-up, and grown-ups do what is expected of them. You have responsibilities now.'

'To whom? To *you*?'

'To this family, Joana.'

'Oh, Papa, what is this? Did we time-warp back to the fifties without anyone letting me know?'

Lukasz threw up his hands and rolled his eyes skyward. He swore his daughter was getting more English every day.

'You have to be reasonable,' he said.

'I'm sorry, Papa, but you can forget it, because it's not going to happen. There's no way I'm moving back home.'

For a moment, Lukasz had a vision of his daughter as a seven year old, sitting at their kitchen table with her arms crossed and bottom lip pushed out, refusing to eat her vegetables. The stubbornness that had been adorable in childhood had developed into an infuriating trait.

'You are my daughter, Joana. You will do as I tell you!' He was trying to keep his voice down because of the guests in the next room, but his growing anger was getting the better of him.

'Are you going to abandon me now? Think of what your mother would have wanted.'

'Did you ever in your life really think about what Mama wanted? Remember those painting classes she signed up for? She loved going to them, and she was good at it, too. But you made her stop so she could be here every night to cook your tea.'

'Joana!'

'The last thing Mama wanted,' she said calmly, 'was for me to turn into your maid. To turn into her.'

'What the hell is that supposed to mean?'

A couple of concerned faces appeared in the doorway, but Lukasz was too worked up by now to take any notice.

'You know what it means. You know what she used to tell me? "I am the fan that the shit hits." I am not going to be your new fan.' She stood up and took hold of her glass.

'You're drunk. You're a disgrace, swearing at your mother's funeral.'

'No, Papa, I'm not a disgrace. Mama was proud of me – and of my studies,' Joana said, before turning her back on him and walking out of the kitchen door.

Lukasz's head was reeling. He grasped the edge of the table, preparing to launch to his feet and fly after her. Then he remembered their friends in the adjacent room. They would all have heard them, of course. They would have heard every word of his and Joana's argument. Was it his imagination, or had the level of noise in the house just dropped? Lukasz slumped back in his chair and massaged his temples with fingers that smelled of tobacco. He remembered the words Ania used to mutter when his temper got the better of him – 'Control yourself, for Christ's sake, you big ox' – and he shut his eyes and drew in a deep, shaky breath. Despite the flap of panic in his chest, he realized that now was not the time. Tomorrow he would try again. He would sit Joana down and remind her of what the doctor had said about his blood pressure. What was it exactly? Whatever it was, it was a serious matter. If he could just make her listen, he knew he could convince her to do what was proper. And if he couldn't – well, that wasn't something he wanted to think about.

Lukasz rubbed his eyes before looking around at the empty kitchen. Briefly, he considered rejoining the others in the sitting room, but he dismissed the idea and instead turned his attention to the bottle beside him.

It was some time before his guests started to leave. Two by two, they padded into the kitchen and bent to embrace their bleary-eyed host. Finally, thought Lukasz, who muttered his thanks and swatted them away. Tomasz and Ewa were the last to go. They came in and hugged him and told him to get off to bed and, just like that, he was alone. He didn't know what had become of Joana.

Lukasz stayed seated at the kitchen table nursing his bottle of brandy until he had drained its contents. Then he rose to his feet and staggered to the sitting room. It smelled of unwashed armpits. It was a tip, glasses everywhere. Someone had taken what little food remained untouched and placed it in the fridge, but all he saw were the plates abandoned on the tabletops, many still smudged with half-eaten slices of cake. A dark splodge bloomed on the beige sofa cushion where someone had spilled a drink. Bloody Tomasz, thought Lukasz, and a new twist of anger unsettled his belly. He prodded the offending spot with trembling fingers.

The room that had been packed with people not long

before suddenly felt far too small for him on his own. It wasn't just the room; the whole house was bearing down on him. He had to get out of there, and quick.

He grabbed a blanket and hobbled on unsteady feet to the hallway, where he pulled a coat and his Leeds United scarf from the cupboard. After slamming the front door behind him, he fumbled with the keys to make sure it was double locked. The street was empty, he was relieved to see, and he negotiated his way across the road to where his car was parked, trying not to slip on the frost that had settled.

He arranged himself as best he could in the back seat, tucking the blanket underneath his legs and draping his coat across his chest up to his chin. The scarf he wrapped around his head. As he lay waiting for sleep, he peered out of the window up at the sky above Elland Road. No stars, not even any satellites. Lukasz smiled sadly into the dead night. He knew that if Ania had been there, she would have found something to gaze at.

Never Said a Word

Daisy Cains

It all came back to me years later when the wrong men were appealing for the third time. I'd missed the first two trials, working hard on the Bar exams, and besides, I'd had my TV knocked off in a break-in one Christmas. But now an ITV reconstruction brought me back to 1974: the gingery men with their wavy, shoulder-length, slightly dirty hair, long leather coats and platform shoes being dragged off to the cells. Seventies footballers or pub bombers, they all dressed pretty much the same. It's a measure of just how wrong the wrong men were, that the six main characters didn't remind me of anyone, just three old men, older than my dad anyway, and three thickset Irish hard cases. No, it was the actors playing the police officers and the journalists who brought back the memories and made me think of the gangs of blokes who sat around our kitchen table drinking over-sugared tea made with sterilized milk while they waited for my father to open his wallet. Scruffy, paint-spattered men who distracted me from my homework and made my mind wander to the Bay City Rollers, Gordon Hill and the pristine copy of *Tammy* waiting on my bedside table.

As I looked at Martin Shaw's bright blue eyes, I was reminded of the sun-bronzed labourers who visited us in the autumn of 1974. I saw Michael leaning down to talk to me in the garage, and I just knew it had been them. I'd never taken much notice of Martin Shaw before – I found *The Professionals* slightly dubious and when it came to seventies cop shows I was always a John Thaw/Dennis Waterman kind of girl. But here was Martin Shaw playing a serious role and I had to take him seriously, particularly those eyes; Michael's eyes.

At eight years old I loved the Rollers and the Villa (Gordon Hill was the exception to my Villa-players-only rule), and each week I read every word of *Tammy*, and *Jackie* if I could get hold of it from my older cousin, but never until I'd finished my schoolwork. But when these tea-drinking, long-haired, foundry-smelling crew with impenetrable accents distracted me, I'd end up showing off my new Bay City Rollers game or my shiny plastic Aston Villa baseball cap or even performing an Osmonds number on the recorder for them. Most of the Irishmen were off the minute they got a sub from my dad; they didn't even stay to finish their tea.

Except one – Michael – who liked to hang around. He'd encourage me to play another tune on the recorder – even though I was, and remain, tone deaf – or he'd help me finish the story I was writing for school the next day. He'd tell me stories of his own, miraculous stories of Irish knights, Brian Boru and Finn McCool. We would read poems together – 'The Hunting of the Snark' and 'The Jumblies' were my favourites – and he promised to buy me a 'monkey with lollipop paws' and a 'green jackdaw'. I pretended to believe him even though I knew he was pulling my leg. But I liked it best when he treated me like a grown-up and we talked about the Villa. One day he brought me a complete set of first eleven signatures on Aston Villa headed notepaper. I realize now that it was a standard Xeroxed copy sent to every fan who sent the club an SAE, but at the time I thought it was wonderful.

My dad was a painter and decorator, and a dodgy one. Not his work, that was always top rank, but he had a relaxed attitude towards tax, health and safety – minor details that ate into his profits – and he employed a lot of Irishmen. All the local firms did, you just pulled up outside a pub and picked them up at the roadside. The usual place to do this was a huge pub by the Seminary on the northern edges of town. The old man or his foreman would roll down the van window and ask: 'Are you a painter, Paddy?'

'No, a brickie's labourer.'

They'd move onto the next and then the next until, with no names asked and no pack-drill, a couple of hungover, so-called painters were bundled into the back of the van where they would either go back to sleep or light a fag and try their hand at having the craic with their temporary employer. Then it was off to some godforsaken, grimy Black Country foundry that was in need of a coat of limewash.

My dad liked his Irish workforce. He'd keep the more reliable of them on to work for him for months at a time and some were even trusted with a van, so they'd become regular visitors to the house, picking up paint and ladders, money and instructions. And so Michael had reason to be around the house, even when my dad was away – and both of them often were.

Watching Martin Shaw, who looked so like Michael, with his brown hair and bright blue eyes, I remembered more and more about what I had seen. And what I had heard, too. I remembered a time when I was hiding under a pile of clothes on the bed. Mom and Auntie Aisling were trying on outfits, flouncing around in front of the cheval mirror, deciding what to wear for a forthcoming wedding. I had burrowed under their discarded clothes and lost myself in a flurry of Estée

Lauder face powder and that perfume Mom used to wear, the obscure Ungaro one, which was virtually impossible to get hold of in the UK, or so Dad claimed when he showed up empty-handed every birthday, Christmas and anniversary. I hadn't moved for ten minutes when I heard Aisling ask, 'How's Michael?'

'Wonderful,' Mom said. 'I think, no I don't think, I know, I love him.'

I couldn't hear Aisling's reply.

'He's so different from Jim. I tried to teach Jim how to love me, but I never succeeded. I haven't had to teach Michael anything.'

I still couldn't hear Aisling's reply.

'Not to make love, just to love.'

Then I felt something lift from me and heard a stifled yelp. 'You asleep, Daisy?' asked Mom, sounding panicked.

I shut my eyes and pretended.

Mom pulled back the pile of clothes. 'Off to bed with you. School tomorrow.'

She tapped me on the backside and I was off like a shot, yawning a lot, probably too much.

I didn't know what to make of what I'd just heard. Michael was better than my dad at something, but I wasn't sure exactly what. Perhaps it was telling stories, but Dad was good at that, so it could have been singing. Dad was a terrible singer. He used to come home from the pub and sing something awful in French about the Knights of the Round Table. But Michael had a beautiful voice. He usually sang David Bowie or T.Rex, but he played up the Irishness for Mom and me, giving us 'The Wild Rover' and 'Whiskey in the Jar'. My favourite was 'The Black Velvet Band' especially when he sang:

She was both fair and handsome
Her neck it was just like a swan

And her hair it hung over her shoulders
Tied up in a black velvet band.

Mom's neck was more like a swan's than mine, pink and chubby as it was, but Michael would sing to me that my eyes 'shone like diamonds' and tell me that I was 'queen of the land'. But he was usually looking at Mom when he sang those words, too – so I was pretty sure that Mom hadn't really meant singing.

These gangs of men in my dad's kitchen were typical of seventies itinerant Irish workers. They'd arrive at Holyhead or Fishguard armed with a tax exemption certificate, which meant they could be paid in cash, the employer had no PAYE problem and the worker would then pay a bit of tax at the end of each year. This system solved the unemployment problem in Ulster and the labour shortage in Britain. Everyone was a winner: the government, the workers and the employers. And my father more than most. If an Irishman entered his employ with an exemption certificate, he rarely left with it: Dad would buy it and use it to siphon large amounts of tax-free cash out of the business. Large amounts of tax-free cash that paid for my expensive girls' school in Edgbaston, my pony and piano lessons, my lacrosse sticks and a brace from a private dentist.

My dad liked these men and he exploited them. They did a lot of work for not very much money, but I now wondered about how they had exploited him too. How they had used his very ordinary dodginess as the perfect cover for their deadly activities. I realized, watching the documentary that evening, that I knew they had, and that I'd always known. And this is how I knew.

*

I'd just saved the dog. My brother had tied Sellotape around his front and back legs, his snout and his tail, and was marching past me with a stapler, intending to staple Copper's ears together on top of his head. I disarmed him and went to free our lovely but stupid dog, which my father insisted on calling 'Chopper' after Ron Harris. I'd looked up Ron 'Chopper' Harris in *Purnell's Encyclopaedia of Association Football* and I hated him. He played for Chelsea, a sixties throwback with no flowing locks and not at all like my dog.

My brother was upset at his game being spoiled, so I took him into the garage. The garage was our forbidden playground. It was where my father stored his paint and his ladders; his spray guns and pressurized pots that blasted concoctions of lime and distemper onto factory walls; asbestos sheets and nasty, sharp fibreglass sheets used for skylights that we made dens with; plus a bright red steam-cleaning machine which was shaped like a steam locomotive. There was row upon row of heavy-duty paint cans: rusty, dusty and stolen paint, expensive industrial paint and specialist chemical paint. Some had been there for as long as I could remember, but they would all apparently come in handy one day. In the meantime, they were great for climbing on and perfect for hiding behind.

I helped my brother aboard the steam-cleaner steam engine, but he scuffed my lacy white socks as he settled into position, so I picked up an oily rag off the floor and chucked it into his face just as he was beginning his Casey Jones impersonation. I stuck my tongue out at him and ducked behind the nearest stack of paint cans. He came after me, grappling for my ponytail. He missed, but connected with a dented tin of red lead oxide. It went flying and the clatter of cans brought us both to a sudden halt.

Then he was heading for the door before I had chance to order him out. I shouted that he could keep running, though I would have preferred him to stay and help. The lead oxide can was large, but grubby and forgotten after its plummet from the back of a lorry. It held five gallons, which was probably more than I could lift unassisted, but it was better that my brother stayed in hiding for now as he couldn't be relied on to stay paint-free. I wasn't sure I was going to be successful in keeping my pinafore clear of incriminating evidence, but I needn't have worried: no paint was spewing out. The lid had gone cartwheeling along the concrete floor and even though the specialist stuff that Dad used could be very thick, some of the tin's contents should have been oozing out. I looked inside. All I could see was an old curtain.

I tugged at the material, but whatever was wrapped inside was too heavy for me to shift, so I pulled back a corner and saw a big lump of brownish clay, like marzipan. I pushed at it and it gave way under my fingers. I pushed my whole hand against it and left a perfect impression. I grinned. This was like modelling clay but not as messy. I remembered the ring I was wearing – my best Mattel Liddle Kiddles ring – it would make a great shape in the marzipan. I took it off and pressed it down, once, twice, then a third time in a circular pattern before I had a frightening thought. Earlier that year, Dad had appeared before the local magistrates on charges of storing dangerous industrial materials in a domestic garage. He'd had to pay a hefty fine and when he told the magistrates the proceedings were 'a load of piffle', they promptly increased the fine. He didn't care and he went on using the garage for storage just the same. So I knew that he kept some really horrible things, acids and chemicals, in there and, knowing my luck, this was probably one of them. I put the lid back on the tin and went to scrub my hands, not forgetting to give my Kiddles ring a good clean with my brother's toothbrush. Well, he hardly ever used it, the stinky sod.

Next morning, the familiar chug of diesel engines and Dad's banter with his sleepy workers woke me but the noise seemed to go on for longer than usual. I heard my dad leave, but one van was still there. I could tell it was the van that the Irishmen used by the splutters and rattles it made as it ticked over beneath my window. My dad's business didn't have any really reliable vehicles, but the one kept for his casual workers was a shocker even given his cavalier approach to MOT standards. The van back-fired away. I thought no more of it and went to clean my teeth, glancing lovingly at my new David Cassidy poster on my way to the bathroom.

School was great that day. I came top of the class in English and history and got a gold star for spelling. Back at home, I ate a Twix and got started on my English homework. I was really excited by our new book – *A Kestrel for a Knave*. A proper book at last, one that had been made into a film for adults, not the stupid kids' stuff we'd done before.

I was alone in the kitchen. Dad was still at work, my brother was probably out torturing toads with his horrible friends and I didn't know where Mom was, shopping or seeing her mother perhaps.

I was reading away when the first van pulled in, followed by a knock at the back door. I opened it and was confronted by a set of nicotine-stained teeth beaming from the soot-blackened face of 'Mick'. It makes me cringe to think about it now but all the Irishmen were known as 'Paddy' or 'Mick', the Scotsmen 'Jock' and the Welshmen 'Taffy'. Over the years my dad had three or four Nobby Clarkes working for him, at least two

Chalkie Whites and – long before Alan Bleasdale – a Yosser Hughes, although this being seventies Birmingham everyone just called him 'Scouse'. I realize now how four men must have been glad of the anonymity that the lazily racist generic provided, but the others – the ordinary, decent, non-bomb-planting Irishmen – didn't complain either, not to us anyway. My father used to put 'Paddy' on their wage packets and no one commented when they collected them.

Mick ruffled my hair, which messed my pigtails up, but I smiled politely back.

'Daddy's not back yet,' I said.

'Not to worry, darling. Why don't you come out to the garage? We've got you a little present.'

I hesitated. 'I'm not supposed to go in there.'

'Oh you'll be all right with us, come on now.'

I followed him and found 'Paddy 1' and 'Paddy 2' smoking at the side of the van. In front of Paddy 1 was a large paint tin that looked just like the one that contained the marzipan and the curtain. Michael came round from behind the back of the van. He looked stern.

I stopped short.

Mick put his hands on my shoulders. 'Don't worry, darling. It's a bit of advice we're after giving you, nothing more.'

Michael took over. 'There's nothing to worry about, lovey, but your da wouldn't be too happy if he knew you'd been messing about with this.' He pointed at the tin. 'It's some dangerous stuff that we use in the building game.'

Paddy 2 snorted. 'More like the demolition game.' He got a kick in the shins from Michael for his trouble.

'How do you know I was touching that tin?' I demanded.

Michael took no notice. My attempt to sound

authoritative didn't work then and it hasn't worked much since.

'See that ring you're wearing, darling?'

I looked sheepishly at the ring finger of my right hand before hiding both hands behind my back.

'Well,' said Michael, smiling and pointing at the decorated corner of the marzipan, 'there it is.'

I bit my lip.

'Ah, there now, darling, we'll say nothing if you say nothing.'

I looked at him and said nothing.

'All right?' he pressed.

'All right,' I stuttered.

'There now, we'll take this away and we'll pretend it was never here. Your da will never have to know. We'll say it was never here and you'll do the same. It was never here and you never saw it. OK?'

I nodded.

Mick let go of my shoulders and ruffled my hair. 'Didn't I say we'd got you a present?' He smiled and handed me a small package. 'Go on, open it.'

I tore at the paper, which had several greasy thumbprints on it, to reveal a Mattel Liddle Kiddles ring. It was 'Harriet', the prettiest one, the one I wanted.

'How did you know this was the one I wanted?' I gasped.

'Your mum must have mentioned it,' Michael said.

'When?'

Paddy 1 interrupted. 'We're good at guessing things like that.' He scowled at Michael.

Mick joined in. 'That's it, luck o' the Irish.'

Michael smiled at me sadly. 'Now be a good girl,' he said, 'and go and put the kettle on. We'll load up and then we'll be in to see your da.'

Mick ruffled my hair again. 'Remember now, you never

saw that tin.' He rubbed the side of his nose, which I thought was a funny thing to do, but I nodded and ran into the house.

It was only when the kettle was boiling that I realized they couldn't come in for a cup of tea with my dad because he wasn't at home. I headed towards the door to tell them, but something made me stop. I stood there for a moment and then went up to my room. I brushed my hair straight after all that ruffling and then I tried 'Harriet' on.

Three days later two concealed bombs tore through two pubs in the centre of town, killing twenty-one people and injuring one hundred and eighty-two others.

Paddy 1, Paddy 2 and Mick stopped turning up to work for my father; the other men said they'd returned to Belfast. They certainly didn't hang around to sell him their tax exemption certificates. But Michael hung around for a little longer. He'd telephone the house and speak to my mom. And once, when my dad was working away – or playing away; I found out as I got older that it amounted to the same thing – he telephoned almost constantly and I heard my mom use the F word for the first time. Apparently, 'the fucking babysitter cried off at the last minute'. She shooed me away before I could hear any more, but soon afterwards a beat-up old Datsun pulled onto the drive and my mom rushed out to meet it. She sat out there in the car with Michael and I leaned on the windowsill, chin in hands and a lock of hair in my mouth, watching. I saw their heads come together and after a while I realized they were kissing, a proper long kiss as well. The lock of hair fell from my mouth and I forgot about my homework as I watched, straining to make out what was going on in the eerie, grey light from our authentic, reproduction carriage lanterns. Michael was unbuttoning Mom's blouse and I watched him put his hand inside. Then her head disap-peared below the dashboard and all I could see was Michael's face, his eyes closed in a funny expression. Just before Mom reappeared, Michael's eyes flew open, those blue Irish eyes I'd seen so often across the kitchen table.

After what had happened, Birmingham was probably the safest place in the country, but Mom refused to go into the city centre and we had to make do with Christmas shopping in Walsall. My brother was disappointed because he had his heart set on the Airfix Stalingrad set, which was only available from Beatties in the Bull Ring. I wasn't too bothered. I didn't feel Christmassy. I'd got 'Harriet', but I'd got her for doing something I shouldn't have done. I'd seen and heard things I shouldn't have, and looking at 'Harriet' made me think of the expression on Michael's face in the Datsun. On Christmas Day I wrapped my new ring in tissue paper and hid it in the bottom of my wardrobe. With it, I packed away the memory of how Michael and the other three men had smiled at me in the garage before driving away with that old paint tin in my dad's backfiring van.

Out of Her Life

Anita Sethi

Sapna Chaudhuri draws back her curtain and sees that the world she knows has vanished. Snow is falling, a white heaven wiping out the dirty streets.

A brown bird hurtles past, so close that she hears through the pane of glass the panicked beating of its wings. But then the bird plummets down into the road, crumpling into a heap of tattered feathers. A car's oiled wheels smash over the bird's broken body, crushing it, until it is nothing three-dimensional. A redness smears the snow.

Then the sky heaves open, pouring snow onto the dead bird. When the snow finally stops, Sapna and Sohni look for traces of the bird in the road but its body has gone.

Sapna wonders if it was her fault that the bird stopped flying. If only she had not opened the curtain, startling the whiteness with the blackness of their bedroom, then the bird might have kept on. She closes her eyes and chants one, two, three, four, five, six, seven, eight, nine, the number of years the twins have been alive, and then opens her eyes, hoping they might have magicked back the bird. But the road is still empty. She draws the curtain, sealing away the white world.

I would like to fall, thinks Sapna, like that bird, out of my life.

*

It is Christmas Eve and the heating has stopped working.

Sapna and Sohni's hands clutch the radiator beneath the window until the last of the heat leaks from it. They clench tighter at a sudden sound behind them of the door being pushed open. It is their mother. Mrs Chaudhuri's voice is low and choked, like the engine of a car when it will not start. 'Heating's still broken. Everything's breaking.' Her daughters turn to look at the small hunched figure, at her watery eyes and the cream-coloured blanket wrapped around her head. Usually the boiler's body is so hot it feels as if it might scald the surface of the palm. But today the twins and their mother touch the boiler and feel that all its warmth has drained away.

'We must have done something bad in a past life to deserve this,' Mrs Chaudhuri mutters, before retreating back into her bed. Mrs Chaudhuri is often talking about how their past lives are to blame for whatever goes wrong. Their past lives, she says, are the reason why she is swollen-eyed for the husband who has left her. He has taken with him the settee, the coffee table with the elephant engravings, and their eleven-year-old son, Ashwin. He has left behind his battered Roget's Thesaurus that he won at school in Delhi, his cricket bat, and their nine-year-old twin daughters.

Sapna and Sohni are not thinking about their past lives, but instead imagining the horrible things that they must have done in their present life to deserve this. If only they had not pulled each other's hair so hard that they screamed, making their dad shake his head and tut tut tut. If only they had not told their mother how their brother had spat in their food, which had made their mother burst into tears and their father start tutting again. If only they had woken up earlier on the day their father left; if they had not slept in, opening their eyes into darkness, but then closing them again. If they had got out of bed that day instead of being such lazy, lazy, lazy girls, they might have been able to wait by the front door and catch their father before he went, like a gust of warm air.

Mrs Chaudhuri doesn't know that her daughters have been finding their father everywhere. They looked for him all over the house and he began to appear. They found stray hairs from his balding head on the sheets in their mother's bedroom, unchanged since he left. They smelled him in the curtains in the hallway near the front door where they hid in case he came back and they could leap out and seize him. They often hear his voice in their heads, too: an echo in there, like the way the doorbell rings inside the mind after the main sound has died down.

Sapna sits clutching the cold radiator and tries to think of her father. Usually he will be with her quickly, like magic he will be in her head, but she can no longer remember what he looks like. She screws her eyes up tight and holds her breath and tries to imagine the shape of his face, his nose, his ears; perhaps if she concentrates on each feature separately, he will be there. But she cannot conjure up anything of him today. The more she tries, the foggier he becomes. All she can see is his bald head, its damp brown skin.

At night she prays like she has been told to do. She prays to God, saying thank you for good things and sorry for bad things and asking for what she would like to happen in the future. But when she thinks of God in her bedroom at night, it is her father she is praying to, his bald skull shining in the blackness.

All over the house, the radiators are draped with clothes, still wet. The wetness is evaporating, letting off a strange, sharp smell; a fishy smell. Hanging out to dry are faded salwar-kameezes, the twins' green school uniforms, and some of their father's great grey shirts. Sapna can almost see his arms in there, outstretched. Mrs Chaudhuri drags herself up to clear away the clothes but when she feels that they are still wet she sinks back into her bed, the cream-coloured blanket still wrapped around her head. Since their father left, their mother has been full of frantic energy that burns itself through the snow and into all of their lives. But then the energy vanishes as soon as it came.

'I'm dying, you know,' their mother whispers. Sapna and Sohni stand over her and prod her arm in an effort to shift her, but she won't budge. Sapna and Sohni often return to their mother's room and check that the air in front of her nose and mouth is warm, that she is still alive and at times they snuggle up against her warm body. 'I'm dying, you know. So you just better learn to look after yourselves because I haven't got much longer to live. You better just pack up your bags and go and live at your father's house. You won't have a mother for much longer.'

Her warmth turns on and off. Today, she is closed tight, as if her hinges have frozen. Some days, however much the twins make a song and dance around her, she stares ahead, her eyes glazed like frost.

The house contracts into itself as the coldness conquers. The molecules on its surfaces swarm together, close in and become a static, frigid mass.

The twins are sitting downstairs in the living room, eyes glued to the TV. *The Snowman* is playing on the static-filled screen: he is walking in the air, partying in the snowy forest and melting with the rising of the sun.

The peace is broken when Sohni notices an empty space on the carpet beside her. 'You've stolen my chocolate Father Christmas,' she screams to her sister. 'You've stolen my chocolate,' she sing-songs. Sapna did indeed steal the chocolate Father, which was standing on the grey carpet. She peeled back the red, gold, glinting foil, and devoured the brown sweetness. Sohni, so fixated on the melting Snowman, did not notice until it was too late, and there was no sweetness left for her.

Sohni dashes upstairs and into her mother's room. She tells their mother about how Sapna stole her chocolate Father Christmas and ate it while they were watching *The Snowman*. But their mother isn't standing for this nonsense. She's given the children everything she has, everything she is, and just bloody look what she gets in return.

The door opens and Mrs Chaudhuri lunges at Sapna, who dashes to her room. Sapna only has time to scramble onto the bed before her mother catches hold of her. In the darkness, lit up by the amber streetlight, her mother looks nothing like herself. Her golden bangles glint and chink. Hands grasp and pull at Sapna's hair so that her head bangs against the wall and her teeth clamp down on her tongue.

'Stop screaming,' Mrs Chaudhuri hisses. 'Who the bloody hell do you think you are, ungrateful thief?' Then she says words that would be banned in the school playground in a pitch of voice like tyres screeching on the pavement, or chalk down the blackboard.

Sohni's voice sounds tiny and faraway as she cries that she doesn't really mind about the chocolate at all. 'Stop it, Mum, stop it,' she says, and Mrs Chaudhuri yells, 'Don't call me Mum. I'm no mother of yours. You both bloody well pack up your bags and go and live at your father's house.'

Then their mother retreats, spitting out her rage and leaving it in the room.

Weak light filters through the living room the next morning. A sobbing noise comes from beneath the Christmas tree where Sohni is crouched. As Sapna stands over her sister, her stomach muscles tighten, and her hand lashes through the air to hit her sister. *Tell-tale, tell-tale, tell-tale*, she shouts. But as soon as she hears the dull *thud* and a whine rise through her sister like a high recorder note blown out, Sapna feels a rotting feeling of shame, as if she has stale banana skins there in her belly.

Soon, silence has grown like a presence itself in the house. Sapna and Sohni together tiptoe to their mother's room, to check she is still alive, that she is still breathing. A soft golden light filters through the thin, drawn curtains, spilling in shadows over the walls which are hung with pictures of Hanuman and blue Krishna playing on a flute, over the clothes-strewn floor, over the bedside table with its dusty framed photograph of the smiling family together, the twins with their black pigtails, their brother with his bucktoothed grin, Mrs Chaudhuri before she hacked off her long flowing hair, Mr Chaudhuri with his arms around his wife. The bed is empty. A note on the pillow reads in their mother's loopy handwriting:

> *I've gone away to escape from evil tongues. Fight each other to death for all I care.*

Sapna and Sohni sit beside the kitchen door and wait. They look down the path that leads past the small rose bush and are united in a game of counting people and raindrops and cars and hours until the numbers get too long and melt away. But still their mother doesn't come back. They make rhymes out of the bad words ringing in their head, to try and hide the bad words: *itch witch bitch stitch glitch*

But soon Sapna cannot say any more rhymes for there is a dull ache rising where her teeth bit down on her tongue. If only she hadn't stolen the chocolate Father Christmas, she thinks. If only she'd given it back to her sister instead of peeling away its foily layers and wolfing it down, the whole of her itching for the sweetness of it until the chocolate was crushed against her tongue and dribbling down the back of her throat, making her feel better for those few moments that the sweetness was inside her.

'I'm sorry for telling tales,' her sister says.

The house starts to heat up of its own accord and soon the radiators are hot slabs again.

*

After she had left her daughter slumped in the darkness Mrs Chaudhuri went back to her room, flung open her wardrobe and pulled out a salwar-kameez, got her toothbrush from the bathroom, shoved her few things into a plastic carrier bag and left the house. Still in her slippers, she walked and walked down the long road, a hunched figure, dragging her shadow through the streets. She didn't feel the cold pinch at her bare legs or nip at her ankles as she wandered, not really knowing where she was going, her slippered feet taking her past the off-licence and the chippy and the pharmacy, towards her friend Priya's house.

She reached the house and pressed her face up against the glass of a more perfect world. There, through the window, she saw Priya nestled on the settee next to her husband. The television flickered away in the corner, ET's heart beating a dangerous red. Priya's children were snuggled up on cushions beside them. A Christmas tree stood in the corner, tall and fat, bearing its baubles with pride.

Then the cold started up in Mrs Chaudhuri. It was in her toes first, suddenly stiff and heavy, before spreading up through her calves, into her stomach and along her spine to pinch the nape of her neck.

Priya heard her friend's sobbing and brought her inside the warm house. She gave her hot chai to drink and dished out aloo gobi for her from a pot in the kitchen. Just the smell of the aloo gobi spread through Mrs Chaudhuri and filled her up. Priya asked how Mr Chaudhuri was, and Mrs Chaudhuri fiddled with the golden ring still clamped around her finger, which seemed to grow tighter and sorer every day. She lied and said that Mr Chaudhuri was at home with the children. She'd just needed to get away, that's all; she just needed to get away from it all, she wasn't feeling too well, not very well at all. Priya nodded briskly as she listened to her friend and noticed how sore the flesh of the finger around her wedding ring had become. They both helped to remove the ring; Priya soaped her friend's fingers in warm water and after a little while, when the skin was relaxed, the ring slid off.

Time vanished as she lay in her friend's house, a muscle throbbing in her leg where the cold had got trapped. She slept a dreamless sleep clogged by the heavy pulsing of her leg. While she was sleeping, Priya kept the ring carefully on the bedside table next to her friend.

When Mrs Chaudhuri awoke she thought of her children, she thought how they must be hungry and need feeding. She slipped out of bed, glanced at the ring, but left it glinting there on the bedside table. Then she walked out of her friend's house, and back down the icy road towards her life.

Old School Entertainment
Nick Walker

Mr and Mrs Edison ran a booth on the station platform. Outside the booth was a billboard. It was Tuesday, so it read:

MAGIC AND ILLUSION
CHAINS CANNOT HOLD HIM. MR EDISON GIVES YOU
A DEMONSTRATION OF THE ART OF ESCAPOLOGY
FIRST TUESDAY IN THE MONTH — ESCAPE FROM
THE TERRIFYING WATERY PRISON

A commuter with oiled hair was intrigued by the billboard and the booth. He had three minutes to spare before his train, so he entered and deposited two pounds in the slot.

A sign was illuminated. ENJOY THE SHOW. Then a timer started and a viewing hatch cranked open.

The customer's eyes widened. Quite rightly. It was a spectacular sight.

Inside the booth, Mr Edison was tightly shackled. Chains and padlocks covered his body. His moustache was waxed. He was spot-lit and a dramatic classic played on a record player. There should've been a watery prison, too, as it was the first Tuesday in the month, but Mr Edison had recently suffered a punctured lung and was waiting for the medical profession to give him the all-clear before he reassembled the tank. Plus, the tank leaked quite badly which had often led to flooding of the booth and shorting of the 'Enjoy the show' sign.

'Sir,' said Mr Edison, 'you see I am chained from head to foot. The padlocks are secure and I can barely breathe.'

The dramatic classic came to its crescendo. Mr Edison's wife, Mrs Edison, worked the volume controls. Occasionally she put her hand to her mouth in dismay, as if this time, for this customer, her courageous husband might just go too far.

'If I haven't freed myself from these bonds before the viewing hatch closes,' said Mr Edison, 'you will win a cash prize.'

'How much?' asked the customer.

'A significant amount,' said Mr Edison.

'Be specific,' said the customer.

'Enough to cause me financial ruin,' said Mr Edison. 'Now, please don't talk to me, it's quite distracting.'

The customer figured it wouldn't take that much to cause the financial ruin of someone who had a booth on the station platform, but he didn't question Mr Edison further.

Mr Edison announced that because the act was so dangerous, he would exchange a farewell kiss with his wife, in case he never saw her again.

Mrs Edison stepped forward. She played the moment well. There was a tear in her eye and a falter in her step. She sighed and clutched her bosom.

'God forfend against it being the last kiss, Roger,' she said.

'Don't use real names,' her husband hissed.

'Sorry,' she said and brought her trembling lips towards her husband's.

'Stop,' said the customer.

The kiss was paused. The Edisons peered at the man.

'Mrs Edison is going to pass the padlock key to Mr Edison during the kiss.'

The Edisons gasped.

'It is,' continued the customer, 'a well-documented sleight of hand. Perfected, I believe, by Harry Houdini and his wife.'

This was the first public unmasking the Edisons had experienced in their booth.

'I assure you, sir,' said Mr Edison manfully, 'that the old and hackneyed tricks of Mr Houdini . . .'

Mrs Edison offered the customer a kiss in order to verify that no such trickery was taking place.

'I don't think that's necessary,' said Mr Edison.

'I don't mind,' said the customer.

'Well, I mind,' said Mr Edison.

'I think it will clear the matter up,' said Mrs Edison, and before Mr Edison could stop her she put her lips to the hatch and the customer with the oiled hair put his lips to the hatch, too, and they kissed.

'I hardly think –' started Mr Edison.

They kissed long and hard. Mr Edison sweated in his straitjacket. Mrs Edison sweated in her period bodice. The customer sweated in his woollen suit.

'All right, yes,' said Mr Edison. 'Well done. We're rumbled. You can stop now.'

But the customer didn't stop. His tongue reached in. He sought out the key. He explored Mrs Edison's mouth. Mrs Edison made tiny little noises.

'It's not that hard to find,' complained Mr Edison.

His wife started panting. She seemed to be trying to find a key in the customer's mouth, too. The dramatic classic soared.

'This is unwanted customer interaction,' said Mr Edison, and he kicked the booth wall.

It didn't seem that unwanted. The customer was feeding

on Mrs Edison. It was more than a kiss now. It was something else. Something primal. They were sucking the life out of each other.

'That's enough!' shouted Mr Edison. He knocked the timer over, stamped on it and the hatch door closed with a slam. Mrs Edison had to jump back before her lips were cut off.

'Show's over,' said Mr Edison.

The customer wiped saliva from his mouth and clapped enthusiastically. Then he exited the booth, adjusting his trousers as he went. He left ten pounds on the seat.

Mrs Edison leaned her head against the booth wall and got her breath back.

Mr Edison struggled impotently in his chains. 'Enjoy that, did you?' he asked.

'Hardly at all,' said Mrs Edison, gasping.

'Let me out then,' said Mr Edison.

Mrs Edison looked at him and chewed her lip.

'You've swallowed the key, haven't you?' he said.

Mrs Edison nodded.

'Oh, you stupid, stupid woman.'

'I did it to preserve the integrity of the act.' The customer's tongue had been like a warm eel and the key had had no hiding place. 'I'm sorry.'

Mr Edison told her to vomit immediately. But she couldn't vomit; she wasn't of a mind to vomit. She still had the taste of the gentleman in her mouth and a tugging in her groin. She hadn't felt less sick in all her life.

The next day, Wednesday, the billboard read:

SIDE SPLITTER
MR EDISON FILLS THE BOOTH WITH GAGS
(MAY OFFEND)

A woman was waiting on the platform and feeling low. Her train was delayed. Perhaps it had crashed. She hoped not because her boyfriend was on it. He was a pig, though, so maybe it wouldn't be such a bad thing after all. Unsettled by this ambivalence, she thought a laugh might help her see things more clearly.

She entered the booth and paid two pounds. The hatch opened.

Mr Edison was still chained up. He looked pale and tired. Mrs Edison, looking pale and tired too, was working the padlocks with a hairpin. She had cuts on her fingers where the hairpin had slipped.

'Is this the right day?' asked the customer.

'Yes,' said Mr Edison. 'This is still the side-splitter day, although there will hopefully be an escape as well. If I do an escape as well then I will ask you to put another pound in the slot.'

'I haven't got another pound,' said the woman.

'Then piss off,' said Mr Edison.

Mrs Edison stabbed him in the hand with the hairpin and apologized to the customer. It had been a long night.

'Has it started?' asked the customer.

'It hasn't started yet, no,' said Mrs Edison. 'Do you know how to break padlocks by any chance?'

'Don't ask her,' snapped Mr Edison. 'No outside help, it's the rule of the booth.'

'It's a silly rule,' said Mrs Edison.

'I don't anyway,' said the customer. 'Know how to break padlocks.'

'Don't bother yourself with showbiz technicalities,' said Mr Edison. 'This is for us to deal with.'

Mrs Edison sighed and put some burlesque music on the record player. It gave the booth a Max Miller feel, albeit a chained up and angry Max Miller.

'Introducing Mr Edison,' said Mrs Edison. 'Hold onto your sides.'

Mr Edison struggled to his feet. He was of the opinion that the show must go on, despite his straitjacket and his wife's bleeding hand.

'Ladies and gentlemen,' he said. 'Or just lady, I should say. I won't say my wife is fat. But when I look at her there's no denying it. It's an empirical fact and it makes me sick. Sick all over the floor. Buckets of it simply pour out of me.'

He waited for a laugh.

'Your wife isn't fat,' said the customer. Mrs Edison smiled at her and mouthed, Thank you.

'Please don't heckle,' warned Mr Edison. 'If you heckle then I'll use my selection of withering put-downs developed during a decade of playing tougher venues than this booth, I can tell you.'

'OK,' said the customer.

Mr Edison continued. 'A funny thing happened to me on the way to the booth today, or rather yesterday. I saw a beautiful woman on the street and I thought to myself, She looks good in a pair of heels. I wish I'd married her. I bet she doesn't go around swallowing keys and kissing men in front of me. Right in front of my face, as if I damn well didn't exist.'

Mr Edison paused. The laugh didn't come. The burlesque music hit a scratch and clicked a phrase over and over. Mrs Edison nudged the record on.

'Here's one,' said Mr Edison. 'A man walks into a pub covered in chains and he says to the barman, "A pint please," and the barman says, "Why are you covered in chains?" To which the man replies, "I've got an idiotic wife." "Really?" says the barman. "Yes," says the man. "Monumentally stupid she is. And do you know what?

Here she is now. You'd better sneak any oily-haired men out the back door because she'll have 'em, she will, the lusty cow. By God, why did I marry her? What misery it's caused.'"

Mr Edison waited for the customer to laugh.

'These aren't jokes,' she said.

'They're structured differently, yes,' said Mr Edison, 'but they're true stories.'

'They aren't funny,' said the customer. 'You advertised side splitting. This isn't side splitting at all.'

Mr Edison jumped at the hatch. His face pressed up against the opening and he hissed, 'I'll split your sides, you picky tart.'

'Roger!' snapped his wife.

'You keep out of this,' shouted Mr Edison, and he continued ranting at the customer, telling her she was just like all the others, sniping away at honest entertainers who were just trying to get by, and he pitied her husband who must be heartily sick of her daily critiques . . .

'I'm not married,' she said.

'That doesn't surprise me in the least,' said Mr Edison, and the customer's lip trembled.

And though his eyes were wild and bloodshot, and his spit had showered the customer, Mr Edison's mind shifted at the trembling lip, and a thought occurred to him. He raised an eyebrow, fancying it might come across a little bit Roger Moore rather than Roger Edison.

'Would you, as an unmarried lady, be interested in kissing me through the hatch?'

'No,' said the customer.

'Really? Because kissing has become *de rigueur* in this booth,' said Mr Edison.

'I'm meeting someone,' the customer said and she wrenched down the hatch cover and put on her coat.

'He won't show!' shouted Mr Edison. 'Who in their right mind would show up for a barren cow like you?'

The customer started crying. 'I'm not barren.'

Mrs Edison cut the music and dragged Mr Edison away. 'You shouldn't call a woman barren.'

'I know that barren look. It's the one I see in your eyes every day.'

'I'm not barren, Roger. We have a son.'

'He's dead.'

'No he isn't.'

'Well, he hasn't been to see a show for years, so he's dead to me.'

Mrs Edison pushed him to the floor and stood on his chest. She prodded open the hatch and through the crack apologized to the customer for any distress caused, and passed her two pounds by way of a refund.

Mr Edison wailed at the loss of two pounds, but Mrs Edison kept her foot on him and said she wouldn't be lectured on the accounts because, by her reckoning, they were still eight pounds in credit from the previous customer, 'which was very much my doing'.

She informed him that she was going to use some of the eight pounds profit on milk of magnesia to ease her terrible stomach ache. She was of the belief that the key had started to rust inside her.

And she asked the customer if she wouldn't mind getting a packet from the station pharmacy.

'Why don't you get your precious son to skivvy for you?' asked the customer as she left the booth.

Mrs Edison was more than happy to answer that question and she delivered an extended monologue on the subject throughout the night and into the following morning, with Mr Edison as her captive audience.

The next day, Thursday, the billboard read:

LA PETITE CHANTEUSE
MRS EDISON SINGS 'FALLING IN LOVE AGAIN' WITH THE
VOICE OF AN ANGEL, ACCOMPANIED BY MR EDISON ON
THE PIANOFORTE
REFUNDS FOR THOSE LEAVING THE BOOTH DRY-EYED

A boy and his father waited on the station platform. The boy asked his father what a petite chanteuse was. The father didn't know. He couldn't read English let alone French, but he'd hidden it from his son for nearly ten years. The boy asked for two pounds to find out. The father paid up. Some of the weekends with his son hadn't been very successful and he was determined that the boy should have something fun to tell his mother about so that she wouldn't be so difficult during access negotiations.

The boy entered the booth alone. He spun the seat to the top and climbed on. He put two pounds in the slot and the hatch opened.

The lighting was stark. Mr Edison had one or two angry sores where the chains were biting into his skin. His eyes were sunken; his chin unshaven.

Mrs Edison was asleep in the corner of the booth. She was surrounded by bent hairpins, broken hacksaw blades and indigestion remedies.

Mr Edison registered that the hatch had opened. 'Help me,' he croaked.

'What's the matter?' asked the boy.

'The key for my padlocks is inconveniently in my wife's stomach,' said Mr Edison.

He'd very much hoped that his wife would have had a bowel movement by now, but she was clogged up. Mr Edison put this down to their starchy showbiz diet. She put it down to the key itself, which was probably being corroded by stomach acid and might well be useless if she ever did pass it.

The boy felt through his pockets and found a handful of raisins. He dropped them through the hatch.

'What the hell am I supposed to do with those?' asked Mr Edison.

'You look hungry,' said the boy.

At that, Mrs Edison woke. She crawled on her hands and knees to the front of the booth and started scrabbling around for the raisins.

'Have some dignity, woman,' said Mr Edison.

'The raisins might loosen me up,' she said.

Mr Edison saw the logic of this and demanded more raisins. But the boy didn't have any more.

'Do you have any other dried fruit products?' asked Mr Edison.

'What's a petite chanteuse?' the boy said instead.

'I'm glad you asked,' said Mr Edison. 'Let's not forget why we're here.' And he shuffled his chair over to an old piano in the corner. On top of it, an Anglepoise lamp illuminated yellow, cracked keys. He leaned over the keyboard and hit the G with his nose. 'There's your note,' he said.

'I'm eating,' his wife replied.

'Get to your feet, woman. The boy wants singing to, don't you, boy?'

'Yes.'

'There you are: a boy who knows what he wants.'

'I want my mum and dad to live together.'

'Well, we can't arrange that, I'm afraid,' said Mr Edison. 'Nor would we want to. Your father is almost certainly better off without her.'

'He cries sometimes,' said the boy.

'Then he's *weak*!' shouted Mr Edison, making them all jump.

Mrs Edison got to her feet. She swayed. 'Give me the G

again,' she said. And, to the boy, 'I'm sure your father isn't weak.'

Mr Edison lunged at the key with his nose; rather too hard this time and he chipped a tooth on the keyboard. Tears poured from his eyes. He didn't cry out, though, as he'd just made a principled stand against weakness.

'La,' sang Mrs Edison unsteadily. She smiled at the boy. She could see his face through the slot. He had nice brown eyes, just like her son Graham. Graham was a train driver.

'Would you like to be a train driver?' she asked him.

'No,' said the boy.

'All boys want to be train drivers,' said Mrs Edison.

'I don't,' said the boy.

'When my boy was little it was the only thing –'

'Leave him alone,' Mr Edison interrupted, the taste of blood in his mouth.

Mrs Edison apologized. She wished Graham would pop into the booth occasionally. Just to say hello. But he never did, even though his train stopped at the station almost daily. That was the thing she'd come to learn about showbiz. It was a family-breaker.

She put a hand on the wall to steady herself.

Mr Edison said he wouldn't be able to accompany her owing to his restricted condition, so she would have to sing *a cappella*.

Mrs Edison felt a sharp pain near her diaphragm and so she decided to use her head voice. It made 'Falling in Love Again' more nasal, but less agonizing.

The boy didn't like her looking so pale and squeaky and he pushed a chocolate toffee through the hatch.

Mrs Edison stopped singing, grabbed the chocolate toffee and stuffed it in her mouth.

'What have you given her?' demanded Mr Edison.

'A chocolate toffee,' said the boy.

'That's dairy,' said Mr Edison. 'You can't give a singer dairy. It clogs the vocal chords.'

The boy had had enough. He decided that a petite chanteuse must be some sort of animal. The booth reminded him of a little zoo. He didn't like zoos. His dad had taken him to a zoo once and a monkey had scratched him while his dad was in the toilets. He wasn't allowed to see his dad for a month after that. He got off the stool and started to leave.

'Don't go,' said Mrs Edison. 'Stay and hear the rest of the song.'

The boy didn't want to.

'Have you got any more chocolate toffees?' she asked him.

The boy shook his head.

Mrs Edison thrust her hands through the hatch and grabbed the boy's arm. He yelped and asked her to let go, but Mrs Edison wouldn't.

'Please stay. Please give me another chocolate. Please talk to me. Are you going on a train today? Somewhere nice. The seaside? Perhaps it'll be the train that my son drives. He drives the train to the seaside. Are you sure you don't want to be a train driver . . .'

The boy struggled and Mrs Edison gripped harder, yabbering about taking a holiday herself, in her son's train, and having tea and cake from the buffet car. The boy cried out.

His father heard the cry and burst into the booth. He saw his son struggling in the grip of a hand sticking out of the hatch. He bellowed at Mrs Edison and prised her fingers open with such force that he broke one of them.

Mrs Edison screamed with pain; a scream which sounded to the boy like a monkey's scream.

The father carried his son out of the booth and onto

the platform, asking the boy, as casually as he could, not to mention that little incident to his mother.

Mrs Edison called out, 'Graham!' And then again, 'Graham!' Even though every cry ripped her abdomen.

She put her broken finger in her mouth and sucked on it. She put her broken finger down her throat and was sick on the floor. Then she rummaged through the sick to look for the key. But there was no key, just chocolate toffees and raisins and bile.

The next day was Friday and the billboard read:

END YOUR WEEK WITH A THRILL
MRS EDISON IS THE LADY IN RED WHO SOON BECOMES
THE LADY IN NOTHING AT ALL
(OVER 18S ONLY UNLESS ACCOMPANIED BY A PARENT OR
GUARDIAN OR SIMILAR)

On the station platform the billboard was noticed by a young man who had just followed his ex-girlfriend to the station and watched her get on a train. She was going to the airport to fly herself halfway round the world where she would, she hoped, discover herself, or at least discover another young man who didn't keep leering at other women quite so much.

The young man told himself he was better off without her as he could now rent pornographic films and watch stripteases without getting a hard time about it at home. Or rather he could have the hard time he wanted, but without someone twittering in his ear about gender politics.

He checked his pockets. He was well financed. He could feed the slot and get a good eyeful.

He entered the booth, deposited two pounds and the hatch opened.

The room was indeed red. The spotlight was red and there were red drapes over the walls. 'Lady in Red' played as advertised.

Mrs Edison, however, was slumped on a chair and already naked. She was also quite pale. One hand fluttered. The other was holding a scalpel. There was sweat on her brow and a stench in the room.

Crouched over her, still painfully bound in chains, was Mr Edison. In his teeth he had a small torch which he was shining on an untidy incision in Mrs Edison's belly. He cursed freely and frequently.

The customer's stomach turned. As did Mrs Edison's.

'Oh good God,' cried the young man.

Mr Edison turned. 'Ah, welcome to Friday's show. In a change to the advertised programme you will see something of an internal striptease by Mrs Edison, followed, I am confident, by a spectacular escape from the chains that bind me.'

Mrs Edison's breath was shallow. She was looking at page fifteen – 'Emergency Obstructions' – of a medical textbook at her feet, but the red spotlight was making the text appear light green and difficult to read. She injected herself with lignocaine and said a little prayer.

'What the hell is this?' asked the young man.

This was a question Mr Edison had asked himself a number of times as he shone the torch into various parts of Mrs Edison's abdomen, a satisfactory answer to which the medical textbook had conspicuously failed to supply. He was hoping he'd have stumbled across the key by now, but had instead been presented with mystery organs.

'Technically,' said Mr Edison, 'given the blood, it's still the Lady in Red, so if you're thinking of complaining to trades descriptions, I shall be able to mount a ferocious legal defence.'

The young man poked his head through the hatch and asked Mrs Edison if she was all right.

'Kindly do not speak to the artiste,' said Mr Edison. He prodded an organ – Mrs Edison's liver – with the torch and she passed out. 'Damn it,' he said. Now who would mop his brow?

The young man became numb and nauseous.

'If you want to ensure the continuation of this unique act,' said Mr Edison, 'I require you to deposit a further two pounds into the slot.'

'I don't want to look,' said the customer.

Mr Edison struggled to his feet and shuffled over to the hatch. He grabbed the hatch with his teeth and pulled and thrashed until it was ripped off.

'There,' he said, spitting teeth. 'Unlimited view. Today only. You may look all you want. In fact, feel free to offer suggestions. I must say we're struggling here.'

The young man rushed from the booth and out onto the station platform where he lit a cigarette with shaking hands.

A group of giggling schoolboys entered the booth thinking they could pass for eighteen as one of them had a fluffy moustache on the way. They emerged ashen and traumatized. One of them was sick on the floor.

The four-fifty to Greenacres had failed to pull away and was still standing at the platform.

The driver of the train stood on the platform, too. It was Graham, the Edisons' only son. He saw the school-boys, the smoking gentleman, and the look of horror on all their faces. He took a deep breath and entered the booth for the first time in thirty years. He emerged a moment later shouting, 'You stupid old man,' and ran to the station phone box where he punched in emergency numbers.

Mr Edison jumped out after him. The light from the

afternoon sun blinding him, the air blowing his hair wildly about his face. 'Graham!' he shouted. 'Graham!'

Graham barged past him and into the booth where he kicked through the dividing wall. He crouched at his mother's side.

'Is that you, love?' whispered Mrs Edison.

'Yes, Mum,' said Graham. 'What should I do?'

'You should take us to the seaside once in a while. Bet it's lovely out.'

'But what about . . . your liver?'

'That can come along later,' said Mrs Edison, 'as hand luggage.'

And even though his mother was trembling with shock, and he was trembling with shock too, that wasn't a bad one; that was old school. And Graham chuckled. And his mother chuckled too, though it caused her to faint again.

'We'll go then,' said Graham to his unconscious mother. 'We'll go to Shoreham and have ourselves whelks.'

Mr Edison lunged back into the room. 'Have you got any bolt cutters? I don't think we're going to get that key.'

'No I haven't got any bolt cutters!' shouted Graham. 'You can stay chained up. It'll give the police one less thing to do.'

Mr Edison paled at the thought of the police. 'Don't split the act, son. It'd break her heart.'

'Rather that than you hacking it to bits.'

Mr Edison had a number of responses to that charge, including, but not restricted to, Graham's complicity in the hacking of Mrs Edison's heart to bits by never visiting despite passing through every day. And they debated the issue for a while, and many views were expressed, and many regrettable things were said. And they only stopped when Mrs Edison's breathing became laboured and rasping.

'Hold on, love,' said Mr Edison.

'Hold on, Mum,' said Graham.

And in that moment they realized they'd found, for the first time in their lives, a bit of common ground between them. Neither wanted this woman's liver to fall out in front of them in a booth on the station platform.

Mr Edison looked at his wife and son, sweaty and covered in blood, and it reminded him of the last time he'd witnessed such a scene. It was at Graham's birth, and on that occasion the billboard had read:

START YOUR WEEK ON A HIGH
MR AND MRS EDISON PRESENT THE MIRACLE OF CREATION
ONE POUND OFF FOR MIDWIVES

Mr Edison remembered how that show hadn't gone terribly well either.

Shooters
Michelle Singh

He said he'd come after midnight because he had a party to go to in All Saints. He said he'd catch the DLR back to Bow Church and walk up to my flat along the Mile End Road. I thought he told me too much. I wondered, does he do this for a hobby? Does he have some other job, or does he just hang around his mum's flat getting her to do his ironing, then take his baby bulldog out for walks, stand listlessly kicking the brick wall under the yellow bridge, waiting for young women to ask him to do them a favour? Because that's what you have to say, Tariq told me. Excuse me. Please would you do me a favour?

He said to leave the money underneath the mat outside my front door. I said, What if it gets nicked? And he said, Nobody goes looking under fuckin' welcome mats on fuckin' New Year's Eve. And I suppose they don't.

I feel hungry. Now that my bleeding's easing off I feel like I want to eat between meals. I put on my shoes and leave my purse behind, taking just the money I need to buy some fried chicken. I'm so tired that my fingers shake when I tie my laces. I want bad food, not the healthy hamper of City fruit that my colleagues sent this morning with their card full of condolences and see you after Christmases.

'Hello, darling,' says Assad. He looks morose. His peaked white paper hat is stained with fried chicken fat. 'What you want today? Not at party tonight?'

'Three hot wings, please,' I say. I put my pound on the counter. It sticks to the laminated yellow menu that declares the existence of the finest spicy halal burger, ever. I point at the small television perched on top of Assad's rusted, humming Coca-Cola fridge. 'That's new.'

The four-split screen shows, in clockwise order, the strip of pavement directly outside the Nice Nice Chicken Shack, the forlorn little kitchen, Assad slouching at the till, and a rear view of me, wearing my long purple coat, hunched at the counter. I stand up straighter and think how fat I look from behind. I turn and look myself in the face, see the black circles around my eyes.

'Yes,' Assad breathes. 'CCTV now.'

'Why?' I turn my pound coin over to see the Queen's nose.

'Naughty black boys,' Assad tells me, shovelling my hot wings into a box, folding the flaps down.

'Why are they naughty?' I keep my face straight.

Assad points at the window. One such naughty black boy is walking past on his way to the bus stop. He looks like the boy who's going to do me a favour.

'They come in here. They just stand in here. They don't buy anything.'

The Nice Nice Chicken Shack is about the size of a toilet.

'Blimey,' I say. 'What, do they just want to keep out of the cold?'

Assad looks wistful, peering at the 277 bus as it pulls in, delivering him fresh customers. Sometimes he can't understand me when I talk too fast.

'People no come when they see naughty black boys in here. That bad for me. Police come, the boys they go, but come back when police leave.'

The grease from my hot wings is seeping through the cardboard box.

'Can I have a carrier bag, please, Assad?'

'Yes, darling.' He passes me a blue and white striped bag, and settles his chin into his cupped right hand. 'No fathers stay, that is what it is. Naughty boys.'

If Ben were waiting for me at home, instead of skulking around the Shanghai office, he would have liked this story when I told it him. Naughty, naughty black boys.

I didn't want Ben to go to China. I told him to tell his boss what had happened to me and that he couldn't go, that it had to be someone else. And Ben said it had been planned for ages, that it had to be him or Tim, and that it was Tim's first baby and it would be his new family's first Christmas together; that I should have a heart.

We'll celebrate Christmas in February when Tim's paternity has finished, he'd said.

Fuck off, I'd said.

I didn't even go to Heathrow to say goodbye. The District Line is freezing first thing and I didn't want to get out of bed.

It happened on my first night alone. Her moaning was part of my dream until it slowly woke me, goosepimpling my arms.

I imagined some beaten Asian wife with rolls of fat sobbing into her apron, being whacked around the head, cradling her face. I pressed my ear against my bedroom wall and felt her voice humming and buzzing, boring down to my eardrum. Is she praying? I wondered. Or is she crying? I stood up, feeling the blood seep out of me and hotly soak my pad. I bent my ear again to the wall and heard the soft slap of skin against paintwork and the guttural oh oh oh panting, and a new noise, a crooning voice, a man's. Then I felt stupid. I pulled my blanket off the bed and dragged it downstairs to sleep in the front room. The second time it happened I slept downstairs again. But the third time I felt crazy. I smacked the palm of my hand three times on the flat of the wall, harsh and loud. Her yowling halted. Fucking shut up, I whispered.

In the morning she was in the hallway at the same time as me, leaving her flat too, dragging a little girl by her hand. She was younger than I'd imagined, heroin-scraggy with a long, scraped back ponytail, ratty pixie face, black padded coat. She stared straight at my face with her glittery green eyes. She was filthy, but her daughter was beautiful with such chocolate-cream skin.

I started talking to Tariq by accident one night on my way into the block after a trip to the chicken shop. I didn't mean to get into a conversation but he held open the outer door for me, reefer sticking to his lip, the earthy smoke haloing his head.

'Thank you,' I said, gazing around at the six boys lolled over the stairs.

'You live next door to Tiffany, innit,' Tariq said. He'd never spoken to me before, but before I had always been with Ben. I guessed he was about sixteen. His face was cleverer than his stupid-faced, floor-staring friends'.

The mention of the name made me feel hot and prickly. So that's what it was. Once through the walls I thought I heard a man shouting Stephanie, not Tiffany. Tiffany, like black-haired Tiff from *EastEnders*. At home, me and Ben used to shout and jeer at the television screen as the show began, the whistle to the aerial view of the East End. Walford; where on earth is this place, where families live together for ever, where the people are white and the doctors are black? Where the West End is as far away as Timbuktu? When Ben worked in the London office he used to say in a solemn voice before leaving for work, 'I'm going up west.' As far away as Mars.

My voice was girlish as I replied to Tariq. 'I don't know. I mean, I know I have a new neighbour. Who is Tiffany?'

The boys all chuckled in a low harmony. 'Boy, Tariq knows Tiffany,' one of them said.

I felt a surge in my pulse and then I knew I was right. She's a fucking prostitute.

On Christmas Eve the screaming started at six in the morning. The sky was a baby blue through my blinds. Tiffany had been quiet that night, no punters, probably because her child was there. I'd heard the little girl's chattering and realized that sometimes she was there, sometimes she wasn't. Everything was completely still until Tiffany started. Her opening line made my stomach curdle.

'Why don't you fack off and die, you little cant? I can't even take a fackin shit in peace.'

'Will you shut up? Will you fackin shut up before I make you fackin shut up?'

'Will you stop talking to me? Will you stop that?'

'Will you listen? Will you listen?'

'Fackin get out of it, fackin come on with your fackin shoes.'

She'd taken the child outside of the flat, I could tell. The echo of the hallway bounced her voice back at her, a thousandfold. Her daughter was screaming, No no no no no. Where were they going, so early?

'Come on, you fackin cant.'

I pulled the covers up to my chin. Should I go out there and make her stop, rescue the poor kid? The cater-wauling grew fainter and fainter until I heard it, shriller now and outside, as Tiffany dragged the child down the stairwell, the sobbing and the roaring receding and then growing clearer the further and closer they were to open windows. I heard the outer door thud back into its hinges and on the street the horror spiralled up into the air, the woman battering and hollering and spanking the girl around the head. I stood petrified and cold at my bedroom window, my little finger prising open a slat, watching them in their neon pink puffa jackets heading for the tube in a slow, stumbling dance, the mother clawing at her daughter's matted ponytail, carrying her down the street like a marionette, feet dangling. She was carrying her by her hair. I would never carry my baby by her hair.

I ran out to the stairs. I didn't know what I was going to do. There was no way I could catch up with her in time. But Tariq was there, on the lowest step, already awake. Perhaps he hadn't gone to bed. He was smoking a bong, alone by the stinking rubbish chute. The aroma of hot new piss lingered on the air and I saw the usual dark dribble in the top right-hand corner of the hallway. I sometimes wondered if the boys urinated in front of each other or if any of them had the presence of mind to retreat to their mother's flat to relieve themselves in privacy. I remember one morning I woke up to four lumps of fresh dog shit punctuating the hallway all the way to the double doors.

'She's a fuckin' loony tune,' Tariq said, whirling his finger close to his temple. 'Must be fun, livin' next to her.'

'I'd pay you a million quid if you could get rid of her.' I forced a smile. 'I can't bloody sleep at night. I feel like I'm going mad.'

'You know, I know people who can shut people up, know what I'm sayin'?'

'No, I don't know what you're saying.'

'Shooters,' he said, more quietly, standing up and moving closer to me. I could smell Quavers on his breath, beyond the aroma of bong. I spied a bright purple crisp packet poking out of his pocket. Suddenly all I wanted to eat, right then, was pickled-onion-flavoured Monster Munch. 'I got a nice lickle friend. He can do you a favour.'

'Oh no,' I said, stepping back from him. 'I wouldn't want to do that sort of thing. *Christ.*'

'That's what you gotta ask. Them words.'

'See you later, Tariq.'

'See you, babes.'

In the toilet afterwards, I thought, when will this bleeding ever stop? The nurse on the telephone at the hospital was kind. She's told me six times that it's normal for almost a month. Then I heard Tiffany's brazen, clanging voice through the walls that feel as thin as a Bible's page. She had returned. I could hear her child's voice, singing.

'If you don't stop fackin singing, I'll come in there, cut your tongue out and take a shit down your fackin throat, you little cant. Fackin Christmas fackin carols.'

I stood up, turned around and vomited into my blood. Then Tiffany started singing.

'Lonely, I'm so lonely, I got nobody . . .'

Shooters aren't too hard to find, really. Not where I live, not even on Christmas Day.

Outside the pub on the corner, a rabble has formed in the beer garden, singing 'Auld Lang Syne' before it's even time. I'm back underneath my blanket on the settee with my lukewarm hot wings on my lap, watching Jools. My ears are straining for footsteps in the hallway. Make sure, I'd said, that the child isn't there. If she is, just walk away. I don't want anything much. Just make her frightened. Tell her to shut the fuck up and let me get some fucking sleep. Some people, I said, don't deserve to be parents.

I've been listening for the little girl's voice all day, but I haven't heard her yet.

Tiffany's first customer of the night is a man who looks like a scarecrow. As he walks along the outside walkway, the Christmas lights from people's windows illuminate his face in greens and reds. Thanks to me, he doesn't stay long, doesn't get his new year's treat. I listen at my bedroom wall for a while to her awful pantings and I slap the wall sixteen times with *David Copperfield* until she stops. She hollers and frightens me so much that I jump. I feel like her mouth is reaching through the plaster, trying to suck me through the wall like a devil.

'You fackin bitch, I'll cut you up if you don't stop knockin. I'll fackin come over there and saw you in half, you fackin hear? Can't even fackin have sex in peace! Fackin fat bitch! Fackin hell!'

Back downstairs I feel a bit shaky and open a bag of popcorn to eat while I watch the television. Suddenly I don't want it. I rub my empty stomach and wish Ben would phone. I hear Tiffany's door ricochet shut as her customer leaves. I wait a long time, still.

When I see him, it's just before midnight. He's massive, like a panther. From the outdoor corridor he disappears from my view. Minutes later I hear bulky fists hammer on Tiffany's door. I wonder why he took so long. Perhaps he had a cigarette.

'Use the fackin bazzz-ar!' Tiffany roars. She is always screaming about the buzzer. She doesn't like her punters knocking. I hear her latch click. Then she's quiet, surprise in her voice. She says a name. His name? Oh God, does she know him? I don't even know his name.

'Hello, babes,' he says. The door shuts. Oh God, was it him? Did I mistake him? Perhaps it wasn't him? I rub my eyes and red leers at me from the inside of my eyelids. I should sleep.

I'm dozing off to the countdown on *Hootenanny* when I hear a noise, like a balloon bursting at a kids' party. It jolts me so much I feel my blood gush out again with the sudden movement. It's the stroke of midnight and outside fireworks sputter up into the sky from the scrub of green outside the flats, with loud cheering from the pub. There's another bang before the twelfth dong of Big Ben and seconds later a shadow is framed in the glass pane of my front door, fingers scrabbling beneath the mat.

'Happy new year, babes,' he says through the letterbox.

I wait an hour before I creep upstairs to sleep in my own bed. I change my pad in the now quiet bathroom, the adhesive suckering off the gusset. I lie in bed making promises. When Ben comes home, I'll tell him we're moving. We'll live somewhere by the sea, somewhere you can get to from Liverpool Street, where you can bring up a baby. I dream of the waves and the seagulls and the ice cream and then I hear Tiffany as if she is gargling with mouthwash, like she's praying.

'Oh God. Fackin God. God.'

She sounds slow and thick as if she's drunk. I kneel up against the wall to listen. There's a rasp in her throat. She is coughing. Then she is quiet. Then she coughs. Then she's quiet for ages. Then she pleads with God to not let her fackin die. Then she is quiet and I hear a high-pitched moan, a bit like how I cried after my operation. Like television static.

I leave the door on the latch and take my yellow Marigolds with me, just in case. Tiffany's door is ajar and I push my way in. Her front room is lit by a naked bulb. Her flat is laid out just like mine, but as if in a mirror, backwards. She lives like a tramp. The floor is covered with junk: a repulsive plastic Santa with muscular thighs, dirty kids' roller skates, cigarettes, empty bottles of WKD, dog-eared tube tickets, sweet wrappers, Rizla papers, a widescreen television on mute, thousands of calling cards with Tiffany bare-breasted and foul on the front, promising Sex Sex Sex.

In her bedroom Tiffany lies on the floor wearing black PVC, a cone-like boob tube, flat on her back, eyes open to a slit. She sees me and her lips move, but with no sound. A quarter of her throat has been ripped out. She lies in a red blossom on her once-cream carpet, a hole torn out of her gut. I feel urine trickling down my leg, taking my blood with it to mingle pinkly with hers on the floor. As Tiffany and I look at each other I have a mad urge to save her and to be her friend.

'Wait here,' I say.

Borges in Buenos Aires
Luke Brown

I'd avoided reading the work of Jorge Luis Borges in the run-up to my trip to Buenos Aires. I had the idea that there would be no better way to appreciate him than after a mid-afternoon ravioli, sipping a *cortado*, a Marlboro Red smouldering in the ashtray as I turned the pages of his labyrinthine stories and chuckled with intellectual delight. Yes, I was thinking in clichés, in the international language of travel and tourism.

The reality was that I was always too strung out from the dirt-cheap cocaine that, as a tourist and a spendthrift, I just couldn't resist – and which brought me back to the hostel in blinding eight o'clock sunshine every morning. It only cost twenty pesos for a *prisé*: £4. And it was three times purer than anything Mani ever sold me back in Birmingham. Some part of me must have believed that if I indulged myself to the full during these three weeks in Argentina then I wouldn't spend any money on drugs for a year back in England. It was deceitful thinking. I flew back, relieved, straight into a debauch at a swingers' club in Aston on Easter Sunday. But that came later.

Fucking Borges! He was unreadable! I couldn't finish the first story's title: 'Tlön, Uqbar, Orbis Tertius'. So I moved onwards to 'The Library of Babel'. Four paragraphs described a series of hexagonal libraries interlocking into infinity. The most overwhelming nausea rose over me. I hurled the book down, horrified, and immediately had to order a Quilmes to go with my coffee. I didn't doubt that Señor Borges was a genius and that I was a decadent, hungover fool, but I had no interest in developing the contradiction. When packing I'd been indecisive and hadn't taken nearly enough books, assuming I'd find an English language bookshop somewhere. And there was one: I heard rumours of it constantly, and made several searches through the narrow side streets it was reputed to exist in. Somewhere, in that labyrinth, it existed, but I began to suspect that if I ever found it, it would stock nothing but English translations of Borges and his experimental contemporaries, and so I gave up and came to rely on the books left behind by travellers in the hostel I was staying in. But it wasn't easy. For all their smugness about expanding their horizons through travel, the books they read were invariably by Andy McNab or someone called Freya North. This Freya North had a whole stable of posh daughters, *Polly*, *Pip*, *Sally* and *Chloe*, and I was almost tempted to return to Emma Zunz, Funes the Memorius and Pierre Menard, author of the *Quixote*. The annoying thing is that I found out later, from my friend Jane, that these books were full of sex. They might have been just the ticket. But at the time, I spent an increasingly panicked hour trying to find something that I might possibly consider reading, eventually reaching a shortlist of *Bleak House* and *Zen and the Art of Motorcycle Maintenance*. Jettisoning the Pirsig after five pages of pious claptrap, I plumped for the Dickens – rambling, sentimental, but readable, and reassuringly overlong – possibly the worst book in the world for the erotic sensation of street life in Buenos Aires. Pages and pages of fog and chancery perfectly expressed my alienation from the life surrounding me, and if ever a pretty girl walked past my table – which happened approximately every three seconds in Buenos Aires – I'd hastily hide the title, presumably suggesting to them that I was reading pornography. Pale and shaky, with large prescription sunglasses that I never took off, I must have looked the type.

All this was going on during the week and a half I had on my own waiting for my friend Dan to arrive in town. He was marrying his Argentinean fiancée in a town a few hours' drive out into the pampas, and meeting up with me and various friends for a three-day bender to lead up to it. I started long before he arrived, hanging out with English, Australian and American young men from the hostel, watching football, drinking the awful national lager all day, before heading down to Mundo Bizarro for a couple of *prisés* from El Coronel, an obnoxious sixty-year-old drug dealer I'd been introduced to by my new friend Arturo on my second night in town.

I'd split up with my girlfriend of nearly three years only two months earlier. This might imply some choice on my part, but it was a clear-cut dumping – and thoroughly deserved. But before I did what I did to provoke this, she'd introduced me by email to an old school friend of hers, Natalie, who lived in Buenos Aires and worked as an English teacher. I'd assumed it would be too awkward to contact her in light of what had happened with Katie, but I ended up ringing her on my first full day there, after a series of dismaying exchanges in which I wasn't understood at all. (I got the hang of it eventually – you had to phrase your Spanish language requests for coffee/beer/directions in the over-dramatized accent of an Italian mobster. English diffidence was incomprehensible to them.) I needed a quick survival lesson. Natalie was very sweet when she picked up the phone, but immediately began asking all about how Katie was, and it became clear she didn't know we'd split up. They were old friends, not current friends, I realized – after all, they lived in separate continents. 'She's fine,' I said. 'Are you missing her yet?' she asked. 'Lots,' I said, truthfully – and we arranged to meet at her flat in Recoleta.

I was still jetlagged and wary of negotiations on public transport, so it took me an hour to walk there from my hostel. I found her apartment and rang the bell, and the most beautiful man I have ever seen opened the door. He was clearly Argentinean and so I can only describe him now, as I apprehended him then, in the international language of travel and tourism – his long, dark, glossy hair, honey-coloured skin, perfect brown pools for eyes, into which one might drop one's soul and never hear a splash. He was smoking a 'fragrant joint'.

'You must be Lee!' he said, reaching out a hand and, when I took it, he leaned forward and kissed me on the cheek. I'd read in the guidebook that this was the way they did hellos and, though I liked it, it surprised me. I didn't know whether to return it, but he left his cheek there for me so I kissed him back. Behind him, a woman who must have been Natalie was lying on her front, her feet raised up and wiggling behind her, while she laughed on the phone and casually waved at me. His stubble scratched against my face as we separated and I immediately wanted to spark a cigarette. Her legs made my initial. Beyond her was an open balcony, with a view out to many more balconies, to the warm dark just beyond in which all the lights seemed to shine more brightly than English streetlights, simply because they weren't English streetlights. Natalie was folded up but looked like she'd be tall when she sprang back. Those legs were full of potential energy.

He was introducing himself. 'My name is Arturo,' he said. 'You have just come to Buenos Aires?'

I nodded. It was calming to be in someone's living room after a few hours in the hostel's communal space listening to non-stop 'electronic tango' – a music that I had loved for nearly fifteen minutes. I was thinking that Arturo had a really good haircut; it was making me insecure. I asked the question I already knew the answer to, 'How do you know Natalie?' and he just smiled and turned around to look at her. I remember the phone she was talking into, an old-fashioned one with a rotary dial. Her legs were tanned and the soles of her feet looked like they would always be dirty. Some men wouldn't have liked that. But not me and Arturo. In fact, I just didn't know who to look at.

He offered me the spliff and, still stunned, I took it and raised it to my lips and inhaled. Twice. Again. And then we were grinning at each other, and embracing, as if enacting the second stage of the unusual hello we'd began before. 'You want a beer?' he asked. He wasn't wrong.

While he was getting it, Natalie hung up and tipped herself from the sofa like a bendy spring taking a stair. 'Lee, it's great you came! – have you met Arturo? – tell me all about your trip! – tell me all about you and Katie!'

Arturo came out of the kitchen with a beer for me and I chose to answer the question about my trip, about a ten-hour wait in Madrid, getting drunk, being poisoned by the food and huddling in my seat while a huge Argentinean party went on around me, on a plane where people stood up and walked around for the whole voyage, a plane like a big pub in the sky. It was the reason I felt so fragile and frightened upon landing; the reason I called Natalie so quickly. It seemed hilarious now, to all three of us.

'This is not normal then?' asked Arturo.

'You tell me,' I said.

He laughed again and was suddenly serious. 'Fuck flying,' he said. 'The peso is too weak.'

I could barely afford to fly myself, and was spending the dregs of an Arts Council grant that I'd hoped would last me until the end of the summer. And I suppose I'd assumed Arturo had more money than me – his T-shirt and jeans looked new and fashionable, his hair was immaculately cut. He looked richer than me anyway, with my northern shagged-out indie-hair, ripped jeans and old Rolling Stones T-shirts. He looked like the kind of man who found himself involved in two-woman threesomes regularly, effortlessly, to whom this had even become a little boring. He told me he worked as a moped courier – he called it a motorbike, but when I saw it later, even with my lack of motor knowledge, I recognized a moped – and played bass in a band. It was lucky I'd called them – they were going away for a few days the day after tomorrow, and I would have missed them.

They took me then to a bar round the corner where we ate pizza and shared litre bottles of Quilmes, which I drank twice as quickly as they did.

I'd gone a bit mad in England leading up to the trip; each weekend (which I defined as Wednesday to Sunday), I was deranged, grief-stricken, booze- and drug-sizzled, completely reliant on pulling new women in order to keep it together, on the drama this caused, the minor intrigues to distract from the major catastrophe: the woman I had thought I wanted to spend my life with. Without my major catastrophe I decided I was nothing, and so I wallowed and drank and ended up in bed with women as impulsive and self-obsessed as myself. I'd got into a state in which I'd forgotten how to talk to girls without flirting, and so it was hard to get into a rhythm with Natalie as Arturo was clearly infatuated with her in a jealous, Latin way and slightly wary of me. He sat with his arm around her, his chin up as he scanned the horizon for pirates and made increasingly uncomfortable jokes about all the male friends she had. When he finally went to the toilet I asked her how long they'd been together: just four months, she told me.

'He's fucking gorgeous,' I said, and she laughed and hit me on the shoulder. At that moment he came back outside and looked at us anxiously.

'Don't,' she said. 'He's dead jealous.'

'What were you talking about?' he asked on sitting back down.

'Lee says you're beautiful,' she said, winking at me.

Arturo frowned, then broke into a grin. 'I like this man!' He laughed, stretching his arm protectively around Natalie.

So I didn't speak to her properly until the day after, when we met for a coffee after one of her lessons. Arturo was out delivering packages on his moped. I waited in the foyer of her college building and watched her appear at the end of a long corridor, her legs glimmering below denim cut-offs as she strode towards me. Whoosh. They really kicked me in the heart. I had to stop staring. As we walked to a café, she told me how much she was looking forward to getting away to the countryside for the weekend, and I imagined her thighs gripping Arturo from behind as they sped (loosely speaking) away from the city. I was smitten; I would have changed place with either of them. It was an immoral passion, driven by the urge to take an undeserved revenge on my ex, to behave like a terrible guest. Or it was just lust, magnified by loneliness and foreign heat. Perspective was impossible in the grip of such want. I couldn't stop thinking about the pair of them fucking, about the shape their bodies made over each other as their skin shone with sweat.

'Lee!' she shouted, breaking my concentration. 'You weren't listening!'

'Sorry, I just lost concentration for a second,' I said.

We were sitting at a café table by then, waiting for ham and cheese toasties, and she smirked and began the story of how she'd met Arturo.

I presume I'd asked her this, although I might not have; I have a talent for eliciting confessions. No one seems to think me capable of making an unfavourable judgement. That's just what I would have done, my face seems to say. You should have stolen her money, you pretty much *had* to fuck his friend while he was asleep, you weren't even lying when you pretended all the drugs were gone . . . Now, shall we do them ourselves, just between us; shall we slip away to yours and get into bed?

Natalie's story was quite boring to begin with: she was in a bar with a colleague, a band began to play, she stared into the good-looking bass player's eyes with the unabashed confidence of the beautiful at the beautiful. I nodded and hmmed, concerned that I hadn't shown her any of my personality so far. I wanted so much for her to find me interesting.

'He really is the most handsome man I've ever seen,' I interrupted.

'God, if you weren't going out with Katie I'd be watching out for you.'

'You *should* watch out for me,' I said, but when she didn't laugh my words hung in the air and sounded sinister. 'Only joking,' I said. 'You can trust me. I'm nice.'

She gave me a brief stare. 'I emailed Katie this morning.'

'Oh! Did she reply yet?'

'Not yet. Aw, you must really miss her. I want to hear about how you two met first.'

Thankfully I could reassure her with a true story here. I'd first seen Katie in Manchester, reading Raymond Chandler's *Lady in the Lake* on her own with a cup of tea. I'd been out on an all-nighter with my best friend, when that was still exhilarating, and I thought I'd seen her giggle at the silly, verbose, performative conversation that we'd been clinging to like a lifebelt. I was probably still drunk when I smiled over at her, caught her eyes and asked the simple question, 'What's your name?'

It was love I remember feeling in those weeks I would wait to see her, different from the lust I felt for Natalie, and it saddens me now that love was no more powerful.

'That's so sweet!' Natalie said. 'So brave!'

'It was easy,' I said. 'She looked so beautiful.'

Natalie pretended to swoon.

'Come *on*. You never finished the rest of your story about meeting Arturo.'

'I can't after that. You'll think I'm awful.'

'This is sounding hopeful.'

She laughed. 'I can't,' she said.

'I promise not to tell a soul,' I said.

'Even Katie?'

'Especially Katie.'

She looked shy for a moment and then continued her story. 'Well, after I'd kissed him, and he is *such* a sexy kisser, and he'd asked me back to his, and I'd refused saying I didn't, not on the first night, but that he could take me out later in the week, and we'd set a date and he'd gone off to drop off his bass and his big amp, I was just so incredibly turned on and I regretted not going with him so much, even though I knew I'd done the right thing. And then the pill I'd taken really came up, and maybe someone offered me a line of coke – well, definitely, a massive line, it was Pedro who gave it to me – anyway, this Pedro ended up chatting me up, he was nice looking too but not as nice, and I was kissing him and in the end I took him back to mine and, well . . . by that time I was in a wild mood. I mean, it's OK to fuck people you don't like, isn't it? It's people you do like who you can't just go round fucking.'

She sat back, contented, at the end of her crazy rant, looking for a reaction. I was really beginning to like her. She had a rigorously logical mind.

'Well, yes,' I said. 'Obviously it's important not to make the wrong first impression.'

'Exactly.' She laughed. 'I knew you'd understand. I couldn't very well have done things any differently. Only thing is, of course, that the guy Pedro turns out to be Arturo's friend. I find this out when he introduces us three weeks later – of course, *we*'ve fucked by *then* – and we have to pretend to be meeting for the first time. Pedro, he goes along with it then and there, but sort of smirking and I can tell Arturo sees there's something funny going on. And I'm always worried that he's asked Pedro when I'm not around and that Pedro's confessed, and now it's this big unspoken thing that neither of us can mention: the reason he's so jealous all the time. What do you think?'

At the time, besides being impressed by her unusual practicality, I was just delighted by the news that she took drugs and might therefore know where to get me some.

'I think they're just very passionate round here, aren't they?' I suggested. 'You know, fiery Latin temperaments. And, of course, you are very attractive.'

'I thought it was Arturo you fancied,' she said.

'No, course not,' I lied. 'I'm just very comfortable with my masculinity.'

'Lucky Katie.'

'Mmm. I'm not sure about that. You better wait and see

what she has to say. By the way, you know you mentioned you were on coke and E . . .'

That's how I ended up that night in Mundo Bizarro with Arturo while Natalie taught her evening class. He brought out a handful of pills and shoved them in my pocket, refusing to take any money for them. 'When I am your guest, you will look after me, yes?'

'Yes,' I said. I didn't want to remind him that he'd admitted he couldn't afford a ticket to England as things stood. Perhaps he thought he was going to go there with Natalie one day. He wouldn't even allow me to get the first beer, and when he brought them back he indicated a man standing at the end of the bar. He looked a bit out of place; he was in his late fifties, wearing a combat jacket and yellow shades in a bar that was mostly full of hip young *porteños* and first-world travellers.

'You see him for the *coca*,' Arturo said 'but he won't sell if you ask him in English. He doesn't like tourists. I'll get you some if you like,' he said.

I knew what I was like with coke, though. I knew that however much Arturo bought me now, I'd need to see El Coronel again. There was still a week to go until my friend showed up.

'Will you teach me how to ask him?' I asked. Arturo's eyes lit up. He must have liked a challenge.

'Dees-coo-pay. ¿Sabay key-enn tea-enn-ay un pree-say, por favor?'

El Coronel screwed up his eyes and looked at me scornfully. '¿Qué?'

I said it again, Mario-ing it up like Joe Pesci. 'Disculpe. ¿Sabe quién tiene un prisé, por favor?'

'No,' he said and turned away.

'Por *favor*,' I tried. This time he blew out impatiently.

'Sí, tengo. ¿Cuánto quieres?'

'Dos, por favor.'

'Vale. Sesenta.'

'Dos, no tres,' I said, wondering why I was pushing it. It was only four quid to me. But Arturo had said it was important that if I wanted to buy off him again to pay the right amount first time or he'd just keep ripping me off more and more.

'Sí, sesenta,' he repeated.

'Quiero tres por sesenta,' I tried.

'Vale.' He nodded and gestured towards the toilet. Inside, I watched my reflection in his yellow shades as he handed me three plastic packages.

When I sat down next to Arturo and grinned, he clapped me on the back. 'You did it, man! My friends, we love to watch the English boys try to buy from El Coronel. He hates you guys! Ha ha ha!'

I wondered if he'd been trying to set me up, but if he had, he'd given me great instructions. Soon, we were blitzed. We went to the toilets together, where I was about to cut a line out on the cistern. 'No,' said Arturo, taking the wrap from me and reaching into it with his house key. 'Like this,' he said, and shovelled a big lump into one nostril. He did the same with the other and passed the wrap back to me with his key. This was fine by me. In England there's too much ceremony with cocaine – all that careful cutting and portioning. Here it was cheap, and you threw it down like tequila.

In an hour's time we were wild with it. Arturo was drinking his beer almost as quickly as me, and teaching me how to make obscene suggestions to young women in Spanish. At some point I asked him whether Natalie was coming along that evening. Perhaps the juxtaposition upset him; he put his arm down firmly on my shoulder and looked at me.

'Natalie,' he said. 'You think she is *pretty*?'

I tried to look as though the thought had never occurred to me. 'I don't really think of her in –'

'Yes, she is,' he agreed solemnly. 'And your girlfriend, *Katie*? In England. She is *pretty* too?'

'Yes,' I said sadly, remembering. 'She's more than that.'

'I am surprised you come here, without her.'

'I didn't want to.'

'So, why?'

I was about to tell him all about it, but then Natalie jumped into our booth with a squeal. Arturo couldn't concentrate on anyone except her when she was around, and as I was getting left out I started drinking faster and went to the toilets for another big keyload of coke. Then there was a round of tequilas, and more tequilas, and the coke was passed around again and again. Natalie ordered yet another round of tequilas for all of us; illogically, so she could catch up, though we were having one for each of hers.

Next thing, I was out in the street, trying to be sick discreetly behind a phone box, before the phone box was revealed to be a policeman's sentry box, and I was forced to flee an angry man in uniform into streets I'd never seen before.

The following afternoon, I woke up in my hostel room, although I had no recollection of returning. Miraculously, it seemed I hadn't been arrested and, even more miraculously, when I rooted through my pockets I found I still had a number of large bank notes and two wraps of cocaine. It was Saturday and Arturo and Natalie would be on the highway by now. My head hurt too much to conjure an erotic fantasy about them, and besides there was something bothering me when I thought about their relationship – as though it had come under particular strain the night before and I was in some way to blame. But, try as I might, I couldn't think my way through the tequila.

Over the next two days I made friends very quickly and forgot them just as fast. I can't remember a single name from then, only faces, accents and their various degrees of success with El Coronel. This was all we cared about, and I was the most successful. Though, on the anniversary of the invasion of Las Malvinas, he refused me emphatically, declaring, 'Las Malvinas son Argentinas.' We had to get an Australian on the case.

By Tuesday I was exhausted and had vowed a day of sobriety. I spent the whole time dozing on the roof of the hostel between long gulps of *Bleak House*. (At one point I tried Borges again and read 'Pierre Menard, Author of the *Quixote*'. I had to hold my stomach for a whole hour afterwards, convinced I would vomit.) As evening approached I was driven back to my room by gregarious Scandinavian youngsters. I was still feeling uneasy about Friday's blackout and, despairing of my small dark room and *Bleak House*, I went down to the lobby and tried to call Natalie. The phone rang out and I left an answer-machine message, trying to sound jaunty and guiltless. There was no way she could call me back anyway, and so I tried again at half-hour intervals until I decided to wait until tomorrow, stop worrying and get drunk in the meantime. My day of sobriety had lasted until about nine in the evening and it's a mark of my weakness of character that I would have felt very proud of my abstinence.

Wednesday lunchtime, and I tried to reach Natalie again – and when there was no answer, I headed out to an internet café, ostensibly to check if she'd written to me but idly thinking I might sting myself back to life by looking at some pornography.

Unfortunately, my computer's screen directly faced the attendant so I was limited to catching up on events in the Premier League. Natalie hadn't written, so I sent her a breezy 'God, I was *so* drunk' email, suggesting we could meet up for a coffee before my friend arrived on Friday. I stared then at the internet browser, with information about all the world at my fingertips, and I could think of nothing that interested me that wasn't obscene. I clicked on the search bar of my email account and typed in Katie's name. A long list of her emails, three years' worth, scrolled down the page. I flicked through some early ones, wounding myself with how coy and witty we'd been with each other, at how successfully we'd flirted, and then, inexorably, I gravitated to the sexy stuff. When I found what I was looking for, I shut my eyes and pictured her, and wished I was back in England. After five minutes I clicked on 'Compose' and began to write to her.

I told her about the local accent; about how you had to dramatize everything; about how everyone on the streets was beautiful, intimidatingly so; that they ate steak every day, but never chips. I told her about the cracked pavements; about the bookshops on every street, the English one hidden at the end of an impenetrable labyrinth; about the inhospitality of the Argentinean literary canon. I told her that you didn't have to always eat steak; there was also ham and cheese. (Katie is a vegetarian.) I didn't tell her how much I *loved* the diet. Particularly about the cocaine – she hated drugs as well as meat; it was one of the reasons we broke up, began to have separate weekends. I did tell her about Arturo, about how pretty he was, about how Natalie drove him crazy, sublimating a description of the intense erotic effect she had on me into his description. And then I confessed that I hadn't told her friend that we'd split up.

That I'd been lonely, and wanting to keep things simple, and how, having not mentioned it at first, I couldn't now. I talked about other things, too – I must have, as I was writing for nearly two hours. And for the first time since I'd been in Argentina I felt I'd achieved something I'd intended to and I *wrote*. After I'd sent it, I refreshed my inbox and there it was: a new email from Katie that must have exactly crossed with mine.

I stared at it for a while. I desperately wanted it to have been written after she'd read mine. In the end I opened it and, after I'd composed a terse reply, I went into the bar next door to drink three beers and chainsmoke Marlboro Reds. I then went straight back to the internet café and wrote to Natalie.

Dear Natalie
You'll have learned by now that Katie and I split up before I came over here. She'll certainly have told you why and – yes – unfortunately, that's me she's describing. I had intended to tell you we'd split up and I'm very sorry I didn't – it just seemed simpler not to. It's hard for me to talk about it.

Anyway, I know now I've caused some friction between you and Arturo. I don't even remember meeting Pedro, let alone encouraging Arturo to punch him. I'm not very good at drinking spirits – I should have warned you.

I really do hope you and Arturo are all right. You were both very welcoming to me, and I valued your friendship. I do hope I didn't betray it and I'm sure I wouldn't have told Arturo what you'd told me about Pedro. I hope I wouldn't. There's something so free about you, Natalie. I know why Arturo gets jealous. It's not your fault, but I know why. If anyone could be immune to that and confident enough to have you,

you'd think it would be him. Or perhaps he's more attractive to men. I don't know; I've never been a woman. Anyway, you'll see now what a lucky escape Katie has had from me.

I just wanted – this is why I'm writing to you – to convince you that the reason I got in touch with you was because I was lonely and the reason I stayed in touch was because you were kind to me, and funny, and great company – it was nothing more sinister.
Love from
Lee

I didn't try to call Natalie again and spent the rest of my time waiting for Dan to show up getting trashed with whoever I could find at the hostel. Everyone was in the same boat; no one knew what to do with themselves.

When Dan arrived I was thrown into an organized schedule of restaurants, bars, a Boca game, a flight to the Iguazú waterfalls and back, and from what I remember it was pretty good fun – and then Dan got married. At the wedding, I had sex with a nice Argentinean girl who was friends with the bride – and you might think that that would be what I remembered most from the trip. It wasn't, of course. I agreed with Natalie. It's easy to fuck people you don't like – but try telling your girlfriend that.

In the last few days of my trip, when I was back at the hostel, skint and waiting for my flight, *Bleak House* still going strong, I couldn't stop thinking about Arturo and Natalie. I'd really liked them, but I'd tried to screw things up for them as soon as I'd had the excuse of being off my head. I kept thinking about the words of Katie's email: 'You will fuck up everything you ever have, Lee, and you will never be happy.'

I hadn't dared to check my inbox again.

On the day before I flew back, I finished *Bleak House* and was suddenly filled with energy. I wanted to dance, but instead began a long walk around some of the sights I hadn't seen. I was just finding my way out of the cemetery in Recoleta when a moped flew past and braked hard. The driver took off his helmet and there was Arturo, shaking his hair loose with a smile and a shouted greeting.

We went for a coffee and, as usual, he insisted on paying. He seemed genuinely pleased to see me and we chatted about the wedding and the Boca game I'd seen at the Bombonera. Arturo was disappointed in me as he was River Plate – a *millonario*. It was a while before I dared to ask him: 'How's Natalie?'

'She's OK,' he said. 'She didn't like me hitting Pedro.' He shrugged. 'But you were right to tell me to. She told me afterwards . . .' He smacked his fist into his palm and grinned. 'I think she is glad I hit him. She says she's not, but . . .' And then he set his features and fixed me with his placid, gorgeous eyes. 'So, Lee, why did you not tell me you and Katie are not together?'

His face was darkening, he looked almost as if he might cry, but I'd adapted by now to the dramatics of his culture and so I played along.

'I don't know, Arturo,' I said, clutching my heart. 'I think . . . I think I just couldn't accept we had split up.'

When he kissed me goodbye I held on to him for too long, until he had to squeeze his way out of my arms and place his hands on my shoulders to hold the distance between us. 'See you in England, Lee,' he said, and we both smiled as though we believed it.

The Argentineans were more subdued on their way back to Europe. I arrived in Birmingham early on Easter Sunday and fell asleep until the evening, when I was woken by a friend hammering on the door. He was DJing at a party his friend was putting on in a swingers' club in Aston – complete with swimming pool, saunas and dark room.

He started to skin up and I fled to the shower then left him downstairs while I went to get dressed. On my bookshelves there was still a card Katie had made me for my birthday. I looked for somewhere to conceal it. It was too early for me to accept that I had to throw her away, that I already had, so I was looking for somewhere to put it where I wouldn't stumble on it by accident. As I searched for the right place I was thinking, This will be the last time. I'll find someone else, someone nearly as good as Katie, and this time I'll deserve her. And any trinkets, love messages, drawings, cards – I'll keep them for a week and then throw them away. Because if I had her, I wouldn't need them. And if I didn't have her, they'd stick in me like splinters that I wouldn't dare to pull for fear of losing all sensation of her.

My friend shouted up the stairs. He was ringing Mani and wondered if I wanted anything. I didn't answer. It was only then, as I was unpacking my bag, that I'd found the perfect place. I folded the card inside *Labyrinths* and wedged the book back into the shelf. Then I pulled on my leather trousers and went downstairs.

About the Authors

Kavita Bhanot currently lives in Himachal Pradesh in India, having lived in London and Birmingham. She has directed an Indian–British literary festival, and worked in Delhi as an editor with India's first professional literary agency. Her short stories have been published in anthologies and journals and broadcast on BBC Radio 4. She is working on her first novel.

After graduating from the University of Leeds in 2000, **Dea Brovig** began her career as an editorial assistant for *The Erotic Review* – where her first short stories were published. She worked in publishing in London until 2008, when she was accepted onto UEA's Creative Writing MA. She is now living in Norwich.

Luke Brown was born in 1979 and grew up in Fleetwood, Lancashire. He lives in Birmingham and on the Euston–New Street train.

Sarah Butler writes novels and short stories. Her fiction has been published in anthologies, journals and online. She runs UrbanWords, a consultancy that develops literature projects engaging with regeneration and urban renewal. She is online at www.sarahbutler.org.uk.

Daisy Cains was born in Lichfield and educated in Malvern and London. She worked briefly as a barrister and then as a teacher before taking up writing full time. Divorced, she writes academic pieces by day and fiction at night.

Katy Darby's fiction has won several awards and has been read on BBC Radio. Her stories have appeared in magazines including *Stand*, *Mslexia* and *The London Magazine*, and online at Pulp.Net, Carvezine and UntitledBooks. Her story 'The Proxy' came second in the 2009 PARSEC Short Story Contest. She teaches short story writing at City University London and co-runs the monthly live fiction event Liars' League (www.liarsleague.com).

Megan Dunn has been settled in the UK for a decade. She has an MA in Creative Writing from UEA. In 2007, she won an Escalator Award from the New Writing Partnership and received Arts Council funding to complete her first novel, *The Prodigal Whore*. This novel and many of her stories draw on her experiences of working in the New Zealand sex industry.

Rodge Glass is originally from Cheshire, but has lived in Scotland since 1997, where he graduated from the University of Glasgow with a PhD. His novels, *No Fireworks* and *Hope for Newborns*, are published by Faber. His most recent book is *Alasdair Gray: A Secretary's Biography*. Published by Bloomsbury in 2008 and winner of a 2009 Somerset Maugham Award, it was informed by the three years that Rodge spent working as personal assistant to Alasdair Gray. Rodge is currently Writer in Residence at the University of Strathclyde, Glasgow.

Iain Grant grew up in rural Lincolnshire, which is not as flat as everyone thinks. His short fiction has appeared in high and low places throughout the last fifteen years. His longer fiction has only appeared in low places. Iain teaches religious education at a Solihull secondary school and is the current chair of the Birmingham Writers' Group (www.birminghamwriters.org.uk).

James Hannah writes at the intersection of the B4364 and the B4373, and at www.jameshannah.com.

Anietie Isong has worked as a journalist in Lagos and has written for several international media. He has won a Commonwealth Short Story Award, a MUSON Poetry Award and the Olaudah Equiano Prize for Fiction. Anietie is a participating poet in the UNESCO-supported project, 'Dialogue Among Civilizations'.

Chris Killen was born in 1981. He currently lives in Manchester. His first novel, *The Bird Room*, was published by Canongate in January 2009. He infrequently maintains a blog (www.dayofmoustaches.blogspot.com).

Amy Mason lives in Bristol. She is part of the storytelling collective Heads and Tales, has written for the theatre company Show of Strength, and runs the outsider fiction website www.scrapscrapscrap.com. She is working on her first novel and was recently nominated for the Jerwood/Arvon mentoring scheme.

Richard Milward was born in Middlesbrough in 1984. His novels, *Apples* and *Ten Storey Love Song*, are published by Faber and he recently graduated in Fine Art from Byam Shaw at Central St Martins in London. He currently lives in Middlesbrough.

David Savill worked as a journalist with BBC Current Affairs television before leaving to become a full-time writer and university lecturer in creative writing. David's short stories have been published in national anthologies, and he recently completed his first novel, the story of a Bosnian and an English man caught up in the Asian tsunami. He is thirty-three years old.

Anita Sethi was born in Manchester in 1981 and grew up in Old Trafford, so close to the football stadium that she could hear when a team scored. She studied English at the University of Cambridge and now works as a journalist, contributing to the *Guardian*, *Independent on Sunday* and *New Statesman* among others, and broadcasting on BBC Radio Five Live. She has received an Arts Council writing award for a novel she is working on.

Kathryn Simmonds is a fan of Alice Munro and Flannery O'Connor. A few of her stories have previously appeared in magazines and anthologies. She also writes poetry, and her collection, *Sunday at the Skin Launderette*, won the Forward Prize for best first collection in 2008.

Michelle Singh lives in rural Essex with her husband and young daughter Ruby. She has a degree in English Literature from the University of Birmingham, where she won the Audrey Pipe award for young writers. She has recently completed an MA in Creative Writing at Birkbeck, University of London. She writes whenever she can, which is not often.

Chris Smith is twenty-six. He graduated with an MA in Creative Writing from the University of Manchester in 2008, moved to a mountain hut in France to work on his novel, and is currently living in South Carolina where he continues to write.

Mehran Waheed, an optometrist, was born in 1979 in Northampton. He spent his childhood in Birmingham, where his father emigrated to from Nairobi. He was a runner-up in the Decibel Penguin Prize in 2006 and is now undertaking an MA in Creative Writing at the University of Lancaster. He has a mentorship with Jill Dawson to help him complete his first novel.

Keelie Walker graduated with a Masters degree from Lancaster University in 2007. She teaches creative writing to adult learners and youth and community groups in Blackpool, and is currently working on a novel.

Nick Walker is the writer with Coventry-based theatre company Talking Birds, which has toured across the UK, Europe and America. His plays and short stories – including *The Bigger Issues* and 'The First King of Mars' – are regularly featured on BBC Radio 4. Nick has worked in television and film, and is the author of two critically acclaimed novels: *Blackbox* and *Helloland*.

About the Editor

Catherine O'Flynn was born in Birmingham in 1970, where she grew up in and around her parents' sweet shop as the youngest child of a large family. She worked in record stores, as a teacher, a web editor, a mystery customer and a postwoman before her debut novel *What Was Lost* was published by Tindal Street Press in 2007. This was listed for every major UK literary prize, including the Man Booker and the Orange, and won the Costa First Novel Award, the Galaxy British Book Awards Newcomer of the Year and the Guildford Festival First Novel Prize. Her second novel, *The News Where You Are*, is published in Summer 2010.

STAR WARS™

THE CLONE WARS™

DEADLY HANDS OF SHON-JU

DESIGNER **KRYSTAL HENNES**

ASSISTANT EDITOR **FREDDYE LINS**

EDITOR **RANDY STRADLEY**

PUBLISHER **MIKE RICHARDSON**

Special thanks to Jann Moorhead, David Anderman, Troy Alders, Leland Chee, Sue Rostoni, and Carol Roeder at Lucas Licensing.

STAR WARS: THE CLONE WARS — DEADLY HANDS OF SHON-JU

ISBN: 9781848568525

Published by Titan Books, a division of Titan Publishing Group Ltd.

144 Southwark Street, London SE1 0UP

Originally published by Dark Horse Comics.

A CIP catalogue record of this title is available from the British Library.

First edition: October 2010

10 9 8 7 6 5 4 3 2 1

Printed in Lithuania

STAR WARS

THE CLONE WARS

DEADLY HANDS OF SHON-JU

SCRIPT **JEREMY BARLOW**   ART **BRIAN KOSCHAK**

COLOURS **RONDA PATTISON**   LETTERING **MICHAEL HEISLER**

COVER ART **SEAN MCNALLY**

TITAN BOOKS

THE RISE OF THE EMPIRE
1000–0 YEARS BEFORE *STAR WARS: A NEW HOPE*

The events in these stories take place approximately twenty-two years before the Battle of Yavin.

After the seeming final defeat of the Sith, the Republic enters a state of complacency. In the waning years of the Republic, the Senate is rife with corruption, and the ambitious Senator Palpatine has himself elected Supreme Chancellor. This is the era of the prequel trilogy.

6

7

8

9

10

11

12

13

15

17

19

20

"I COULD DO THINGS WITH THE FORCE THAT THE OTHER STUDENTS COULD NOT...CHANNEL IT IN WAYS THEY COULD ONLY *IMAGINE.*

"AND YET, YEAR AFTER YEAR I WAS PASSED OVER FOR GRADUATION WHILE OTHER ...LESS QUALIFIED STUDENTS WERE ADVANCED.

"EVENTUALLY THEY TOLD ME I WOULD *NEVER* GRADUATE TO KNIGHTHOOD.

"THEY SAID THAT I WAS TOO FOCUSED ON USING THE FORCE AS A *WEAPON.* THAT I WAS *TOO OLD* TO CONTINUE THEIR TRAINING...

"...THAT MY CURRENT PATH WOULD NOT LEAD TO ENLIGHTENMENT.

"SO I LEFT...

"...ANGRY, BITTER, DETERMINED TO PROVE THEM WRONG. I CONTINUED MY STUDIES IN EXILE.

"THE JEDI GAVE UP ON ME, BUT I DIDN'T GIVE UP ON EXPANDING MY LEARNING, ON HONING MY ABILITIES...

"...ON DEEPENING MY CONNECTION TO THE FORCE.

"OVER TIME MY ANGER COOLED AND I FOUND TRANQUILITY. BALANCE.

"I FORSOOK THE LIGHTSABER AND LEARNED INSTEAD TO DIRECT THE FORCE INTO MY HANDS...

"...TO DO *INCREDIBLE* THINGS.

25

26

"*ATTUMA DUUM* -- PIRATE, WEAPONS DEALER, AND WAR PROFITEER.

"HE AND HIS BLACK-MARKET OPERATIONS HAVE BECOME A THORN IN YOUR REPUBLIC'S SIDE OF LATE.

"HIS HEADQUARTERS IS SHIELDED AND HIDDEN WITHIN THE ASTEROID BELT THAT RINGS THIS MOON, MAKING IT PRACTICALLY *UNTOUCHABLE* BY YOUR STANDARD BATTLE CRUISERS.

"BUT NOT BY A SMALL STRIKE TEAM.

"I'VE DEDUCED THAT'S WHY YOU'RE HERE. THERE'S NO OTHER REASON."

27

YOU'RE RIGHT -- I CAME HERE WITH A SMALL ESCORT OF ELITE CLONES...

"...WE CAME TO APPREHEND DUUM AND TAKE HIM BACK TO CORUSCANT, WHERE HE WOULD STAND TRIAL FOR HIS WAR CRIMES. BUT WE WERE *BETRAYED*...

"...DUUM HAS OPERATIVES EVERYWHERE. HIS UNDER-GROUND SPY NETWORK ALERTED HIM THAT WE WERE COMING. WE WERE AMBUSHED...

"...IT WAS A SLAUGHTER. I WAS THE ONLY ONE TO SURVIVE."

28

29

SHE TRIES TO SHRUG THEM OFF, BUT SHON-JU'S WORDS LINGER IN HER MIND...DREDGING UP FEARS SHE HAS KEPT BURIED.

HAS SHE BEEN ABANDONED IN HER TIME OF NEED? FORGOTTEN BY THOSE SHE TRUSTS?

THE FORCE PROVIDES!

THERE'S NO WAY FOR HER TO ANSWER THESE QUESTIONS NOW, SO SHE PUTS THEM AWAY...

...AND PRAYS THESE EMOTIONS WON'T INTERFERE WITH HER MISSION.

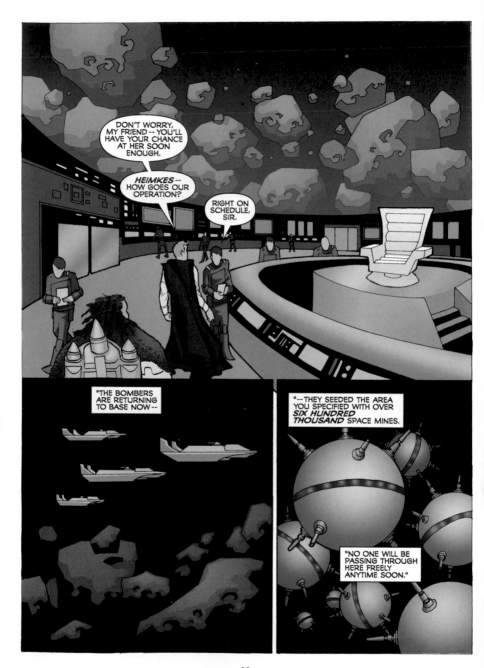

32

34

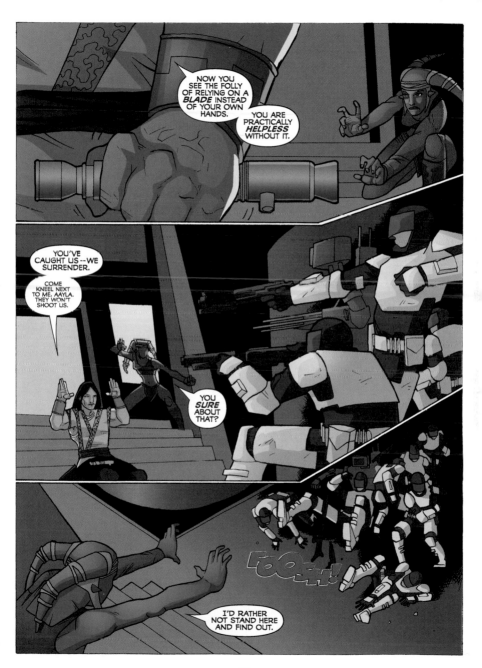

37

39

40

WHAT DO YOU THINK-- SHOULD I TELL HER? KNOWING WILL DRIVE HER CRAZY.

WERE IT ME, I'D PROBABLY LOSE MY POODOO.

I'VE BEEN FEEDING INTEL TO THE REPUBLIC FOR MONTHS -- GIVING THEM THE LOCATIONS OF THE CONFEDERACY'S SUPPLY LINES, AND SO ON. RELIABLE INFORMATION.

BUT *TONIGHT* THE COORDINATES I'VE GIVEN THEM ARE FALSE...

"...TONIGHT I'M LURING THEM INTO A *MINEFIELD* I'VE LAID RIGHT OUTSIDE MY WINDOW."

42

NO,
I REALLY
DON'T.

GOODBYE,
SWEET JEDI.
SABAT -- SHALL
WE?

NAW, I'M
STAYING HERE.
I DON'T TRUST
THESE TWO TO
STAY PUT.

SABAT -- I
DON'T KNOW IF
THAT'S DEDICATION
OR *PARANOIA*...
BUT THAT'S WHY
I LIKE YOU.

I'LL
HAVE HEIMKES
PATCH THE FEED
DOWN TO YOUR
MONITOR SO YOU
CAN WATCH
FROM HERE.

IN THE
MEANTIME,
THOUGH...

43

46

47

49

52

54

55

56

58

59

AMIDST THE CHAOS, AAYLA BARELY CONSIDERS HER OWN SURVIVAL.

INSTEAD, SHON-JU'S VOWS OF REVENGE AGAINST THE JEDI REPLAY IN HER MIND. THE LOOK IN HIS EYES HAUNTS HER.

AAYLA WAS ONCE BROUGHT BACK FROM HER OWN DARKNESS. SHE WONDERS...

...CAN SHE SAVE SHON-JU FROM HIS?

62

63

64

65

68

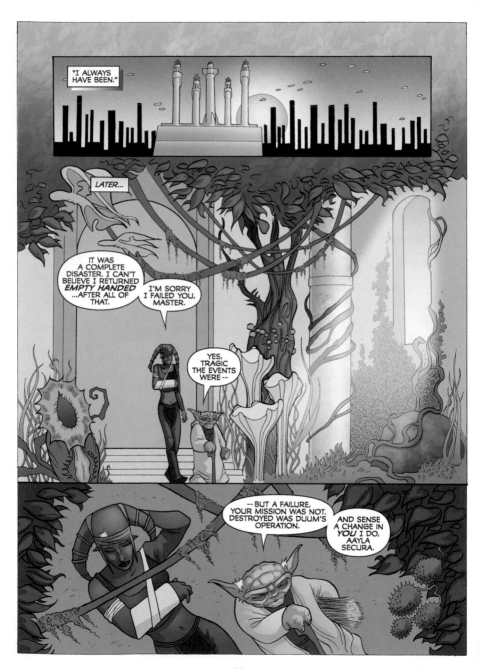

72

75

ALSO AVAILABLE NOW:

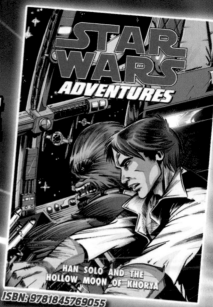

STAR WARS ADVENTURES

HAN SOLO AND THE HOLLOW MOON OF KHORYA
ISBN: 9781845769055

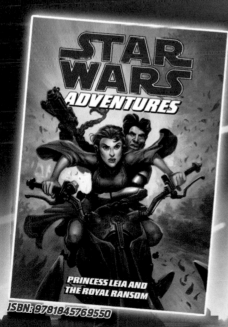

STAR WARS ADVENTURES

PRINCESS LEIA AND THE ROYAL RANSOM
ISBN: 9781845769550

STAR WARS ADVENTURES

LUKE SKYWALKER AND THE TREASURE OF THE DRAGONSNAKES
ISBN: 9781848564008

WWW.TITANBOOKS.COM   WWW.STARWARS.COM

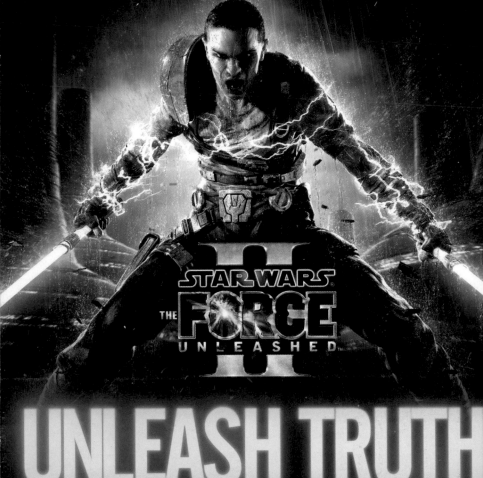

STAR WARS

THE FORCE UNLEASHED II

UNLEASH TRUTH

BETRAYED BY DARTH VADER FOR THE LAST TIME,
STARKILLER HAS ESCAPED AND FACES A NEW JOURNEY TO FIND HIS TRUE IDENTITY.

OUT NOW

WWW.UNLEASHED2010.EU